UNBREAKABLE

Special Edition

USA TODAY BESTSELLING AUTHOR

For Margaret

"Some people don't understand the promises they're making when they make them," I said.

"Right, of course. But you keep the promise anyway. That's what love is. Love is keeping the promise anyway."

JOHN GREEN

CHAPTER 1

Sylvia

IN HINDSIGHT, I should not have had that fifth mimosa at Breakfast with Santa.

Or the sixth, seventh, and eighth.

In my defense, I would like to say that they were incredibly tasty and *deceptively* strong. In fact, I'm pretty sure the bartenders began adding more alcohol to them as the event wore on.

And I needed it.

It was the first time Brett, my ex-husband, and fucking *Kimmy*, his soon-to-be-next-wife, and I were all in a room together. They were seated at a table with Whitney, our newly thirteen-year-old daughter, and Keaton, our ten-year-old son, along with another family from the country club. Back in August, when we'd made the reservations, I'd assumed it would be *me* sitting in the seat now occupied by Kimmy. Of course, I'd been totally unaware at the time that Brett had already hired a divorce attorney, established residency in Nevada so the whole thing could be done quickly, and purchased a love nest for himself and his little side dish.

I was only attending this breakfast because my daughter had begged me to come. She couldn't stand Kimmy, and she was furious with her dad. I was careful not to badmouth him in front of the kids, but I probably didn't even need to worry about it. He'd never been Father of the Year. In his mind, paying their private school tuition bills, buying them expensive birthday presents, and taking them on fancy trips made him a good dad. He never spent any real time with them, and he blamed his work schedule for missing out on their activities.

I'd practically been a single parent anyway the last few years, and when he left for good, the kids had made it clear they were staying with me. They tolerated weekend visits with their dad—when he didn't cancel—but there was never any question where their loyalty lay. And when I'd floated the idea of moving to Cloverleigh Farms, my childhood home in northern Michigan, where they'd spent some fun summer vacations over the years, they'd both voted yes. They might have been young, but they knew I needed to get away from here in order to put the pieces of my life back together.

Every night I lay awake wondering if I was being too selfish, taking them from the only home they'd ever known, but then I'd think about having to run into Brett and Kimmy all over town, or drive by my dream house and see the For Sale sign out front, or endure the pity of people who'd pretended to be my friends yet ditched me entirely when I'd needed them most. I wanted to be around family, around people I could trust, in a place that felt like home. I needed a safe harbor.

And the kids did too.

Ever since Brett left, Whitney had been wearing more and more makeup. I wasn't sure if she was just a normal thirteen-year-old girl experimenting or if it went deeper, but it worried me. When I tried to talk to her about it, she claimed she just really liked makeup. Brett hated it, of course, so maybe it was her way of defying him? Of saying *fuck you for leaving* with her loud red lips? Part of me admired her for that. Did I really need to take it away from her?

Keaton, for his part, seemed to be eating his feelings. He was hungry all the time, and even though I didn't keep junk food in the house, he would manage to buy it somewhere. Recently he'd started hiding it—I'd found a bunch of candy bar wrappers shoved under his pillow last week. When I'd checked his desk drawers, I discovered even more. I'd asked him about it, and he'd blamed a friend. I hadn't had the heart to call him out.

I prayed every night that Cloverleigh Farms would heal our aching hearts—or at least make me a better parent.

Tipping up the sixth mimosa, I turned around, setting the empty champagne flute on the bar. "I'll have another, please." What the hell, it was Saturday, right?

"Yes, Mrs. Baxter," said the bartender.

Mrs. Baxter. What a joke.

"Sylvia! So nice to see you!" Tippy Hewitt Hamilton air-kissed my cheek and gestured to the drink the bartender handed me. "I'll have one too."

"Yes, Mrs. Hamilton."

I took a sip of my drink, fortifying myself for a conversation with Tippy, the gossipy queen bee of the Ocean View Country Club set, women I'd considered friends until recently. But many of them had known Brett was cheating on me, and none of them had said a thing. Their excuse? They didn't want to upset me.

It was bullshit.

There was politeness, and there was loyalty, and I knew the damn difference, even if they didn't.

"So I hear you're moving back to Michigan," Tippy said with a toothy smile.

"Yes."

"You poor thing. Hard enough to have to leave that big,

beautiful home, but moving to Michigan at the start of winter? It's practically inhumane!"

"Actually, Tippy, I didn't *have* to move. I'm choosing to. The weather might be cold in Michigan, but the people there are a lot warmer."

The barb went right over her head.

"And you grew up on a . . . *farm*, right?" She made a face that told me she equated *farm* with *disease-ridden, backwater swamp*.

I saw no point in telling her that Cloverleigh Farms was actually one of the most beautiful places on earth in any season. That people came from all over the country to stay at our inn or get married in our orchard. That our vineyard rivaled anything I'd ever visited in Napa Valley, and our wines won awards all over the world. She wouldn't have believed me. "Yes."

"How quaint." She patted my arm condescendingly. "I'm sure you'll be very happy there."

I took another sip of my drink as we were joined by three other women, whose gossip antennae had no doubt communicated to them the opportunity to get a good scoop.

"Sylvia, darling, you look wonderful." Hilly Briggs air-kissed my cheek. She was wearing so much perfume—an attempt to mask the fact that she smoked to stay skinny—I nearly choked.

"The decorations are the best we've ever had," said Liz Dunham, whose carefully applied concealer couldn't quite mask the needle marks where her dermatologist had recently injected something to combat her wrinkles and plump her cheeks.

Looking thin and young was a competitive sport around here.

"Who are you sitting with, dear?" asked Jane Blythe Miller. I could tell she felt sorry for me from the tone of her voice and the tilt of her head—and also that she kind of enjoyed it. "Do you have a table?"

"I'm sort of just floating," I said, attempting to smile. "I'm not very hungry anyway."

They all nodded, their matching haircuts swinging. They were dressed alike too, each wearing some version of a twinset or turtleneck sweater and skirt of a "proper length," per club rules. Pearl necklaces hung around every one of their necks. I'd noticed Kimmy was wearing a pearl necklace too, and I'd wondered if Brett had purchased it for her. It was the kind of thing he liked to do, buy people's affection.

"You're better off," said Jane with a sigh. "I shouldn't have eaten that giant slice of coffee cake. It probably had a thousand calories."

"Don't be ridiculous. Sylvia doesn't have to worry about her weight," said Hilly with a touch of envy. "She's already so nice and thin these days."

I was actually *too* thin, and I knew it. But the stress of the last year or so had robbed me of my appetite and caused vomiting episodes when I did manage to finish a meal. Deep down, I'd known for a long time that my passionless marriage was disintegrating. I'd just been too scared to do anything about it.

"Good thing," said Tippy, lifting her mimosa to her lips. "After all, she's back on the market. She needs to look her best."

"The *market*?" I blinked at her. "I'm not for sale, Tippy."

"Relax," Tippy said, patting my arm. "It was a compliment. You're beautiful, Sylvia. It won't take you any time at all to find a new husband."

"Who says she even wants a new husband?" asked Jane. "Marriage can be such a pain. Sometimes I wish Richard would leave me just so I could get a moment's peace! You must have tons of time for yourself now, Sylvia."

I could have answered that I hadn't been looking for any

time to myself, I had zero peace whatsoever, and I actually missed my children terribly over the weekends they spent with Brett, but I didn't.

"Another mimosa, please."

My former friends exchanged glances as I downed it in a few gulps. I didn't usually drink this heavily, but it was either swallow it or throw it in their faces, and I didn't want to make a scene—not yet, anyway.

Then Hilly glanced toward Brett's table. "This must be so difficult for you, Syl."

The others murmured in agreement.

"I just don't know *how* you're keeping your cool," Liz said, the look on her face telling me she kind of wished I might lose it. "I heard about the baby."

"Baby?" My stomach tightened. "What baby?"

"You don't know? Well, apparently, Kimmy is pregnant," Jane said, gleefully breaking the news. "She told everyone at the Ladies Auxiliary Lunch yesterday that she's four months along."

"Four months?" I did some quick math—not easy after the amount of alcohol I'd consumed—and realized he had to have knocked her up over the summer, *long* before he told me he was leaving. "Oh my God."

"It did cause quite a stir," Hilly said, "but I'm sure no one there believed those other things she said."

I stared at her. "What other things?"

"Oh, you know, the usual insults the Other Woman lobs at the First Wife. That Brett was miserable with you for years because you're such an ice queen. That he told her you were boring in bed. That you didn't excite him anymore. That he couldn't even get it up for you."

I felt like I was melting into a hot, horrifying puddle of humiliation. I couldn't breathe.

"God, it's just so crass," Tippy said before sipping her drink. "I mean, who says those things out loud at lunch?"

As if she hadn't hung on every single word out of Kimmy's mouth—as if *all* of them hadn't!

"Crass and ridiculous," Liz huffed. "I mean, she's practically half his age! But her skin is just perfect. And I bet her boobs don't sag at all."

"Well, I haven't seen her boobs," I told her, suddenly tired of taking the high road and staying quiet when I wanted to scream. "But maybe if we ask her, she'll flash us. Clearly she has no problem getting naked in front of other people's husbands."

Liz appeared offended. "I only meant that it must be hard for you to see him with someone like her."

"Because I'm so old and saggy?" I tossed back the rest of my mimosa and ordered another, although the room was already spinning.

"How many of those have you had?" asked Tippy with a judgmental quirk of her brow. "Maybe you should drink some coffee instead."

"And maybe *you* should have told me my husband was fucking the salesgirl at J.Crew with the perky tits," I announced, then glared at the rest of them. "All of you."

"Sylvia, that's not really fair," Tippy said, smoothing her cardigan over her stomach. "I didn't know for sure. I'd only heard rumors about the—you know . . . divorce." She whispered the last word, as if by saying it out loud she might manifest its monstrous presence and it would eat all of their marriages alive.

"Same." Liz nodded. "We didn't want to say anything because we didn't want to cause any unnecessary *drama*. We were only thinking of you."

"Yes, and I think it's really a shame that you're blaming *us* when this isn't our fault." Hilly pouted. "We were trying to be good friends."

"How?" I cried. "You let me look like a fool! And you completely stopped calling or including me!"

"We didn't know what to say, Sylvia," Jane replied, looking uncomfortable. "It's just so *awkward*."

"And did any of you stand up for me yesterday? Did any of you come to my defense and shut down the ugly gossip she was spreading?" I looked every one of them in the eye, knowing the answer already.

"Well, we couldn't really take sides, could we?" Hilly smoothed her hair. "After all, our husbands are all close with Brett. We'll have to go to their wedding. We're still going to have to socialize with them, no matter how terrible it will be to have to make conversation with that *infant* he's marrying."

"I'm sure you'll manage. You're all excellent at pretending to be someone's friend." I grabbed my fresh mimosa, spilling some over the side of the glass. Then I tipped it up and slammed it.

When the glass was empty, I set it on the marble bar with a clank and tossed my hair. "And now, if you'll excuse me, there's something I have to do."

Not one of them stopped me as I made my way through the country club dining room, but they followed behind like a pack of hounds. I stumbled once, catching myself on the back of someone's chair, but eventually made it to Brett's table, where I grabbed a silver pitcher full of ice water.

"Ice queen, huh? I'll give you ice queen." Then I dumped the entire thing in his lap.

"Sylvia, what the hell?" Brett jumped up and tons of little cubes fell to the floor, but the crotch of his pants was soaked. "Have you lost your mind?"

"No, actually. I think I just found it." My adrenaline was pumping—I felt like I could do anything at that moment. "I must have been crazy to think you'd be faithful to me, or to keep the promises you made. You're nothing but a liar and a cheat." God, it felt glorious to say the words right to his face! Next, I looked at Kimmy. "And you're an idiot to think he's going to be any different with you, but that's your problem."

"Enough," Brett snapped, straightening his tie and glancing around the room. People were staring.

"Actually, I'm just getting started." Fueled by mimosa and the fury of a woman scorned, I charged for the dance floor at the front of the room, where Santa was standing in front of a red velvet throne and speaking into a microphone. A line of children wound toward the door, eager to sit on his lap, and two teenagers dressed as elves were doing their best to keep the impatient kids under control.

"Ho, ho, ho," Santa bellowed, brandishing an old-fashioned scroll. "Let's see who's on the Nice List this year—and who's on the Naughty!"

I marched up to him and grabbed the mic from his hand. "Let me help you with that, Santa."

The bewildered old man just blinked at me.

Turning toward the crowd, I brought it to my lips. "Excuse me, ladies and gentlemen. I've got something to say."

The room hushed. Expressions ranged from curious to concerned to shocked—I was generally a quiet, dignified sort of person. Not at all the type of woman to commandeer Santa's mic and lecture a room full of people just trying to enjoy their Bloody Marys and quiche.

"For any of you who don't know me, I'm Sylvia Baxter— at least, I've *been* Sylvia Baxter for the last fifteen years. And Sylvia Baxter is classy. Sylvia Baxter takes the high road. Sylvia Baxter *behaves*." I paused. "Sylvia Baxter is on the Nice List."

A disapproving murmur rippled through the room.

"But there are some people in this room who are *not* on the Nice List. In fact, there are some people here at the *top* of the Naughty List."

A child in line to see Santa burst into tears.

"Philandering husbands who cheat and lie about it— *they're* on the Naughty List." I glared at Brett and then at Kimmy. "Naive salesgirls from J.Crew who spread nasty gossip—*they're* on the Naughty List." I stared down Tippy and the rest of my former confidantes. "Disloyal social climbers who call themselves friends even as they stick knives in your back—*they're* on the Naughty List."

At that point, Brett left his table and was starting to walk toward the dance floor.

Oh, *hell* no. I would *not* let that man silence me.

But I knew I should probably wrap this up.

"The rest of you are probably on the Nice List," I said, talking more quickly now that Brett was headed my way. "And if you want to make sure you stay there, it's actually really easy." I shrugged. "Don't be an asshole. Merry Christmas, everybody. Peace out."

Then I held out my arm and dropped the mic.

It sounded terrible. It looked ridiculous. Santa was going to switch me to the Naughty List, and people around here were going to talk shit about me for years to come.

But it felt really badass.

And that was worth it.

CHAPTER 2

Henry

"HEY. YOU STILL HERE?"

I looked up from the oak barrel I was working on, surprised to see Declan MacAllister walking across the stone floor of the cavernous winery cellar. As the CFO of Cloverleigh Farms, he didn't poke his head back here too often. "Hey, Mack. What's up?"

"I saw your car in the lot. It's Saturday night, DeSantis. You're a swinging single dude now. You're supposed to be out hooking up with chicks, not here in this bunker giving your wine a massage."

I laughed. "Bâtonnage, not massage."

"Whatever," he said, watching me insert a long metal baton into the hole in the barrel's side. "God, I really want to make a sexual joke right now. Would that be considered workplace harassment?"

"Listen, this is about as sexual as my Saturday night is gonna get, so no jokes, please." I worked the baton back and forth, scraping its curved metal foot along the bottom of the barrel.

Mack shook his head. "That is depressing as fuck. I can't even bring myself to make fun of you for it."

"Thanks, asshole."

"Come on, you need to get out of here. Let's go to my house for a beer and some dinner. Frannie has a roast in the oven."

"No way. I'm not intruding on your Saturday night with your wife." But my mouth watered at the idea of a roast. I hadn't eaten a home-cooked meal like that in forever. But Mack, a single dad of three girls, and Frannie had just gotten married a couple months ago—right about the time Renee, my ex-wife, had served me with divorce papers and left for good.

"Are you kidding? I've got three kids, DeSantis. There is no Saturday night that does not involve intrusion. And what else are you gonna do tonight, huh?"

I hesitated. The truth was, tonight's itinerary looked something like this:

1) Eat some shitty leftovers straight from the carton.

2) Watch some terrible porn that didn't even turn me on.

3) Jerk off anyway.

4) Go to sleep.

But I couldn't say that. And I didn't want to be anyone's Saturday night charity project. "Actually, I've got a lot of work to do. I'll be here for a while."

Mack wouldn't give up. "Listen, Henry, I've been the divorced guy. I know all about the crappy takeout food and talking to your TV and feeling like everybody else in the fucking world is having a better time than you." He gestured toward the barrels. "Although, in your case, it might be true."

Laughing, I pulled the baton out, replaced the air lock valve, and moved on to the next barrel. "I actually enjoy my work."

"But you've been in here nonstop since the harvest," he went on. "I'm beginning to think you're sleeping here."

"I go home eventually." But the truth was, I preferred the bright, open spaces of the winery to the dark, empty rooms of my house. As head winemaker, I always had something to do here. We were a small operation, but I was involved in every single step of the process, both out in the vineyard and here in the cellar. And we did everything by hand, at my insistence, which meant a lot of extra patience and skill and time, but I wouldn't have it any other way. At home, all I did was sit around and wonder where the fuck I'd gone wrong.

But that wasn't Mack's problem.

"What are you still doing here anyway, if Frannie's got dinner in the oven?" I asked.

"I had to bring a bunch of Christmas presents from Santa to my office to hide. The girls are constantly on the hunt for them."

Hiding presents from Santa—just one more rite of fatherhood I wouldn't get to experience.

I buried the thought before it got to me. "They still believe in Santa, huh?"

Mack pulled on a knit winter hat. "Winnie does for sure. She's only five. Felicity's eight and suspicious of everything, so that's a maybe. Millie is thirteen, so probably not, but she's putting on a pretty good show. Frannie told her anyone who doesn't believe gets three fewer gifts so she wouldn't ruin it for her sisters."

"Smart."

"She is."

"How'd you get her to marry you, anyway?"

Mack looked genuinely perplexed as he shook his head. "Seriously, I've got no fucking idea."

After Mack left, I finished up my barrel work, returned some emails, tasted some riesling from the tanks, made some notes, straightened up the lab, and looked around to see if there was anything else that needed to be done before I headed home.

There wasn't, but I didn't feel like facing my empty house yet, the one I'd hoped would be full of family by now. So instead of going out to the parking lot, I zipped up my coat, pulled on a hat and gloves, and went out to the vineyard.

It was cold, late December in Michigan cold, but I didn't mind. I liked the smell of winter, the sharp sting of the air in my lungs, the crunch of the snow beneath my boots. I walked the rows of dormant vines, thinking over the past season, getting a feel for the energy of the upcoming growth, contemplating new strategies for each block of vines. I was always happiest out here in the vineyard, no matter the season. The vines could be cooperative or temperamental, fragile or hardy, but they spoke a language I understood, and I knew how to nurture, shape, and renew them into something beautiful year after year.

If only I'd been half as successful as a husband.

I exhaled, my breath a cloud of white in the icy night air. For the millionth time, I wondered if there had been something more I could have done to save my marriage. The real enemy had been infertility, which had eaten away at our happiness little by little, until there was nothing left. Despite what Renee said, I'd never blamed her, but she'd felt crushed under the weight of knowing it was her endometriosis causing the problem. She said she felt like a failure as a woman, and as a wife. No matter how many times I tried to convince her otherwise, she refused to listen or get therapy. The hormones were hell on her, and I tried hard to be sensitive to her feelings, to remind myself that this wasn't what either of us had planned.

The only times I got angry with her were when we'd fight about adoption—she wouldn't consider it. Had I called her stubborn? Unreasonable? Closed-minded? Unfair? Had I said things I regretted?

Fuck yes, I had.

But I'd said those things from a place of frustration and exhaustion and fear. I wanted to be a father, dammit, and I saw my chances slipping away because of her relentless determination to "become a mother the *real* way." I *did* blame her for that. Had I been wrong?

In the end, maybe it didn't matter.

After five failed rounds of IVF, our savings were drained. After years of trying to get the timing exactly right for conception, sex became a chore. After months of endless fights and sleeping on the couch and apologizing the next day for whatever I'd said that made her cry all night long, I'd given up on having children and just wanted peace.

I wanted to talk about something other than fertility. I wanted to stop being unable to go places as a couple because seeing a pregnant woman—or worse, hearing one say *we weren't even trying*—would put Renee over the edge. I wanted to *want* sex again, to take pleasure in it for its own sake, for the release, for the connection, for the fucking fun of it. My dick had become a clinical piece of machinery, just another cog in a mechanism that refused to work. And eventually, it was clear Renee had no use for it if it wasn't going to get her pregnant.

We grew resentful of each other. We grew distant and angry. We grew apart.

Then she said she was leaving. That my presence in her life was a constant reminder of her childlessness, she wasn't in love with me anymore, and she couldn't stay. She took off one afternoon in early September, and I hadn't heard from her since.

I'd been hurt, of course. Angry. Bitter. Resentful. But also . . . relieved.

Because I couldn't honestly say I was in love with her anymore either—it felt shitty, but it was the truth. The years we'd spent trying and failing to start a family, the fights, the cost, the blame . . . all of it had taken a toll. I had no idea how to make her happy, and I wasn't sure I ever would.

Frankly, I wasn't sure I knew how to make *any* woman happy. My whole experience with marriage had taught me that you could never really know a person. What you thought someone wanted, what you thought you could offer, it could all change. Life was unpredictable, and just when you thought you had it all figured out, just when you thought winter was over and spring was right around the bend, you got hit with a late frost that killed every bud on the vine.

So when people said things to me like, "Oh, you're still young, it's different for a guy, you'll be fine . . ." I kind of wanted to fucking punch them in the face. It wasn't that easy to just pick up, move on, and start over. I didn't trust anyone or anything to turn out like I thought.

Plus, it's not like this small town was overrun with hot single women banging my door down.

I was closer to forty than thirty. I was a farmer and a science nerd. I got excited about things like soil and microclimates and carbonic maceration. I loved getting my hands dirty.

I had a pretty decent body (thanks to hours spent working off tension at the gym), but I wasn't ripped. I had a career I loved, but I wasn't rich—and I was never going to be rich. I drove a beat-up truck, tracked mud in the house, and got a fourteen-dollar haircut.

Did I own a suit and tie? Yes, but three-hundred sixty-five days a year, I went to work in frayed jeans and shirts with holes in them, and I liked it that way.

Back when she gave a fuck, Renee used to say I was good in bed—I *never* took a woman's pleasure for granted—but those days were long gone.

Christ. Would I ever have sex again? I missed everything about it—the smell of perfume in the dark, the feel of soft curves beneath my palms, the taste of a woman on my tongue.

I nearly groaned aloud as I reached the end of one row and started down another. But there was no use getting worked up about it. I wasn't ready to date anyone, and I wasn't the type to jump in bed with some random woman I didn't know.

I told myself to be grateful for what I did have—a nice house, a great job, some good friends. Sure, my sex life was depressing as fuck and my first Christmas alone was going to be hard, but I'd get through it. Maybe I'd buy myself a present—a new truck, a nicer watch, a fishing boat.

At the very least, a subscription to a better porn site.

I was going to need it.

CHAPTER 3

Sylvia

ONE WEEK after the Breakfast with Santa debacle, the kids and I caught a 5:50 A.M. flight to Salt Lake City, then a 9:35 A.M. flight to Detroit before finally hopping on a small plane that took us to Cherry Capital Airport in Traverse City. By the time my dad picked us up, we'd been traveling for almost ten hours. We were exhausted, grouchy, and starving.

"Should we stop for dinner on the way home?" I asked him as we waited for our mountain of luggage. Each of us had two huge suitcases, and what winter clothing we hadn't been able to fit in those, I'd boxed up and shipped here. Once the house sold, I'd have to go back and ship our summer things. I planned on leaving almost everything else in the house for Brett to deal with—I wanted no reminder of my old life here.

"Nope, your mom was ordering pizza when I left the house. Should be there by the time we get back. And she's all excited about baking cookies with the kids tonight." He put an arm around Whitney and squeezed her tight. "We're so glad you guys are here. Did I tell you I bought a new sleigh?"

Whitney beamed up at him with her bright red lips. "The kind the horses pull?"

"Yep. This one is even bigger—it's got three rows of seats, so you can take a ride together with your cousins. Doesn't that sound nice?"

"Yes, it does." I smiled, even as my throat tightened, overwhelmed with gratitude and relief at coming home. "Thanks, Daddy."

My parents had said we could stay at Cloverleigh Farms as long as we needed to, and they certainly had the room. Back when I was growing up, it had been just a small family farm, but in the last thirty years, my parents had expanded the farmhouse into a thirty-room inn with a bar and restaurant. In addition, there was now a winery, tasting room, a brand new distillery, and it was consistently named one of the top wedding venues in the state. My sister April was the event planner, and I'd never seen anyone bring a bride's vision to life the way she could. My sister Chloe was the new CEO, slowly easing into the position as my dad "retired" at a snail's pace.

"Is anyone else coming to dinner?" I asked as we started on the thirty-minute drive from the airport to the farm.

"I think April might come by."

"No wedding tonight?" I was surprised, since Saturday nights were always booked.

"It was an afternoon wedding, so she thought she'd be done around seven. But the whole family is coming for Sunday dinner tomorrow, and then we'll have the big party at the inn on Tuesday."

I nodded. My parents always threw a big Christmas Eve party at the inn for staff, extended family, and close friends. It had been a few years since I'd attended one, since Brett had preferred Aspen to Cloverleigh Farms for the holidays, but I remembered them from my youth as warm, noisy, fun gatherings full of people in high spirits. Part of me was looking forward to it and part of me dreaded having to explain over and over again where Brett was.

But that would be my reality, at least for a while.

When we pulled up to the house, I got a little teary-eyed at seeing it blanketed with snow and covered in lights. It was beautiful and familiar, reminding me of Christmases from my childhood—I'd missed it.

My mom misted up as well when she greeted us, and she gave me an extra long hug. "It's going to be okay, darling," she whispered, squeezing me tight. "You're home now. You belong here."

"Thanks, Mom." I hoped with all my heart she was right.

Later, April and I snuck over to the bar at the inn for a glass of wine, and I told her about Breakfast with Santa.

"Wait—you did *what*?" Seated across the high-top table from me, April paused with her glass halfway to her mouth.

"I got drunk at Breakfast with Santa, dumped a pitcher of ice water in Brett's lap, took the mic right out of jolly old St. Nick's hand, made a kid cry, and told the entire country club not to be an asshole." I cringed. "Then I said 'peace out' and dropped the mic."

She burst out laughing. "You did not!"

"I did," I admitted, wrinkling my nose. "It was pretty bad."

"What possessed you?"

I told her the news about Kimmy's pregnancy, how she'd said terrible things about me in public, how my former friends had failed to have my back. "I just couldn't take it anymore," I said. "I've kept my cool this whole time, but I finally had to let it out."

"I don't blame you. How did the kids react?"

"I'm sure they were embarrassed, but neither of them wanted to talk about it when they got home."

She shrugged. "Well, parents have been embarrassing their children since the beginning of time. They'll live. They might need therapy," she added, "but they'll live."

"Yeah. I think we'll all need some therapy. Including Santa." I winced a little as I recalled the old man's befuddled face when I went charging up to him.

"Santa will get over it. Your kids are the only people you need to worry about. How are they doing?"

"Hard to say for sure," I fretted. "They don't talk much about their feelings."

"No?"

"No, I think they're coping in other ways—Whitney has taken to wearing a lot of heavy makeup."

April smiled ruefully. "I noticed that. Looks like you during your black eyeliner phase. Mom hated it so much, remember?"

I exhaled. "I do, and part of me says she's just acting like a normal thirteen-year-old girl. But another part of me wonders if it's some kind of mask she's trying to put on for protection."

"Hmm." April's forehead creased. "That's a tough one."

"And I don't want to forbid it or tell her it looks ridiculous, because that's what her dad does. She's not even allowed to wear makeup at his house."

"Dickhead," my sister muttered. "As if lipstick and eyeliner are more inappropriate than his pregnant girlfriend?"

"Exactly." I slowly spun my wineglass around by the stem. "I want to be understanding of her age and what she's going through, but also still a responsible parent. Like, what's the balance?"

"Beats me." Her expression was sympathetic. "You're in a tough spot there, hon. I'm sorry. What about Keaton?"

I sipped my pinot noir. "Keaton's coping mechanism is food. He's been sneaking it."

"Oh, no. Have you talked to him?"

"A little. But I don't want to punish him, you know? I just sort of keep trying to encourage him to talk to me if he wants to."

"He seems happy about the move."

I nodded. "They both claim to be good with it. They've always loved our summer visits here, and Whit is already asking if they can have a horse. It also helps that Mack's daughter Millie is about the same age as Whitney. They hung out a lot when we were here for the wedding, and they text all the time. Keaton seems to get along well with his daughter Felicity too—she's kind of a science geek like he is, I guess."

"That's all good stuff."

"Still . . ." I set my glass on the table. "There's no way being deserted by their father isn't going to cause lasting damage, and I worry it's more than I can handle. He didn't fight me on full custody, he didn't fight me on this move, and I had to talk him into letting them come stay with him the second half of their winter vacation. He thought a weekend would be plenty."

April gasped. "What a jerk! Do the kids know that?"

"No, and I hated covering for him. But what was the alternative? Let him crush my children's feelings the way he crushed mine?"

She reached across the table and put a hand on mine. "You're doing the right thing, even though he doesn't deserve it. When do they go back to see him?"

"A week from today—the twenty-ninth. Then they're back here on the fifth, the day before school starts."

"And you're going to stay at the house with Mom and Dad for a while?"

I nodded. "Until I find something to buy, but I probably have to wait for the Santa Barbara house to sell first. Brett practically emptied our joint accounts, so I don't have a ton of extra cash lying around, and I'd rather die than ask him for money."

"Mom and Dad would help you out, wouldn't they?"

"They offered, but I don't want to take their retirement money. They've earned it." I gathered my hair over one shoulder. "No, I knew this wouldn't be easy, but I want to do it on my own. When the California house sells, which shouldn't take long, I'll find something small and secluded, maybe on a little bit of land. I'd like the kids to be able to have a horse, and maybe we could get a few other animals too. Brett never wanted pets in the house, but I think it's important to grow up caring for animals. And I think it will be good therapy too."

"I think you're right, and that all sounds perfect." She tilted her head. "But why the seclusion? Are you hiding out?"

"At least for a little while. I feel like my life has been upside down for months—I want to get through the holidays, and then all I want is a fresh start with the new year. For all of us."

"I get it. And speaking of the holidays, all your boxes with the kids' gifts in them arrived safe and sound. They're all wrapped up and ready to be torn open by eager little hands."

"Thank you." I smiled at her, grateful again to have such a supportive family. "I was dreading this Christmas, but being home again, seeing the house with all the lights on it, and the snow on the ground, it feels nostalgic in a good way. I want to take the kids sledding and ice skating and build a snowman by the barn like we used to."

"Yes! You have to." April looked excited. "Remember the snowball fights we used to have? Those were epic. We need to do that again."

I laughed. "My kids would be all in for sure. And they could use the fun. But enough about us. How's everybody else? Dad's health seems good."

April nodded. "Mom and Dad are doing great. Enjoyed their cruise and are considering spending a month or so in Florida over the winter, maybe even buying a place down there. Dad's not a hundred percent retired yet, but he works much less. He walks on the treadmill or outside every day, and he's at Mack and Frannie's house a lot—loves being a bonus grandfather. Mack's girls even call him Grandpa John."

I smiled. "That's so cute. And Frannie's doing well? I can't believe she's a stepmom of three—our baby sister! She's not even thirty yet!"

"I know. And she's a natural. I bet they have their own kids soon too."

"Wow. Hard to imagine. Time flies, doesn't it?" I shook my head. "How about Chloe? Have she and Oliver set a wedding date?" Chloe, the second youngest Sawyer sister, had gotten engaged to her childhood nemesis, Oliver, at the end of the summer.

"Possibly next summer, but they're still arguing about it. He wants sooner, she wants more time to plan." April laughed and shook her head. "Those two get off on bickering, I swear to God. It's like foreplay to them."

I squinted. "Foreplay? What's foreplay? I vaguely recall it might have something to do with sex, but . . ."

April's eyes closed. "Tell me about it."

"How about Meg? She's back home for good now?" Our middle sister had been living in DC for years but had come home for Frannie's wedding and promptly fallen head over heels for her old friend Noah, a sheriff's deputy in town.

"Yep. She moved back right before Thanksgiving, and she appears to be going through the *motions* of looking for a place to live, but she and Noah seem pretty darn cozy in his house. I'll be surprised if she ever moves out." She sighed. "All three of our little sisters seem happy as can be."

I heard the wistful tone in her voice. "What about you? Are you seeing anyone? Got a hot date for New Year's Eve?"

She shook her head. "I wish, but no. I've just been working a lot."

"Even in December?"

She shrugged. "Well, Mom and Dad were gone on their cruise for three weeks, so we all had to pitch in to cover. And there have been a ton of holiday parties this month. Chloe is running ragged trying to get the distillery going while still managing the tasting room and prepping to take over for Dad full time. The Christmas Eve party is coming up Tuesday, and the New Year's Eve dinner is the following week. January will be a little break, at least, but we've got some corporate events. And in February, we'll get busy again for Valentine's Day and Presidents' Weekend."

"Sounds like you should hire some help."

"It's on my list. I'm actually interviewing someone right after the holidays, another event planner."

"I can help out in the meantime."

"I might take you up on that," April said. "Or if you want to freeze your ass off in the vineyard, you can help Henry with the pruning."

"Oh, that's right. Pruning starts soon."

"Twenty thousand acres, all done by hand." April imitated Henry's deep voice. "It's an art form."

I laughed. I didn't know Henry all that well, but I knew he was *very* serious about his vines. "Poor Henry. Does it bother him that you guys tease him so much?"

"Nah." She waved a hand in the air. "He's like the honorary Sawyer brother—he can take it. And he knows we're kidding."

"Dad emailed me a link to a magazine article about him a few weeks ago. Like a 40 Under 40 Tastemakers in Wine kind of thing?"

April nodded happily. "Yeah, that was really cool! I was so thrilled for him. He's *so* good at what he does." Then she sighed. "And he needs the positivity these days. He's going through a divorce too, did I tell you that?"

"Oh no, is he?" My heart ached a little in sympathy. "I remember him saying at Frannie's wedding that he and his wife had separated. I was hoping it would work out."

April shook her head. "I guess she'd already left and filed for divorce by then. He sort of hid it for a while. She moved to Chicago."

"Was there someone else?"

She lifted her shoulders. "Henry just says they just grew apart, and I haven't wanted to pry, but I think there's more to the story."

"How long were they married?" I tried to picture them together, but it had been a while—maybe a Cloverleigh Christmas party years ago? I remembered her as acting sort of quiet and sullen that night, in contrast to Henry's easygoing, friendly personality.

"I'm not exactly sure. They were married when he took the job here, which was nine years ago, so at least that long. He seems okay day to day, but he works a *lot*. His truck is always there when I leave work late at night after a wedding."

My heart went out to Henry. Maybe he was working constantly to distract himself, or to avoid going home alone. I understood that—there was nothing worse than the silence of an empty house.

"Well, all I want to do is *drink* wine these days," I said with a sigh, "but I'll get out there in the cold and prune vines if I must. I remember Dad making us learn how to do it when we were kids, and then we'd go in and chug gallons of hot chocolate afterward. Remember how Mom used to make it from scratch on the stove top? So good."

April laughed. "Yeah, but this time we'll spike it."

Smiling, I clinked my glass against hers. "Sounds like a plan."

Just after eight, April headed home to her condo in Traverse City and I took the private corridor that led from the inn's lobby to my parents' house. I found my kids wrapped in blankets on the couches in the family room with my dad watching *It's a Wonderful Life*. My mother, of course, was cleaning up the cookie mess in the kitchen by herself.

"Let me help you," I said, rolling up my sleeves. I inhaled the scent of cookies baking. "Mmmm, smells delicious."

"Thank you, darling." My mom cradled my cheek for a moment. "But aren't you tired?"

"A little. But please don't tell me I look it. I'm going to lose my mind if one more person tells me I look exhausted. Or skinny. Or worried. I'm working on all of it."

"You look just beautiful to me." She smiled and went back to work.

We got the dishwasher loaded and running just as the first batch came out of the oven. I grabbed the bowl of dough from the fridge. "Want me to put in a second batch?"

"No, no," she insisted, shooing me out of the kitchen. "You've had a long day. Go watch the movie or curl up with a book and a cup of tea somewhere."

"Thanks." But I didn't really feel like watching a movie or reading a book. After a long day of sitting on planes and then stuffing my face with pizza, I felt like I needed a little exercise. "Actually, I think I might take a walk. Get some fresh air."

"Okay, sweetheart. Dress warmly."

"I will." From the closet in the front hall, I grabbed my winter coat, zipping it all the way up. I tied a scarf around my neck, and tugged on a hat, my snow boots, and mittens. Then I slipped out the front door, pulling it shut behind me.

The air was bracingly cold, but I didn't mind. I shoved my hands into my pockets and followed the snow-kissed brick path around the back of the house, past the old red barn and the stables, past the new white barn that served as a wedding reception venue, and over toward the winery and vineyard.

Right away I saw the pickup truck in the winery's parking lot, and I assumed it was Henry's. I hadn't brought my phone with me, but I knew it had to be almost ten o'clock. What was he still doing here this late? I recalled what April had said and wondered if he could use a friend.

Moving a little quicker, I followed the path to the winery door. Lights were on inside, but the double doors were locked. I pressed my face to the glass and peered into the tasting room, but I didn't see anyone, so I knocked a few times. No one answered. I knocked again, a little louder.

Five seconds later, Henry appeared, a confused expression on his face as he crossed the tasting room floor from the direction of the cellar, peering out the window. When he saw me, he hurried to the doors, unlocked them, and pushed one open. "Sylvia?"

"Hi, Henry."

"Come on in."

"Thanks. It's freezing out there." I moved inside the bright, open space, grateful for the warmth.

Henry shut the door behind me. "I'm sorry if you were waiting outside for long. I was in the cellar and it's hard to hear from there. I wasn't expecting anyone." He ruffled his hair in a boyish gesture that made it messier rather than neater. It was walnut-colored and thick, with just the tiniest hint of gray at the temples. A short layer of scruff covered his jaw.

"Oh, that's okay. It was only a minute or so." I gestured toward the parking lot with a mittened hand. "I was out taking a walk and saw your truck. I thought I'd come in and say hi. See how things are going."

"Things are going well, thanks."

"Did the grapes have a good year?"

"Yeah," he said, nodding. "I think it's going to be a nice vintage."

After a somewhat awkward pause, I glanced toward the cellar. "Working late, huh?"

He shrugged. "I'm kind of a night owl these days."

"Me too." That is, if you could call lying awake panicking about your hot mess of a life being a night owl.

"Did you just get in?" he asked, crossing his arms over his chest. He wore jeans, work boots, and a thick gray henley with the sleeves pushed up, revealing muscular forearms and solid wrists. His henley had a hole on the chest, and a white undershirt peeked through.

"We got in earlier tonight. I don't know if you heard, but the kids and I are moving here." There was another awkward moment of silence before I added, "Brett and I split up."

He nodded, looking a little uncomfortable. "I did hear that, from April, but I wasn't sure if I was supposed to know or not. So I didn't want to say anything."

I looked at the floor and shuffled my feet before peeking up at him. "Um, is it weird if I say the same thing? That I know about your divorce too, but I'm not sure if I'm supposed to?"

"It's fine." Then he surprised me with a smile, his green eyes crinkling at the corners. "But clearly, if we ever have a real secret, we should not tell April."

I smiled too. "Clearly."

We stood there grinning at each other for a moment, and my body warmed as I suddenly found myself wondering what kind of secret the ruggedly handsome Henry DeSantis and I might have.

It awakened something small and fluttery inside me.

CHAPTER 4

Henry

I'D FORGOTTEN how beautiful she was.

I hadn't spent any extended time with Sylvia, the oldest Sawyer daughter, since she'd lived in California as long as I'd worked here, but I'd met and chatted with her a dozen times over the years. She had always struck me as elegant and kind, maybe a little reserved—friendly, but not as outgoing as April, Chloe, or Frannie, whom I knew much better because they lived or worked here. So it surprised me that she'd wandered in here tonight to say hi.

The last time I'd seen her was at Mack and Frannie's wedding. She and her husband had been seated at our table, but he was the kind of guy who liked to dominate the conversation, and all I could think of was that I finally had to explain Renee's absence. I hadn't told anyone yet that she'd already moved out. But I remembered thinking that Sylvia had looked sad that night—stunning, as usual, but sad.

One year, Renee had pitched a fit about my talking to Sylvia too long at the Cloverleigh Christmas party, not just because Sylvia was attractive, but she had two perfect children as well. So not only was her face superior, but her uterus was too.

"You're being ridiculous," I'd told Renee after she blew up at me on the ride home. "She asked me about this year's crop because of the wet spring weather. We were talking about wine."

"You don't think she's pretty?" Renee accused.

There was *no* good way to answer that question. "Listen. In all the years we've been together, I've never once been tempted by another woman's face—let alone another woman's uterus."

It was true. I'd never been unfaithful to Renee, never even thought about it.

But standing here looking at Sylvia's wide-set blue eyes, her cheeks pink from the cold, her long blond hair tumbling around her face from beneath her winter hat . . . I didn't blame Renee for being jealous.

Of course I thought Sylvia was pretty—who wouldn't?

She glanced around. "So what's new and exciting? I haven't been in here in a while."

I wasn't sure how to answer that, since my idea of exciting wasn't always the same as other people's when it came to wine. Before I could decide if hearing about our new bottling line would send her racing for the door, bored to tears, she asked another question.

"What's in the barrels?" She moved toward the large windows overlooking the cellar, which was one level down and lined with huge steel tanks and rows of big oak barrels.

"Several things." I walked over and stood at her side. She smelled like cookies, and my stomach growled. "Chardonnay, cabernet franc, pinot noir."

"And in the tanks?"

"Riesling."

"Oh, I love riesling."

"Want to taste some?"

She faced me, her eyes lighting up. "Sure."

"Follow me." I led her through a door at the back of the

tasting room and down the stone steps into the brightly lit cellar. From an antique cabinet over on one side, I grabbed two glasses. "So the wine is going to be a little bit cloudy because it's not filtered yet, and it's also freezing cold, but—"

"Oh, wow. There's ice on the tanks." She took off her mittens and hat, shoved them inside her coat pockets, and fluffed her hair a little.

"Yeah." Momentarily distracted by the feminine gesture and all that golden blond hair, I paused for a second before recovering. "This is what's called cold stabilization, where the wine is stored just above its freezing point."

"Really? Why?" Then she grimaced. "Sorry. I'll just warn you now, all my questions will probably sound stupid to you. I love wine, but despite growing up here, I'm pretty ignorant about the process."

"That's okay." I turned the spigot on one of the tanks and filled one glass halfway, handing it to her. "I'm happy to teach you about it—you just have to let me know when I'm getting boring. I could talk forever about making wine. Renee used to —never mind."

She put a hand on my arm. "No, tell me. Renee used to what?"

I filled the second glass, sorry I'd opened my mouth, but at the same time thinking how nice it was to feel her touch. "She was just over it after a while. She got sick of hearing me talk about what I do."

"But you love what you do."

I exhaled as I straightened. "It was part of a bigger problem. Anyway, I'm happy to answer your questions. If you start to snore, I'll stop talking."

She laughed. "That won't happen." Lifting up her glass, she looked at the riesling, which was pale yellow and slightly opaque. Her fingers were slender and graceful on the stem, her fingernails painted a soft pink. "Why do you have to keep it so cold?"

"To prevent crystallization of the bitartrates—what we sometimes call 'wine diamonds.'"

"Wine diamonds." Her plush lips curved into a smile. "That actually sounds beautiful."

I laughed. "Maybe, but you don't want them in your glass. Next week we'll filter this and get it ready for bottling."

"Got it." She lowered the glass and peered into it. "So am I supposed to sniff this first?"

"You can, sure." I watched her stick her nose inside the rim and inhale. "What do you smell?"

She picked up her chin and looked at me, her expression concerned, like she was figuring out a math problem. "I don't know. Something fruity? I'm not good at this."

Smiling, I swirled the wine in the glass. "You're not wrong."

"What do *you* smell?"

"Orchard fruits like apple, peach, apricot. A little honey. Maybe a little petrol."

"Petrol!" She looked horrified.

"It's normal," I assured her with a laugh.

She sniffed again. "I don't smell that at all, and how the heck do you pick out individual fruits like that?"

"Training. Experience. I also happen to have a very sensitive nose. I'm good at picking up different scents. Now taste it."

She took a sip, and her eyebrows rose. "It's actually so cold I can't taste anything."

"Yeah, the cold numbs your taste buds. Try this—don't swallow it right away. Keep the wine in your mouth for a few seconds. Let it warm up on your tongue." I hadn't intended for it to sound suggestive, but her cheeks grew a little pink.

"Okay."

We sipped at the same time, giving the wine a moment to lose its chill in our mouths, and I found myself thinking about her tongue. *If I kissed her right now, I know exactly how she'd taste.*

Ashamed, I pushed the thought from my head.

"So what do you think?" I asked, stepping back from her slightly. "Can you detect any specific flavors?"

She swallowed and waited a second. "Maybe citrus?"

"Very good."

She beamed, lighting up the entire room. "Yay! I got one right!"

Laughing, I sipped again. "Do you like it?"

"I love it. And how cool that these grapes were grown right outside!" She pointed in the direction of the vineyard.

"It is cool—at least, *I* think it is. What you're tasting is totally unique to the soil here, to *this* vineyard, to the way *we* make wine. And what we're tasting this year will be different than what we taste next year from the very same vines. Wines tell a different story with every vintage."

She looked surprised, then delighted. "I love that—the idea that wines tell a story."

"That's how I look at it." I couldn't help feeling excited to have someone to talk to about what I did—someone who *wanted* to listen and learn. "And it's a story you don't just read—you need more than just sight to really understand and appreciate it. You need smell, taste, touch—the feel of the wine in your mouth is just as important to the story as its scent or flavor."

"Wow." Sylvia blinked at me. "You're *really* good at this. You make tasting wine sound very . . . um, sensual."

"It should be sensual. But sorry." I laughed self-consciously, shrugging my shoulders. "I tend to get carried away."

"Don't apologize, I love that you're so passionate about what you do." She lifted the wine to her lips again, finishing the glass. "This is really good. I can taste it better now that it's warming up a little. And I'm sure I'll need plenty of wine to get through all these Cloverleigh holiday parties. Can't say I'm looking forward to all the questions about my ex."

I finished my glass too. "I hear you on that. I'm tempted to skip them altogether."

"Don't you dare!" Her expression was outraged. "Don't make me be the only freshly-divorced person there. We can hide out together if it gets bad."

"Oh yeah? Where?"

"I don't know. The attic. The basement. The roof! We'll watch for Santa Claus." She frowned with pursed lips. "Although I don't know that he's speaking to me these days. Pretty sure I'm on the naughty list."

"Why is that?" I could not imagine this woman being naughty in any way, shape, or form.

Well, I *could*, but I was trying not to.

She bit her bottom lip. "I got drunk at this event at our country club called Breakfast with Santa. I stole Santa's microphone. I said 'don't be an asshole' to everyone in a room full of kids."

My eyebrows shot up. "Wow."

She sighed, looking into her empty glass like she hoped more wine would magically appear. "It was not my finest moment."

"Well, everyone has to let off steam now and again. Want a little more wine?"

She grinned and nodded, rising up on her tiptoes. "Yes, please. Thank you."

I refilled our glasses with a small pour and handed hers back.

"What about you?" She took a little sip. "Throw any public tantrums lately?"

I laughed. "Can't say I've thrown any public tantrums, but every couple days I beat the hell out of the heavy bag at the gym. That seems to help."

"I get that. Punching things probably feels pretty good."

"I can confirm that it does."

"Do you feel like . . ." But then she shook her head. "Never mind. I should stop bothering you and go home." She lifted her glass to her lips.

"No. Go ahead." I surprised myself by pressing the issue—talking about my feelings was my *least* favorite thing to do. Renee and I had talked them to death, on our own and with a counselor. But talking to Sylvia felt nice—I didn't want her to leave. I surprised myself again by touching her shoulder. "What were you going to ask?"

She stared into her glass as she twirled the stem. "I was just going to ask if you felt like your friends abandoned you after your wife left. If you felt like people didn't care about what you were going through and you had nobody to talk to."

"Oh." I thought for a second. "Not really, I guess. But . . . I'm more of a private person. I didn't really want to talk about it. It was done, and there was nothing anyone could say to change that."

"I know, but . . ." She looked up at me, her expression serious. "Didn't you ever feel so lonely you wanted to scream?"

I felt a sudden compulsion to put my arms around her, and had to force myself not to. "That's when I go punch things. You should try it sometime."

She tipped up her wine again, finishing it. I finished mine too and reached for her glass. "Here, I'll take that."

She followed me to the sink at the back of the cellar. "I've actually never thrown a punch at anything in my entire life."

"What?" I pretended to be shocked as I washed our glasses. "You've never been in a bar fight?"

She laughed, sticking her hands in her coat pockets. "Never."

"No sparring with your sisters when you were young? My brothers and I beat the hell out of each other."

"Nope. I think Meg and Chloe went at it a few times, and

April and I definitely got into screaming matches over who stole whose lip gloss or hairbrush or jean jacket, but nothing physical."

"Not even *one* playground brawl to brag about?" I teased, setting the glasses on the rack to dry and wiping my hands on the bottom of my shirt. That's when I noticed the hole—fucking hell, did I have to be wearing a shirt with a hole in it the one time Sylvia Sawyer came in here to talk to me? I felt like I should apologize or something—she was always so well-dressed and perfectly put together. And there was no way she hadn't noticed it—it was right fucking there on my chest. I put a hand over it, but she wasn't looking at me.

"You know, there *was* this bully who shoved me off the swings once in third grade, but I didn't fight back," she said distractedly.

"Why not?"

"I was scared. She was bigger than me."

"That's why you need to learn to throw a punch," I told her. "You should come to the gym sometime. There's a great coach there who works with beginners, and she has a lot of female clients. I think there's also a self-defense class too."

"Really?" She perked up a little. "That might be good. I'll be living alone here and everything, and even though this town isn't very dangerous, you never know."

"Exactly."

"And I think it would be great to feel . . . stronger. More confident. To know that I can take care of myself no matter what. Chances are, I'm never going to have to throw that punch, but if I did . . ."

"You'd know what to do."

"I'd know what to do." She smiled at me, a gleam in her eye. "You know, I already saw the hole in your shirt."

"Can't we pretend you didn't?"

Laughing, she tugged my hand off my chest. "I saw it, and

it's fine, Henry. You don't have to feel bad for dressing comfortably at work. I crashed *your* space."

"I'm glad you did."

Our eyes locked, and a moment passed during which I wondered what life might have been like if our timing had been different. Would I have kissed her on a night like tonight? Would we have been good together? Would we be home in bed by now, wrapped up warm and close beneath the covers?

The thought made the crotch of my pants feel tight.

It also made me feel like a jerk.

Sure, she was lonely, just like I was. But she was also really fucking vulnerable, and she was in here with me—*alone*, at *night*—because she trusted me to keep my hands to myself. I was a family friend and an employee. Only a total asshole would take advantage of her in this situation. Not to mention that it would jeopardize my job, my relationship with her family, and my professional reputation.

I took my hand from hers. "It's getting late. Let me walk you back."

She pulled her mittens from her pockets and put them on. "You don't have to walk me back. It's late, and I'm sure you're anxious to get home."

"Let me rephrase that," I said firmly. "I'm going to walk you back now."

She narrowed her eyes at me as she tugged her hat on, but she smiled too. "Bully."

"So fight me."

She sort of slapped at my chest with her mittened hands, and I grinned as I backed toward the stairs. "That's it? You really do need that class."

A few minutes later, we were walking along the path toward the house, snow falling softly around us.

"Are you coming for dinner tomorrow night?" she asked.

"I don't think so."

"Why not?"

"It's just family, isn't it?"

"You're practically family, Henry. And I'm inviting you. I'm surprised my mom didn't already."

"She did."

"There, see?" She nudged me with her elbow. "You're coming. It's settled."

"You know, April once mentioned you could be a bossy know-it-all. I didn't believe her."

She put her nose in the air. "I'm the big sister. I get to be bossy sometimes."

"You're not *my* big sister."

"True," she said. "Although it is my house. That should count for something. Come on."

"I will think about your invitation," I told her.

"Oh, you're one of *those* guys, huh?" she asked as we reached her parents' front porch.

I climbed the steps next to her. "What guys?"

"One of those guys who can't give in to a woman." She faced me in front of the door and poked my chest, her expression playful.

With my hands safely clenched inside my pockets, I looked down at her and fought every male instinct in my body, the ones that knew exactly what to do when you walked a pretty girl onto her front porch at night, and her face glowed faintly in the dark, her long, gossamer hair was dusted with snowflakes, and her warm, soft lips were *right fucking there*, so close all you'd have to do was lean forward and you'd know what they felt like on yours.

"I can give in to a woman," I said quietly.

The smile slid off her face, and her mouth opened slightly.

"Goodnight, Sylvia." Quickly, before I could do something I'd regret, I hustled down the steps and started out on the path toward the winery again. I didn't hear the Sawyers' front door open or close, so I assumed she stood there for a bit, watching me walk through the snowy dark, but I didn't turn around and look.

Fuck yes, I could give in to a woman.

What I couldn't give in to was myself.

That night, I dreamt about her.

We were tasting wine in the cellar, but she was naked, and she let me pour the cold wine over her skin and lick it off. At four A.M., I woke up with a massive erection that refused to go away. I tossed and turned for another hour, then I gave up and slid my hand down inside my boxer briefs. Maybe it would get her out of my head.

As I stroked myself, I imagined my warm tongue running over her throat, her breasts, her stomach, her thighs. I heard her sighs and moans echoing off the stone walls. I felt her fingers fisting in my hair, her legs wrapping around my head, her body going rigid with tension. I made her come just like that, the wine dripping off her body as she pulsed against my tongue, and I groaned as my own orgasm made my cock throb inside my fist.

But I shouldn't have done it. I felt terrible about it. Because now when I looked at her, all I'd be able to think about was her naked body on the stone floor.

There was no way I was going to her family dinner tonight.

To make sure I wouldn't even be tempted, I wore my grubbiest jeans and my ugliest flannel shirt with the most holes to work, the one my ex had always begged me to throw out. I didn't shave, and I threw a cap on my head rather than comb my hair.

At the winery, I did grunt work and heavy lifting all day

long, ensuring that I'd work up a sweat. I was by myself, since I'd given my assistant Mariela the week off, and the tasting room was closed for the week, so no one would care if I smelled bad.

Around six o'clock, I was outside stacking new bins on the crush pad when I heard someone call my name. Surprised that anyone would be out here at this hour in the frigid dark, I walked around to the front of the winery.

Sylvia stood near the tasting room door, shivering in the cold without a fucking coat on, arms wrapped around herself. "Hey!" she called, spotting me. "I was looking for you!"

I jogged toward her, unzipping my jacket. "What's going on? Everything okay?"

"Yes, but my God, it's freezing!" She hopped back and forth from one foot to another.

Quickly I took off my Carhartt and held it out for her to slip her arms in. "Put this on. Don't argue."

She shrugged it on, and we hurried inside the tasting room with her swimming in my giant coat. After shutting the door behind us, I switched on every single light—I did *not* trust myself alone in the dark with her.

"Sheesh!" Sylvia blew on her hands. "It's even colder than last night! I can't feel my face! What is it, like ten below?"

"It's actually about twenty-five, but it's still too cold to be running around without a coat." I set my hat and gloves on a high-top table and ran a hand through my matted hair. "What were you doing out there?"

"Looking for you. We're all at my parents' for dinner and someone asked where you were. I volunteered to come get you."

"Without a coat?"

"The house is *roasting*—I've been cooking all day and I was so hot. And don't change the subject." She fished a hand out of the sleeve of my jacket and scolded me with one finger. "You said you'd come to dinner."

I crossed my arms over my chest. "I said I'd *think* about it."

"And did you?"

"Yes. But I can't come."

"Why not?"

I shrugged. "I'm working."

Sylvia rolled her eyes. "It's Christmas, Henry! Take a break!"

"It's not Christmas yet."

"It is in our house. Starting today, the inn is officially closed to guests for a whole week, and that means Christmas vacation at Cloverleigh Farms starts right now." She held up both hands, but they were lost in my sleeves. "I can appreciate that you want to wait for Jesus's actual birthday to celebrate, but I feel certain he will not mind if you come have dinner with us tonight. In fact, he wants you to. He told me."

I laughed. "Jesus told you he wants me to come have dinner with you?"

"Yes. He said you've been working too hard."

"I feel like Jesus has more important things to worry about."

She shook her head. "We can't question, Jesus, Henry. Now let's go. I bet you haven't eaten yet, and I've had sweet and spicy party meatballs in the slow cooker all day."

My mouth watered. "Meatballs, huh?"

She saw my weakness. "Yes. And that's just an appetizer. There's a ham in the oven, and honey-roasted butternut squash, crispy Brussels sprouts with bacon and pecans . . ."

Real food.

I groaned right along with my belly. "You're killing me."

"Good. Come and eat."

"Look at me. I'm a mess, Sylvia."

"Doesn't matter what you're wearing, tonight is casual."

I was trying to think up another excuse when she moved closer. For a second, I was scared to breathe. Because whether she smelled like cookies or party meatballs or perfume, I was going to want some.

"Hey," she said quietly. "I know you don't find big social gatherings much fun these days. I don't either, and I will totally understand if you'd rather go home. But I had a really nice time talking with you last night, and—" She stopped.

"And what?"

She lifted her shoulders. "I guess that's it. I had a really nice time talking with you last night." Then she began shimmying out of my coat. "Look, don't worry about dinner. It's totally understandable that you'd rather be alone, and I didn't mean to—"

"Sylvia." I grabbed the sleeves of my Carhartt on her upper arms before she got it off, effectively trapping her. "I don't want to be alone tonight. It's not that."

"So what is it?"

"I just . . ." But how was I supposed to finish the sentence? I just think you're too beautiful? I just can't stop thinking about kissing you? I just had this dream about you last night that made me come so hard, I don't trust myself alone with you, and would you mind stepping over here beneath the riesling spigot so I can show you what I did?

She was completely still and looking at me like she was half hopeful, half scared.

For a few crazy seconds, I thought, *Fuck it. Just kiss her.*

Suddenly the door to the winery flew open. "Hey! You guys coming or what?" It was April, bundled up properly in a long puffy jacket. "Mom sent me to come find you."

Letting go of Sylvia, I stepped back and tried to breathe normally.

"He's giving me a hard time," Sylvia said. But her voice shook a little.

"Screw that." April pointed at me. "You're coming to dinner, Henry. It's Christmas."

I gave up the fight. "Okay, but I need to run home to shower."

"Take your time," April said. "We're not going anywhere. Mack and Frannie and the kids just got there, and Chloe and Oliver haven't even arrived yet. Meg and Noah are running late too."

"What can I bring?" I asked her.

April shook her head. "Nothing, just come."

I wouldn't show up empty-handed, but I could worry about that later. "Okay, I'll see you in a little bit."

"Good," April said. "Coming, Syl?"

"Yes." She started to remove my Carhartt again, but I reached out and stopped her.

"Wear it. It's too cold for you to be out there without a coat."

Her face flushed as she zipped it up. "Okay. Thanks. See you in a little bit."

I watched them walk out and wondered if it was normal to feel like a fifteen-year-old boy in a grown man's body. Hormones I'd forgotten I had were surging through my veins, and my heart was beating way too fast. She was so fucking pretty.

It's fine, I told myself as I got ready to go. *It's normal. It's a biological response. She's a beautiful woman paying a lot of atten-tion to you, and you haven't had sex in a really long time.*

But letting her wear my coat was as far as this could go.

CHAPTER 5

Sylvia

HENRY'S JACKET was thick and warm and smelled really good—not like fancy cologne or aftershave—but something earthy and wintry and masculine. I'd smelled the same scent last night, standing close to him in the winery. As I walked, I dipped my chin deeper inside the collar and inhaled deeply.

"What are you doing?" April asked.

"Nothing."

"Um, it looked to me like you were sniffing Henry's coat."

"What? That's ridiculous."

"Really? Because it *also* looked like something was going on between you two just now in the tasting room."

My stomach hollowed. "Like what?"

"I don't know. It seemed like I was interrupting something."

"That's even more ridiculous."

But was it?

Ever since Henry had walked me home last night, he'd been on my mind. Not in an obscene way or anything, just . . . there. I'd had such a nice time with him. I couldn't even remember the last time I'd talked so openly and easily with someone, let alone a man. Brett was a talker, of course, but it was always totally superficial. And if I tried to steer the conversation somewhere deeper and more meaningful, if I tried to hint at the fears I had that our marriage was coming apart at the seams, or ask him how he was feeling, he would just change the subject. After a while, he wouldn't even look me in the eye.

Henry had looked right at me. Listened to me. Made me feel heard and understood. Plus, he was smart and passionate about what he did, and he was *really* hot. I don't know how I hadn't noticed it before. He was like a cross between a rugged outdoorsman and a sexy professor, right at home in jeans and boots with dirt on his hands, but intelligent and articulate and sensitive too. I'd almost died when he told me to let the wine warm up on my tongue—it was probably an innocent, wine-industry kind of thing to say, but it made me hot all over.

I wondered what he thought of me. Did he find me attractive?

God, it was such a juvenile thought—*Do you like me? Check yes or no*—but I had to admit, part of me hoped he did, even if nothing could come of it. It had been a long time since I'd felt beautiful in a man's eyes.

"What's so ridiculous about it?" April challenged. "Henry is very handsome."

"He is," I agreed carefully.

"He's also a great guy. And you've both been through a lot."

"That's just it," I said. "It's way too soon to even think about . . . moving on. My divorce is barely final."

"Doesn't seem to be holding Brett back," April observed wryly. "And I'm not saying you need to *marry* Henry. Just get to know each other better, especially since you're moving here. Be his friend. There's no harm in that, is there?"

"No," I admitted.

"That's all I meant."

We walked up the steps of the front porch, and I thought of what Henry had said to me last night.

I can give in to a woman.

I shivered inside his coat. He hadn't said it salaciously or even flirtatiously, but something about the words themselves or maybe the quiet, serious way he'd delivered them had made my rusty, out-of-use core muscles clench up tight.

And April wasn't entirely imagining things, of course—there *had* been a moment there in the winery when I'd had this crazy feeling Henry might try to kiss me. What was even crazier was that I'd kind of hoped he would, even though I didn't think I was ready for it, and something told me he wasn't either.

But I'd wanted it.

Hell yes, I'd wanted it.

Inside the house, it was noisy and chaotic—everyone had arrived, the dining room table was laden with platters and bowls and chafing dishes, Christmas carols were playing on wireless speakers, a fire roared in the fireplace, five kids were running in circles, and everyone was in a good mood. It made me so happy to see Keaton and Whitney enjoying themselves, I didn't even care that their dinner would probably consist of cookies, chocolate, and candy canes. The adults poured drinks, filled plates, and sat around in the great room addition off the back of the house, eating and sipping and catching up. It felt so good to be surrounded by family again, it nearly put a lump in my throat.

Taking my plate over to the couch, I sat down and chatted with Meg and Noah about getting involved with a charity they loved, since I'd been on the board of several philanthropies in the past and had experience with fundraising and special events. At the bar, I spoke with Mack about the schools my kids would be attending, got the scoop on the administrators and teachers he liked and disliked. Back in the great room, I took a seat near my dad and asked him if he had ideas about neighborhoods to search for houses in, what the prices and taxes might be like, whether or not I should use an agent or do it on my own. Chloe asked if I had any time to help out in the tasting room next week, since the inn would be booked and she was short-staffed while employees were on vacation. I told her I'd be glad to.

My appetite was good, and I was back at the table for seconds of dessert when I heard a knock on the front door. My stomach jumped, and I quickly checked my sweater for spills and rubbed my lips together, hoping they still had a little color. Setting my plate aside, I went to answer it.

When I pulled the door open, I wasn't prepared for the way my body reacted. At the sight of Henry freshly scrubbed, hair neatly groomed, scruff trimmed, wearing a dark wool peacoat and holding a bottle of wine, my face warmed and my pulse zoomed.

"Hi," he said, his breath cloudy in the cold air.

"Hi. Come on in." I moved aside so he could come into the house and caught the scent of his cologne as he passed by. My dormant lady parts tightened. "Can I take your coat? I promise to give it back—along with your other one—when you go."

"Sure." He stomped the snow from his boots and handed me the bottle of wine. "That's for you."

"Thanks." Setting it on the hall table momentarily, I hung up his coat in the closet and turned to face him. He wore a thin charcoal-colored sweater over a navy dress shirt and dark jeans. "You look nice."

"Thanks. I figured I'd wear a shirt with no holes this time. Try not to look like a hungry college student." He looked at my angora sweater, skinny dress jeans, and high-heeled boots. "You look nice too."

"Thank you." Grabbing the bottle of wine he'd brought, I glanced toward the back of the house, where all the noise was coming from. "Ready?"

"Do I have a choice?"

Smiling, I took his arm. "No. But I'll stay with you, and I promise it's going to be fine. Come on."

If Henry was anxious walking into a room full of people, he didn't show it. Of course, it helped that the only people there were my family members and their significant others, and everyone knew not to ask about Renee or say anything that might make him feel uncomfortable. He seemed right at home hanging out with Mack, chatting with Oliver about progress at the distillery, laughing with Chloe about some obnoxious wine industry asshole who'd toured the vineyard and cellar last week and had all kinds of opinions on why Henry's preferred sorting method was a waste of time. And he gobbled three full plates of food like he hadn't had a decent meal in ages.

Later, he joined me, Chloe and Oliver, Mack and Frannie, and all five kids in a competitive game of Hedbanz, and I was surprised at how easily he interacted with both Mack's girls and my two children. He seemed to really enjoy playing the game and went out of his way to make them laugh. It made me wonder if he'd ever wanted kids.

After the game, while he talked with my dad about the upcoming growth season over cups of coffee laced with Irish whiskey and topped with cream, I helped my mother and April clean up the kitchen. By then, Mack and Frannie had taken their kids home, my kids had gone up to their bedrooms, and Meg and Noah had disappeared without even saying goodbye.

"They've probably banged like five times already," April whispered as we dumped leftovers into plastic containers.

I groaned. "Stop. It was torture watching them all night. They can barely keep their hands off each other."

"I know. And you should hear her stories about the sex." April shook her head. "It's insane. Like, *handcuffs* insane."

"I've heard some of them." I glanced at my mom to make sure she couldn't hear us. "I'm actually kind of jealous. I've never done anything like that. Have you?"

"Nope. Where do you even *find* guys like that—good guys who'll treat you right but have that alpha male attitude behind a closed door? Is it a law enforcement thing? Maybe I should start hanging around the fire station."

I shook my head. "I have no idea. I really don't. In my experience, it's been one or the other—or neither."

When the leftovers had been put away and the dishwasher started, April yawned and asked if it was okay for her to take off.

"Of course," my mother said. "I can handle the rest."

"I'll help you, Mom," I said. The only thing left to do was the serving pieces, which had to be done by hand. "I'll wash and you can dry."

"Thanks, honey."

We said goodnight to April and got started, the conversation in the family room carrying over the quiet hum of the dishwasher now that the music had been turned off. I heard Henry's deep voice and glanced over my shoulder. He was sitting on the couch opposite my father, leaning forward with his elbows on his knees, like he was listening really intently.

I smiled and turned back to the sink. "Henry's so into his vines. It's cute."

My mother glanced at me. "He is. Into his vines *and* cute."

I wondered if I'd gone too far, so I bit my lip instead of asking what I really wanted to know—what was his wife really like? Had their marriage been that bad? Why didn't they ever have kids?

My mother helped me out. "It's so nice to see him

enjoying himself," she said. "He's been so down the past few months."

"Well, divorce will do that."

"Yes. It was nice to see *you* enjoying yourself too. Did you have fun?"

"Yes," I said. "My favorite part was seeing the kids having a good time. They really get along well with Mack's girls."

"Mack's girls are darling."

"I hope Keaton makes a few guy friends here too."

"He will. As soon as school starts, I'm sure he'll have no trouble."

I scrubbed the bottom of a sauté pan. "I worry about him, not having a father around. I mean, I worry about both of them not having a father around. But then I remember what kind of man Brett turned out to be, and I think maybe it's better to have no male influence than *that*."

"They'll have plenty of healthy male influence around here," my mother assured me. "Your dad, Mack, Henry. Oliver and Noah are around a lot too."

I saw the opening and took it. "Henry does seem great with kids. I wonder why they never had any."

My mother was silent for a minute, and I figured maybe she didn't know. But after I handed her the pan for drying, she spoke up, a little quieter than before. "They tried for years," she said. "That was part of the problem. Renee had endometriosis, so they were hoping IVF would work, but it didn't."

"Oh no." Immediately, I understood their situation better. I, too, had struggled to get pregnant. After a couple years of being unsuccessful spontaneously, we'd turned to IVF and gotten lucky twice.

I knew how grueling the experience could be. And I knew the toll it could take on a woman's psyche, on her body, and on a marriage. I suddenly felt sorry for Henry's ex—I could empathize with her. I felt awful for Henry too.

"That's so hard," I said. "Is that why the marriage fell apart?"

"I never asked, but I think it had a lot to do with it." She took a platter from my hands and began drying it. "I only know what I know because Renee confided in me a little. I've never said a word to Henry about it."

"I won't either," I promised.

My mother changed the subject to tomorrow night's party, fretting about the endless to-do list she had. As we finished the washing and drying, I assured her I'd be around to help. "In the morning, just give me a list of things I can do. And don't worry, it's going to be a fantastic party. It always is."

As we were putting the dishes we'd washed into the cupboards, Chloe and Oliver came through the kitchen to say goodnight. After they'd gone, my mother wiped her brow and fanned her face. "Darn these hot flashes. I may need to go up to my room and put the fan on."

I smiled and grabbed the sponge to wipe down the counters. "Go ahead. I'll finish up."

"Thank you, dear." She poked her head into the family room and said goodnight before going upstairs, and a moment later, Henry and my dad came into the kitchen with empty cups.

"Well, I guess I'll head up to bed too." My father set his coffee mug in the sink and kissed my head. "The fire is almost out in there. Are you going to be up for a bit or should I take care of it?"

"I'll take care of it. Night, Daddy."

"See you, John," Henry said. "Thanks for everything."

My father gave us a wave and headed for the stairs, and then it was just Henry and me left in the kitchen. "Glad you came?" I asked him.

"Definitely." He came around the island and set his glass mug on the counter. "Everything was delicious. Thank you so much for coming to get me. I'd have gone home and eaten Fritos for dinner."

I grinned and shook my head. "How can you be so picky about wine and eat such terrible food?"

"Good question. Probably because I'm good at making wine but bad at making food."

I smiled, turning off the faucet. "Want a little more coffee? There's probably half a pot left."

He hesitated. "Are you going to have some?"

"Sure. Grab the whiskey from the bar, would you?"

While he retrieved the whiskey bottle, I poured us each a mug of coffee. He added a shot to each glass, and I spooned some of the leftover whipped cream on top. "There. Perfect."

"Do you want to sit down?" he asked, glancing down at my shoes. "You've been working in here for a while."

"Definitely. Let's go into the family room."

The fire was low but still crackled in the fireplace, giving the room a cozy glow. I took a seat at one end of the couch, and Henry settled at the other end.

Tugging off my boots, I tucked my legs beneath me. "Looks like it's still coming down out there," I said, glancing out the sliding glass doors toward the patio. "But I like having a white Christmas."

"Me too," he said, sipping his coffee. "You must have missed that in California."

"Well, we usually spent the holidays in Aspen if we didn't come here." I felt embarrassed saying it. It sounded so preten-tious to me now.

"That must have been nice."

"It was nice," I said, "but being home for the holidays is better."

He nodded, and I realized I had no idea where home was for him.

"Where did you grow up?" I asked, bringing my cup to my lips.

"On a farm in Iowa."

"Really?" For some reason, it made me smile, picturing him as an Iowa farm boy.

He looked amused. "Does that surprise you?"

"Kind of. And I don't know why it should—you're still *kind of* a farmer."

"Oh, I'm definitely still a farmer."

"Is your family still in Iowa?"

He sipped his coffee before answering. "No. My brothers are spread around the country—one in Indianapolis, one in Fargo, one in Seattle—and my parents are both gone. I've got some cousins there, but I don't see them too often."

"Does the farm where you grew up still exist?"

"It does, but my dad sold it, and it was incorporated into a large-scale operation."

"Why'd he sell it? I mean, why not give it to you?"

"I was still in college at the time, and I wasn't really interested in farming corn and soybeans anyway. Actually, I wasn't interested in farming at all. I thought I'd major in biology and go on to medical school."

Intrigued, I tilted my head. "What made you change your mind about medical school?"

"I took a viticulture class at Cornell and fell in love with it, much to my mother's dismay. I think she'd quite looked forward to bragging about her doctor son."

I grinned. "Any regrets?"

"None. What I do still involves a lot of science, and I much prefer wine to people. Well, *most* people."

"Me too. Sometimes I wonder if I was more tolerant of jerks when I was younger, or if there are simply more jerks around now." I sighed. "Or maybe I just attract them."

Henry smiled kindly. "I don't know about that."

"I'm telling you, Henry, I can't name one single person in my life—that I'm not related to—who supported me like I'd have supported a friend in my situation. And I *trusted* them. I thought they cared about me. I must be the world's worst judge of character." I shook my head. "Well, duh. Look who I married."

"Don't be so hard on yourself," Henry said quietly, the logs on the fire snapping softly. "You see the good in people. That's a nice quality."

"I guess. I feel so stupid, though." I set my mug on the end table and wrapped my arms around my knees. "Everyone knew Brett was cheating on me—even *I* knew it. But we all pretended we didn't."

"Why?"

"My so-called friends claim they didn't want to upset me. And why did *I* pretend?" I felt my throat catch and hoped I wouldn't embarrass myself by crying in front of Henry. I didn't even know why I was telling him this stuff, but something about the warmth of the fire, the late hour, and the silent house seemed to invite confession. "I guess I was scared. I didn't want him to leave me. I didn't want to be single with two kids at thirty-seven. I didn't want my kids to grow up in a broken home. So I pretended to be happy."

"That had to be really hard."

"It was." I hesitated before asking the next question, but some gut instinct told me to ask it. Maybe he wanted to confess too. "Did *you* pretend to be happy?"

Henry stared into his cup without saying anything. For a second, I was scared my gut had been off and it was too personal a question for him to answer. He'd told me last night he was a private person, hadn't he?

I backtracked. "I'm sorry, I didn't mean to pry into—"

"I'm not good at pretending," he said, interrupting me. "With me, what you see is what you get, and I won't lie. Maybe that was my problem."

I rested my chin on my knees. "How so?"

He tilted his coffee this way and that. "We couldn't have kids, and she wouldn't adopt. I wasn't going to tell her that was okay with me. I was angry at her for that. I wanted a family. We argued, and I'm sure I said things I shouldn't have."

"I'm sorry." I thought about telling him I understood because I'd faced infertility too, but decided against it. This wasn't about me.

He shrugged. "There were other issues too."

"Of course. Any marriage has its problems."

"But not being able to have kids really changed us, and it fractured the relationship beyond repair."

"Did you try counseling?" I asked.

He nodded slowly. "We did. But I think it was too late by then."

"Brett refused to try counseling, although I'm not sure it would have helped us either. His girlfriend was already pregnant—not that I knew it then."

Henry's jaw dropped, then he pressed his lips together and shook his head. "You deserve a lot better, Sylvia."

We were both silent for a moment.

"How long were you married?" I asked.

"Ten years."

"Do you miss her?"

Exhaling, he sat back, staring into the fireplace. "I don't know. I don't miss the fights or the tension. I guess I miss some things about being married, but I sure as hell wouldn't go back to the marriage I had, not the one I had in the end, anyway."

"Same," I said. "There are things I miss too, but I don't miss *him*. It's more like I miss the life I thought I had, if that makes any sense. Or the life I thought I *would* have. But can you miss something you never had in the first place?"

"I think you can." He looked down at his coffee again. "I know I do."

My throat tightened up. What was the right thing to say here? I didn't like it when people said, *Oh, you're still young and beautiful, you'll meet someone else,* because to me it was dismissive and insensitive, so I didn't want to say it to Henry. But I didn't want him to give up on his dreams of fatherhood either. He'd be such a great dad. "Have you thought about adopting a child on your own?"

"No. I don't even know if a single man *can* adopt, and I don't really want to be a single parent anyway." He looked up, his expression contrite. "Sorry—I know you're in that position right now."

"Not by choice, believe me. So I understand." I took a breath. "Sometimes I want to kick myself for feeling so complacent. I thought I had everything figured out, you know? I mean, by the time you get to this age, aren't you supposed to? And now . . . here I am starting over again."

Henry studied me for a moment. "I think it's really brave, what you're doing."

"Thanks, but I don't feel brave. I just feel . . . broken."

"You're not broken, Sylvia." His voice was firm.

"No?"

He slowly shook his head. "No."

My heart skipped a beat. I wanted to believe him. I wanted to thank him for listening to me and talking openly about himself. I wanted him to set his coffee cup down, move closer to me, put his hands in my hair.

Was he thinking about it too?

"I should go," he said, rising to his feet.

Reluctantly unfolding my legs, I stood up too. "Here, I'll take your cup."

He handed it to me, and our fingers touched, sending a hot little current buzzing up my arm, which then shot directly between my legs. Immediately—and I swear to God, I have never done this before—I looked at his crotch. His *crotch!* What the hell was wrong with me?

Quickly I turned around and headed for the kitchen.

"Thanks again for inviting me," he said, following behind.

"Thanks for coming." I set our cups in the sink, nervous to turn around and face him because he'd see how flushed I was. Had he seen me looking at his zipper? I tried to make my voice sound normal. "You'll be here tomorrow night, right?"

"I was planning on it."

"Good." Forcing a smile, I turned around and hoped my face wasn't as red as it felt. "Let me get your coat." I had to pass him in order to reach the front hall, but I was careful not to brush against him. I wasn't sure I could handle it.

From the closet, I pulled his wool peacoat from a hanger and while he put it on, I took out the Carhartt I'd borrowed earlier. "Thanks for lending this to me."

"No problem." He buttoned his coat. "Don't let me catch you outside without a coat again. You're not in California anymore."

I laughed nervously. "No."

He pulled his gloves from his pocket and slipped them on, then he took the Carhartt from me, folding it over one arm. "I'll see you tomorrow."

"Okay."

For a moment, we just stood there in the darkened hall-way. Facing each other. Nearly chest to chest. The house was silent, but my heart was pounding like a jackhammer. I held my breath. *Kiss me,* I thought heedlessly. *I don't care if I'm ready or not, I just want to be kissed by you tonight. Held by you. Desired by you.*

"Mom?" called a voice from the top of the stairs.

Henry and I sprang apart, although we hadn't even been touching.

I moved to the landing and peered up at Whitney, who looked like a ghost in her white nightgown in the dark. "I'll be up in a minute, Whit. Everything okay?"

"Yes. I just need some water."

"I'll bring you a glass. Go back to bed."

She disappeared down the hallway, and I turned around to find Henry pulling open the front door.

"Goodnight," he said, without looking back.

"Night." I stayed put on the landing.

Only once he'd pulled the door shut behind him could I breathe again. After making sure the door was locked, I leaned back against it.

Holy shit.

Holy. Shit.

If Whitney hadn't interrupted, would something have happened between Henry and me? Would we have kissed? Would we still be standing here in the dark, wrapped in an embrace?

I closed my eyes and imagined it. Chills swept over my skin. I placed a hand over my heart and felt it thumping hard. What would it be like to feel his beating against it?

Then I forced myself to stop being ridiculous, go get my daughter some water, and put myself to bed. It was late, and I was acting like a delusional teenager, not a responsible mother of two.

I could not have a crush on Henry. I could not kiss Henry. I shouldn't even allow myself to fantasize about it.

But I did.

All. Night. Long.

CHAPTER 6

Henry

I **GOT** out of bed early Tuesday morning and went right to the gym, thankful as hell it was open for a few hours on Christmas Eve.

I needed to let off some steam.

And not the angry kind of steam I was used to letting off during a workout, not the kind that made me want to punch things and kick things and make my muscles suffer to take my mind off a deeper kind of pain—no. This was something else entirely.

This steam was tension. This steam was need. This steam was born of an attraction to Sylvia so fierce I could feel it in my bones. All day yesterday at work and all throughout a second sleepless night, I'd thought of nothing but her and the chance I'd blown to touch her the night before. Kiss her. Take her in my arms and make her feel good again. Make her forget that her asshole ex ever existed, even if it was just for a little while. Make her feel brave and beautiful and sexy—all the things I saw when I looked at her.

But did she want me to?

There were moments when I was pretty sure she did—I could see it in her eyes, sense it in her body language. But then it was almost like she caught herself thinking something naughty and shut it down.

And maybe it was just wishful thinking on my part. Maybe she was just being nice, staying up late with me, talking to me, trusting me with her feelings. After all, she was still pretty messed up over her divorce. She flat out *told* me she felt broken. Even if she didn't appear at all that way to me, what kind of monster would I be if I took advantage of that?

In any other situation, I'd have made a move last night at the door. If she were anyone else. If the circumstances were different. Maybe even if it were a year from now, when our wounds weren't still so raw.

Because I didn't fully trust *my* motives either—sure, Sylvia was funny and sweet, she was a great listener, and I loved making her laugh, but I wasn't up all night imagining jokes I could tell her.

I was up thinking about all the things I wanted to *do* to her.

Delicious things.

Dirty things.

Things that a woman like Sylvia—classy and refined Sylvia—had probably never even imagined.

Was I just too hard up for sex to see straight? Maybe this whole thing was one-sided, and I'd earn myself a great big kick in the nuts if I tried something with her.

But I could think of nothing I'd like more for Christmas than to make her come while she screamed my name.

I moaned as I pulled my truck into a parking space at the gym, my cock rock hard in my pants. Now I'd have to sit here until it went away, and who knew how long that would take?

I forced myself to think of unsexy things. Mold on the vines. Insects. Hormone tracking devices measuring peak fertile days. When I was positive I could walk in without embarrassing myself, I got out of the truck.

I needed to fucking sweat.

"Henry! You made it!"

Later that evening, Daphne Sawyer kissed my cheek and took my coat. Her husband shook my hand, clapping me on the back. "I hope the drive wasn't too bad."

"Not too bad. Looks great in here." The lobby of the inn looked like an old Hollywood Christmas movie set—fire blazing in the huge stone fireplace, a massive evergreen in the corner decked out with so many lights and ornaments you could hardly see the branches, a hundred or so well-dressed people sitting in groups on the lobby couches and chairs, or standing in clusters near the tree, all holding a drink of some sort or balancing a plate of food on one hand.

"Thank you, darling." Daphne patted my lapel. "You look wonderful. Go get yourself a drink. Bar's open."

I was heading in that direction when I spotted Sylvia.

My knees went weak. She wore a deep red strapless dress that clung to her curves like an apple skin. The front of her hair was pulled back off her face, and the rest fell in loose waves around her shoulders. Her lips were painted to match her dress. Normally, I didn't like a lot of makeup, but I couldn't take my eyes off her mouth from across the room. God, the things I wanted to do to that mouth.

Whiskey. Whiskey would help.

Since the party was already in full swing, I was able to slip through the crowd without her seeing me. But along the way, I was stopped several times by party guests I hadn't seen since last year. Almost all of them asked me where Renee was, and their awkward *I'm sorrys*—or worse, the dead silences— when I told them we were now divorced were nearly enough to make me regret coming. Finally, I made it to the bar, where I ordered a High West Double Rye, neat. I was planning to take my drink and hide out in a dark corner for a while when I felt a tap on my shoulder.

"Hey, you."

I turned around, feeling like the wind had been knocked out of me. She looked like an angel—albeit one who might be tempted to do bad things with those ruby lips. "Hey," I said, my voice cracking. I cleared my throat.

Sylvia smiled seductively, her eyes traveling over my suit and tie. "You look fantastic."

"Thanks. So do you." But fantastic wasn't even close to how delectable she looked—I wanted to lick her like a candy cane—but I tried to tamp down the thought. "Can I get you something to drink?"

"Sure. I'd love a glass of wine. Maybe the sparkling white?"

"You got it." I ordered it for her, and when it arrived, she picked it up and tapped her glass against mine. "Merry Christmas, Henry."

"Merry Christmas." I took a sip of whiskey and watched her lift the wine to those sexy red lips. My dick stirred, fully prepared to deck her halls.

"So many people out there," she said, setting her glass down on the bar and sliding onto a stool.

"Yeah." I could smell her perfume. Jasmine. Almond. Cocoa. I nearly drooled. There were times having a sensitive nose didn't make life easy.

"I didn't even see you come in. My mom told me you were in here. Are you hiding out?"

"Kind of."

She toyed with the edge of a cocktail napkin. "Are people asking about Renee?"

I nodded and took another drink. "What about you? People asking about Brett?"

"Yes." She sighed. "But we were expecting it, right?"

"Right. How are the kids doing?"

"Pretty good, although they tried to call their dad earlier, and he didn't answer and never returned their call. I think they were bummed about that."

I drank again. It wasn't fair that a fucking asshole like that got to have kids when he didn't deserve them. And they were great kids too. Polite and friendly and good-natured, especially considering what they'd been through. It was a testament to Sylvia's parenting that they were so well-adjusted.

"Anyway," she went on, waving a hand in the air, "I don't want to talk about that. But I did want to tell you that I had such a nice time last night, and I hope I didn't talk your ear off."

"Not at all." I studied her hands for a moment, imagining those pale, graceful fingers wrapped around my cock.

"It's been so long since I've had a heart-to-heart with a friend."

Knock it off, asshole. She's talking to you. She's calling you her friend.

I forced myself to look her in the eye. "Same here."

She wrinkled her nose. "I might have gone a little overboard with the sharing."

"If you did, I did."

She shook her head. "You didn't at all. I was glad you told me those things. I mean, I'm so sorry you went through them, but I'm grateful you trusted me enough to talk about them. It made me feel less alone, like I'm not the only one still making mistakes and tripping on the path to wherever it is I'm going."

I swallowed more whiskey. "You're definitely not the only one."

"Good. Any time you want to talk again, I'm here."

I could think of plenty of things I'd rather do than talk with her, but I kept my mouth shut.

"So what are your plans for this week?" she asked brightly. "Since the inn and winery are closed, you've got time off, right?"

I nodded. "More or less."

"What will you do? Go visit family?"

"No, I'm not planning any travel. I've got some projects around the house I've been putting off, but I'll also probably come into work."

"Work!" She looked at me like I was nuts.

"There are things that have to be done or checked every day, and I gave my assistant the entire week off, so . . ." I shrugged. "I need to do them."

"Do you want help?" she asked, sitting up straighter in her seat. "Maybe you could teach me . . . some more things. I've always wanted to learn more about the winemaking at Cloverleigh, and I really enjoyed the lesson on tasting the other night. Plus I told Chloe I'd fill in while she's short-staffed in the tasting room next week. I'd be happy to come in and assist you during the next few days—if you need the help, I mean."

What I *needed* was for her to get out of my head, and spending more time with her—especially without other people around—wasn't going to help whatsoever. But she looked so eager, I couldn't bring myself to say no. "Uh, sure."

Her face lit up. "Great! I'm excited. And it will be such a good distraction for me too."

Distraction? How about the way she was crossing her legs toward me? Or the way her thick dark lashes framed those light blue eyes? Or the way her bare shoulders seemed to shimmer a little in the bar's low light? My skin felt hot beneath my suit. My shirt felt too tight on my chest, and the crotch of my pants was definitely snug.

I downed the rest of my drink and set the empty glass on the bar. "Could I have another?" I asked the bartender, loosening the knot in my tie.

Sylvia laughed. "Is it the prospect of spending more time with me?"

That actually made me crack half a smile. "You have no idea."

Sylvia and I pretty much hid out in the bar all night. Occasionally one of us would get up—I'd bring back a plate of food for us, she'd check on the kids—but mostly we just stayed on those two stools at the end of the bar, drinking whiskey and wine, pretending we were the only two people in the room, maybe even in the world.

We talked a lot about the vineyard, the upcoming season, what happens at the winery during the winter, but also about vineyards she'd visited in California and Europe. We'd been to some of the same ones in northern France, and I told her about how I'd adapted some of the techniques I'd learned from working the harvest there. She listened attentively and asked intelligent questions, and I knew she'd learn quickly.

"Did you ever think about going into the wine industry after college?" I asked her.

"Not back then." She swirled the wine in her glass. "I was going to be a photojournalist."

"Really?"

"I wanted to travel the world and tell stories with pictures," she announced grandly, making a sweeping gesture with her hand.

I sipped my whiskey. "What happened?"

She sighed. "I got married. Had a family. I don't regret it, because my kids are the best thing that ever happened to me, but I do sometimes miss that feeling of being creative."

"Do you still take pictures?"

"Not too much anymore. Nothing artistic anyway. Mostly I took them for social media, so I could continue fooling everyone into thinking my life was perfect." She shook her head. "So stupid."

I'd seen her photos on social media, and they *had* made her life look impossibly perfect. But still, she had an eye for beauty. "You should get back into it. Even if it's just to be creative."

She smiled and laughed softly. "Thanks. Maybe I will."

The hours flew by, and the more I talked to her, the more attracted I was to her. But Sylvia wasn't the type to openly flirt, and I was careful to keep my words clean, even though my thoughts drifted. Her leg brushed against mine once or twice, which nearly made me lose my cool, but overall, there was nothing suggestive about either our conversation or our body language.

So when the party wound down and the bar was closing up, I was more than a little surprised when she asked if I'd like to come back to her house for one last drink.

"Don't you have to put the kids to bed?" I asked.

"Yes, but then I have to wait for them to go to sleep, so I can play Santa." She stifled a yawn. "If I can stay awake."

"Ah. So my job is to make sure you don't fall asleep?"

"Exactly. And to carry the heavy boxes in from the garage." She laughed, squeezing my bicep through my suit coat. "I need those muscles. I don't have any."

"You're going to get some, remember?" I said, growing hot under the collar at her touch. "You're going to the gym."

"That's right." She nodded defiantly. "Getting stronger is New Year's resolution number one."

"What's number two?" I asked.

She thought for a second. "Find a way to be happy on my own. But I think they're related, you know? I'm going to need strength—physical and emotional, to start over."

I nodded slowly. "That's true."

"What about you?" she asked, getting to her feet. "Have you thought of any resolutions yet?"

"I'm not much for that stuff."

"Well, I am. And I have one for you." She lifted her chin.

"Oh yeah?"

"Yes. You should look into adoption as a single dad."

"I think you've had too much wine." I got to my feet and adjusted my tie.

She laughed. "That's entirely possible. Come on, it's almost midnight. Let's get the kids and sneak out of here."

While Sylvia was putting her kids to bed, her parents came in. I was a little embarrassed to be standing there alone in the kitchen.

"Sylvia asked for help playing Santa," I explained. "She's getting the kids settled."

"I don't blame her," said Daphne softly, pulling off her heels. "I wish I could stay up and play Santa again, but I'm plum worn out. Plus I want to get up early and make waffles for everyone. That's what I always did Christmas morning for our kids."

"I don't mind staying," I said.

"Can I pour you a drink?" asked John. But he looked just as exhausted as his wife.

"No, thanks. I'm fine."

"In that case, I'll head up too," he said, yawning loudly. "Those parties are fun, but boy, they're a lot of work."

"It was a great party," I said. "Thanks again for inviting me."

"Merry Christmas, dear," Daphne said on her way out of the kitchen. "If you're not busy tomorrow, come for waffles."

When I was alone again, I wandered into the family room. It was silent and dark, lit only by the Christmas tree in the corner. I switched on a lamp and went over to the built-in shelves lining the fireplace wall to study the framed photographs.

There was a wedding portrait of Mr. and Mrs. Sawyer and one of Mack and Frannie as well. Baby pictures of Keaton and Whitney. Graduation photos of all five Sawyer sisters. In addition, there were more informal pictures taken around the farm—three little blond girls swimming in the creek during the summer, a gap-toothed Chloe grinning down from a perch in a tree, April swinging tiny Frannie around by the hands with the vineyard in the background.

I heard a noise behind me and turned to see Sylvia coming into the room, still wearing her dress and heels, carrying two glasses of amber liquid. "Hey," I said quietly, wishing more than anything I could reach out, put my hands on her hips, and pull her flush against me.

"Hey." She smiled. "I'm glad you're still here. Sorry it took so long—the kids made me recite *The Night Before Christmas* like I used to do when they were tiny."

"You can recite it from memory?"

She shrugged. "One of my hidden talents. Here. I poured us a little scotch from my dad's secret stash in the library. Don't tell on me."

I laughed, taking the glass from her. "Thanks. And speaking of talent." I gestured toward the photos. "Did you take these?"

She glanced at them. "Yes. A long time ago."

"They're beautiful, Sylvia. You have a gift."

"Thank you." She sipped her scotch. "I was thinking of maybe talking to my parents about taking some photos for the website and social media. Do you know who runs those accounts?"

"At one point, I think Frannie, but after she left to start the pastry shop, I think social media has sort of been neglected. Talk to Chloe—I bet she'd know."

"I will. There has to be *some* way to make myself useful around here, right? I'm just not good at too many things."

She said it as a joke, but I got the feeling there was something serious in her words too. "Sylvia, you're good at a lot of things."

"Like what?"

"You're an amazing mom. You're a talented photographer. You're a fast learner. You're good with social media. You're good with social anything—and you can talk to anyone."

She shrugged it off, like it was nothing. "Talking to people isn't that hard."

"Are you kidding? It is hard, and you make it look easy. The other night I overheard Noah telling Meg to make sure you get on the board of his Veterans and service dog charity because he's positive you can talk people into writing big fat checks."

She giggled and sipped her scotch again. "I *am* pretty good at that."

"See?" I elbowed her gently. "So don't sell yourself short. You've got a lot to offer."

"I'm looking forward to working in the winery," she said. "I'd love to be good at that. I know I'm not qualified to replace Chloe as the manager, but maybe in the future . . ."

"I can easily see that in your future. Your life here is just getting started, Sylvia. You can do anything you want."

She looked up at me, and my blood rushed faster. My arm was still touching hers. I dropped my eyes to those sweet cherry-red lips and imagined the taste of scotch on them.

Her chin lifted slightly. I inclined my head and heard her quick inhale.

Then I came to my senses and lifted my glass, finishing my drink in a couple quick swallows. "Should we get started?"

"Oh. Yes. Good idea." She seemed a little flustered as she set her glass aside.

Removing my coat, I draped it over one arm of the couch before following her through the kitchen and out to the garage. Together we brought in more than a dozen presents, already wrapped and labeled for her children from Santa Claus.

"What's the big one?" I asked, pointing at a large rectangular box designated for Keaton.

"A telescope," she said. "Keaton has been dying for one. He's into astronomy. I think it's the whole Star Wars thing."

"Hey, if Star Wars gets kids into astronomy, that's pretty fucking cool."

"I'm just hoping I can figure out how to set it up. I'm not too mechanically inclined, and neither is my dad, no matter what he tells you."

I laughed. "I'd be glad to help. Just let me know."

When everything was arranged beneath the tree, we stood side by side, looking at it all.

It reminded me of my childhood, of coming downstairs and seeing the piles of gifts for my brothers and me—not as many, of course, and not as beautifully wrapped, but evidence that Santa was real and that I'd been good enough to deserve presents from him. We'd rip them open all at once, and the living room would be a chaotic mess of shredded paper and ribbon, but even my fastidious mom wouldn't care. She and my dad would sit on the couch with their coffee and act surprised by every gift we opened, asking to look at it more closely, saying of course it was okay if we played with it now. Then they'd go into the kitchen and make breakfast together—she'd scramble the eggs and fry the bacon and he'd make hash browns from scratch. Best Christmas mornings ever. I fucking wanted that feeling back, and only family could deliver it. How the hell had Sylvia's husband thrown it away?

For a moment, I allowed myself a little fantasy—Sylvia was *my* wife, we were in *our* home, and we were up late playing Santa for *our* children.

This is what it would be like, I thought, coming in from the party in our formal clothes, quickly and quietly getting the gifts under the tree, laughing a little because we were tipsy and it was Christmas and we had everything we could ever want. And when we were done, we'd go upstairs and I'd unzip that red dress and she'd unbutton my shirt and we'd make love even though it was late and we were tired and we'd be up at the crack of dawn tomorrow to watch our kids open their presents in wide-eyed delight. Maybe her hair would be a mess and she'd have mascara under her eyes, but I'd look at her and know I was married to the sexiest, most amazing woman in the world.

I saw it way too clearly. That was *fucked up*. What was in that expensive scotch, anyway?

Next to me, Sylvia sighed. "I don't even know for sure if they still believe in Santa Claus, but I'm not about to ruin it for them. They've had enough taken away from them this year."

"Yeah."

"Hey. Everything okay?" Sylvia tugged on my sleeve.

"Yeah."

"What are you thinking about?"

I faced her. Spoke quietly but firmly. "What a good mother you are. How lucky your kids are to have you."

She looked down at her feet. "I don't know about that."

"I do." I put my fingers under her chin and tilted her head up. "I know a lot of things."

"Like what?" she whispered.

"I know your husband was the luckiest son of a bitch in the world. I know you're the most beautiful woman I've ever met. And I know I should leave right now, before I do something stupid."

Her lips opened. She sucked in her breath, her chest rising. "Like what?"

"Like this." Sliding both hands into her hair, I crushed my mouth to hers. It was not the first kiss I'd imagined the other night in the winery—a sweet and gentle tasting of one another, a tentative meeting of wine-drenched tongues. This was a hot, searing, scotch-fueled, red-dress kiss that ate up all the oxygen in the room. My lips opened wide and slanted over hers, my tongue lashing between them. My body curved above hers, my heart thundering in my chest. Her spine bowed slightly, and I felt her breasts pressing against me. Her hands moved up my sides and around my back—then she shocked me by sliding her palms down over my ass and pulling me tighter to her. My dick was getting harder by the second, and she moaned slightly as she felt it pushing against her pelvic bone.

If there had been any doubt in my mind that she'd wanted this too, it was gone now—but did that make it right?

God, this was so fucking *unfair*.

I wanted to be the good guy for her, the patient gentleman, the anti-asshole. But I also really, really liked the feeling of her hair in my fingers and her tongue in my mouth and her hands grabbing my ass. It had been so long since someone wanted me this way—for no reason other than raw, unfiltered desire—and it felt so fucking good.

My mouth traveled across her cheek and down her neck. I inhaled the scent of her perfume and wished I could swim in it. Stroking her throat with my tongue, I reached down and hitched up her dress, bringing one of her legs up to my hip, gripping her thigh with my fingers.

"Henry," she whispered. "I—"

But whatever she was going to say next was swallowed up by the loud chime of a clock on the mantle.

We jumped apart.

CHAPTER 7

Sylvia

"OH MY GOD." I placed a hand over my racing heart, my lungs working overtime. "That scared me!"

"Me too." Henry grabbed the knot of his necktie and loosened it. "God, Sylvia. I'm so sorry. That won't happen again."

Wait—he was *sorry*?

Before I knew what to say, he was grabbing his suit jacket from the couch and shrugging it on. "Fuck. I left my overcoat at the party."

"I can go back with you to get it," I offered, although my legs felt so wobbly I wasn't sure I'd make it.

"No." He put a hand out, as if to stop me from coming closer to him. "You stay here. I'll go back and get it."

"Okay." I twisted my fingers together at my waist. My insides were all tangled up. "Can I at least walk you out?"

"I'm good. I know my way." Clearly wishing to keep his distance—and for me to keep mine—he gave me a wave and headed for the front hall, where a door would lead him down the private corridor to the inn's executive offices.

I heard it open and close softly.

He was gone before I could even say goodbye. Or tell him not to be sorry. Or beg him to kiss me again.

What the hell?

Left standing there alone on trembling legs, I wrapped one arm around my jittery stomach and placed one hand over my mouth. A minute ago, Henry's lips had been on mine. His hands had been on my skin. The hard length of his dick had been trapped between the heat of our bodies.

And I'd loved every second of it.

My God, how long had it been since I'd been kissed like that? Touched like that? Wanted like that? Because there was no doubt in my mind that Henry had wanted me—I'd felt it. I wished I could have felt *more* of it.

I glared at the mantel. *Fucking asshole clock.*

Lowering myself gingerly onto the couch, I took a few minutes to catch my breath. As my pulse slowed, my senses returned.

Maybe it was for the best that we'd been interrupted. After all, it's not like we could have taken it much farther. Were we going to take our clothes off in front of the Christmas tree? At my *parents'* house? With my *children* asleep upstairs?

No. Of course we weren't. And that was a good thing.

Because as intoxicating as it had felt to be thoroughly ravished by Henry tonight, I wasn't ready for more. And given the way he'd hustled out of here tonight, muttering apologetic words—*that won't happen again*—he wasn't either.

But damn.

The man could kiss.

Christmas morning, the kids woke me up before eight, bubbling over with excitement because they'd peeked downstairs and it was clear that Santa knew they'd moved to

Cloverleigh Farms—there were all kinds of presents under the tree for them. Even if they no longer believed, they faked it convincingly and enthusiastically, maybe even just for me. But it made me happy.

Shoving my feet into fuzzy slippers, I threw on a robe and followed them downstairs, inhaling the smell of coffee brewing. My parents were in the kitchen, my mother mixing up waffle batter and my dad slicing bananas for a fruit salad. There was a fire going in the fireplace, and Bing Crosby crooned "White Christmas" over the speakers.

"Morning," I chirped, reaching into the cupboard for a coffee cup.

"Morning, dear." My mom smiled at me. "How'd you sleep?"

"Great," I lied. In truth, I'd lain awake for hours reliving that kiss—and the things Henry had said to me right before it. But I didn't feel groggy or anything. In fact, I felt pretty damn good. He'd told me I was the most beautiful woman he'd ever seen. Even if it wasn't true, I'd loved hearing the words from his lips.

My dad came over and mussed my hair. "It's so good to have you guys here on Christmas morning. It's been a while since we've had kids in the house."

"It's good to be here, Daddy." I kissed his cheek and poured myself some coffee, wondering what Henry was doing this morning. It made me feel sad to think of him all alone, especially since I knew now that he wanted children. His first Christmas on his own, without even a wife for company, was going to be hard, wasn't it?

The thought stayed with me as we drank coffee, watched the kids open presents, stuffed ourselves with waffles and eggs and bacon and fruit salad, and cleaned up piles of bows, boxes, and torn wrapping paper. But I wasn't sure what to do about it—call him? Invite him over? I didn't even have his number. And I had the feeling that even if I did, he'd refuse to come. He'd say he didn't want to intrude on family time.

Could I convince him he wouldn't be an intrusion? Would he even want to come here? Maybe he just wanted to be left alone. Maybe it would just be awkward to be in the same room together today, after what we'd done last night. The thought made me sad—I didn't want things to be awkward between us. Henry was the closest thing I had to a good friend here. I liked and respected him. He made me laugh. We understood each other.

Had the kiss ruined everything?

When the mess was cleaned up, I went upstairs, showered, and got dressed. Mack was due over with the girls around two, and my dad had promised to take everyone out in the new antique sleigh. We'd had plenty of snow overnight, and the whole farm looked magical, like something inside a snow globe.

Once I was dressed, I told Keaton and Whitney to get upstairs and do the same, then told my mom I was going for a walk.

"Want company?" she asked from the couch, where she was relaxing with another cup of coffee and a new paperback I'd gotten her.

"No, that's okay. I won't be long—just need to burn off some calories before Christmas dinner." It was partly the truth, but I also wanted to see if Henry's truck was in the lot.

"Sounds good. Bundle up," she admonished, ever the mom.

"I will." After pulling on all my winter gear, I left the house and wandered down the brick path again, as I had the other night. But this time, Henry's truck wasn't there.

I was both happy and sad—it was good that he wasn't so miserable at home alone that he'd come into work on Christmas Day, but I also wanted to see him. I walked back home and asked my dad, who was helping Keaton unpack his telescope, if I could borrow his car.

"Sure, honey. Keys are on a hook in the mudroom. Be careful—the roads are still slippery."

"Thanks, I will." I ruffled Keaton's hair. "I won't be long."

"Okay," he said. "Can we call Dad when you get back? I want to tell him what I got."

"You can call him whenever you want, buddy. But remember the time difference—it's only about eight A.M. there right now. He might not be up yet."

"Okay."

Praying Brett wouldn't ignore a call from his children on Christmas morning—but not putting it past him—I grabbed my dad's car keys off the hook near the back door and headed out to the garage.

While the car warmed up, I called April.

"Hey," she said after the first ring. "Merry Christmas."

"Merry Christmas."

"Did Santa come?"

"He did. The kids are happy."

"I didn't even see you before I left last night. Did you sneak off to get the presents under the tree?"

"No, actually, I was in the bar most of the night talking to Henry. And then he walked back to the house with me and helped me get the gifts out after the kids went to bed."

"Aha. *Interesting.*"

"It wasn't like that," I scolded, although actually, it was exactly like that.

"I'm only teasing. You know I adore Henry and think you two should be friends."

"Yeah." I bit my lip. "Speaking of that, you don't happen to know his address, do you?"

"I probably have it somewhere. Hold on."

I waited, trying to think up a good reason why I'd need

his address right now and coming up short. Maybe I'd get lucky and she wouldn't ask.

Nope.

Right after she recited it, she asked, "What do you need his address for?"

Sighing, I decided to be honest—or close to it. "Because I feel weird about something that happened last night, and I think he might too. And I don't really want to deal with it over the phone, not that I even have his number."

April was silent for a moment. "What happened last night?"

I hesitated.

"Sylvia, you cannot do this to me. What *happened*?"

"Okay, okay." I took a breath. "He kissed me. We kissed."

Her gasp was audible. "You said it wasn't like that! And wait, those are two different things. He kissed you? Or you simultaneously kissed each other?"

"What difference does it make?"

"You're not seriously asking me that, are you? It's a huge difference! Who made the move?"

"He did."

April squealed so loud I had to hold the phone away from my ear. "Details!"

"There aren't that many. We were standing in the dark next to the tree, and he said something really sweet, and then the next thing I knew, he kissed me."

"Did you kiss him back?"

"Um, yes. *Very* enthusiastically. I'm actually a little embarrassed at how enthusiastically I kissed him back."

"Why?"

"Because I totally grabbed his ass."

Another squeal, possibly louder than the first. "So what happened after that?"

I closed my eyes and shook my head. "Grandma Sawyer's clock on the mantel went off and scared the shit out of us."

"No!"

"Yep. We jumped apart, he apologized, and then he practically bolted out the door."

"God, it's like Cinderella! The clock struck midnight, and the spell was broken."

"Pretty much."

"So what are you going to say to him today?"

"I don't even know exactly what yet—I just feel like something needs to be said. I don't want things to be awkward between us. We've gotten to know each other so much better over the last few days, and I really do want to be friends."

"And there's no chance you could be more?"

"No way. Not right now. I have so many other things I need to focus on—finding a house, a job, getting the kids settled . . . and the thought of starting up a relationship again absolutely terrifies me. Not just with Henry, with *anyone*."

She sighed. "I get it."

"I agree he is a great guy, and very attractive, and *such* a good kisser, but I need to keep my head on straight and my feet on the ground."

"God, you're so mature and responsible. Anyone else would be like, 'Give me all the hot rebound sex right now!'"

Laughing, I put the car in drive. "Yeah, that is not my style. But I better go. I have to be back by noon."

"Okay. I'll see you at Mack and Frannie's for dinner."

"Bring wine. And wish me luck!"

Fifteen minutes later, I found Henry's house without a problem and pulled into his driveway. For a moment I sat in the car and looked at his house—a brick ranch with an attached garage, black shutters, and a bay window in the front. I wondered about the first time he and his ex had pulled up in front of it. Was it their dream house? Had they imagined the rest of their lives here? Did Henry plan to stay here by himself? If so, would he eventually remarry and try again to have a family? Or would he change his mind and maybe attempt to adopt?

It's none of your business, Sylvia. You've got your own life to put back together—Henry isn't your next good cause. He's a grown man, and when he's ready to move on, he will. Just go in there and make sure he knows you're still his friend.

Turning off the engine, I got out of the car and hurried onto the front porch. After a deep breath, I knocked a few times on the thick wooden front door, which was painted black to match the shutters.

Henry pulled it open, looking rugged, rumpled, and sexy in jeans and a black T-shirt with a hole in the sleeve. His feet were bare and his hair was damp, like he'd just gotten dressed after a shower. His expression told me he was surprised to see me. "Sylvia. Hi."

"Hi. Can I come in?"

"Of course." He swung the door open wide, and I stepped into the front hall. Right away I could smell coffee brewing and the scent of burning wood.

I glanced around. To my left was an office, and to my right was the dining room. Straight ahead appeared to be a family room, where a fire was lit in the fireplace. From what I could see, the house had oak floors throughout, so I took off my snowy boots and left them on a rug that said WELCOME.

Henry shut the door behind me and messed with his hair a little. "I'll take your coat—glad to see you're actually wearing one."

I laughed and shrugged it off. "Thanks."

After hanging up my jacket in the front hall closet, he turned to me. "Can I get you something? Coffee or tea?"

"Coffee sounds good." I followed him back into the family

room, which opened onto a kitchen and breakfast nook on one side, and possibly the master bedroom on the other. "I like your house. It's got a nice open feel."

"Thanks." He went into the kitchen and took a white mug with the green Cloverleigh Farms logo on it from the cupboard. "We did some pretty extensive renovations when we bought it."

I glanced around. "No Christmas tree, huh?"

"I decided not to bother this year. I'm really not home that much anyway." He poured me a cup of coffee from the pot. "I'm sorry, I don't have cream, but would you like sugar?"

"Just a little, thanks."

"Go ahead and sit down. I'll bring it to you."

I wandered over to the dark brown leather sectional and lowered myself at one end, facing the fireplace. Looking around, Henry's house seemed just like him—the decor was rustic in a masculine way, but beautiful too, with touches here and there suggesting he liked the occasional luxury. On the coffee table in front of me were several oversized hardcover books on wine. The mantel was made from what might have been reclaimed wood, and upon it were a few black and white photographs, a pair of wrought-iron candlesticks, a stack of old books, and a small plant. Actually, there were several plants around the room. The wall to my left was all wooden shelves—his television was mounted in the middle, and the rest were filled with books, framed photos, and what looked like mementos from his travels.

I wanted to study them all and ask about them—where had he gotten that old map? What place in the world did he love best? Did he like vineyards more than beaches? Did he like upscale hotels in the city or small cabins in the mountains? Was he an ocean or lake person? Did he prefer snow skiing or water skiing? If he had all the money in the world, would he still live here and do what he did?

On the other end of the couch was a chunky double-knit

throw blanket in a soft camel color, and I wondered if someone had made it for him. For a moment, I let myself imagine the two of us on a wintry afternoon like this one, wrapped up in it and each other, right here on the couch. I missed that feeling of just being close to someone, that effortless, easy affection. Would I ever feel that again?

A moment later, Henry came over with two cups of coffee and handed one to me. "Here you go. Let me know if you'd like it sweeter."

"I'm sure it's fine." I sipped it, scorched my tongue, and suffered silently, totally unsure how to start this conversation. I was having trouble focusing on why I'd come here—all I could think about was his body pressed close to mine in the dark. "So you're probably wondering why I'm here."

He lowered himself onto the opposite end of the couch, as far away from me as possible. "I've got a pretty good idea."

I took another scalding sip. "I thought maybe we should talk about what happened last night."

His expression was something between a frown and a grimace. "I'm sorry about that. It was totally out of line."

"Henry, it wasn't."

"Yes, it was, and I've been kicking myself for it ever since I left your house."

"Please don't." I set my coffee cup on the table in front of me and scooted closer to him. I put a hand on his arm—his skin was warm. "It's okay. You don't need to be sorry. I'm not."

"You're not?"

"No." I sat back. "Do you know how long it's been since someone kissed me that way?"

He shook his head, almost looking frightened to know the answer.

"A *really* long time. And it felt good. So good I didn't want it to end." For a split second, I almost thought he was going to smile.

"I still shouldn't have done it." The frown was unyielding. "I work for your family. You're going through a rough time. I don't know what I want."

"Because it's too soon to know that, Henry." I sat back, placing my hands in my lap. "You and I, we're still healing. And that's okay. But for me, part of that healing process means learning to feel good in my skin again. You made me feel beautiful and sexy and *desirable*."

"You are all of those things," he said quickly.

I smiled, warmth humming beneath my skin. "You are too."

He gave me a look like he was in pain. "Jesus Christ, Sylvia. You shouldn't say that stuff to me."

"Why not?"

"Because it puts ideas in my head."

"Ideas aren't going to hurt us. And I trust you to behave."

"Maybe you shouldn't do that either."

"I can't help it." I smiled, in spite of everything. "You know I tend to trust everyone. And if you turn out to be a giant asshole, I'll be mad. But my heart is telling me you are *not* that guy."

He took a deep breath and exhaled slowly, messing his hair. "I'm not that guy. I just . . . lost control temporarily. But like I said, it won't happen again."

"But we can still be friends, right?"

"I guess so." He didn't look entirely sure.

"I hope so, Henry." I leaned forward again, placing my hand on his leg this time. "Because I could use a friend like you."

His eyes were on my hand. "Okay, but you *really* have to stop touching me."

I laughed and took my hand off him. "I can do that."

"And don't wear that red dress around me again."

"Deal."

"And maybe not that perfume either." He inhaled a shuddering breath. "It smells too fucking good."

I held up both hands, palms toward him. "I will keep my hands to myself, wear only rags, and stick to unscented soap. Does that work?" But my toes were tingling—he liked my dress! He liked my perfume! He was tempted when I touched him!

I felt like the girl who gets the note back to find the "yes" box was checked—he liked me!

"Could you wear a bag over your head too?" he asked.

I laughed. "You know, *you* don't make it easy, either."

"I don't?"

I shook my head. "No, you are too handsome and too smart, and every time you do something like give me your coat or tell me I'm beautiful, it makes me melt."

"That's why I want you to wear the bag. If I can't *see* how beautiful you are, maybe I'll forget."

Heat crept into my cheeks as I smiled at him. "You did it again."

"I'd say I was sorry, but you know I'm not much of a liar."

"I know." I moved back to my end of the couch and picked up my coffee, which was now cool enough to drink. "I like that about you—your honesty. I've heard enough lies to last my entire life."

He sipped his coffee too, and I figured maybe now was a good time to move forward. Try to get to a place of normalcy, a place where we could converse without feeling nervous or awkward.

"Thanks again for helping me with the gifts last night," I said. "The kids were thrilled this morning."

"I was glad to help. Did Keaton like his telescope?"

I nodded. "He's all excited to set it up."

"And how about Whitney? What was her favorite gift?"

"Probably the ridiculously expensive eye shadow palette. I'm a little scared about her appearance at Christmas dinner."

He chuckled. "You're going to Mack's house?"

"Yes. Are you?" I asked, excited by the prospect.

"No. I'm going to another friend's house."

"Oh." I tried not to feel too disappointed. Of course he had other friends. "Mack is bringing the girls over to take a ride in the new sleigh this afternoon. You should come."

"Thanks, but I've got some things to do."

"I doubt any of your things are as fun as a ride in a horse-drawn sleigh with hot chocolate afterward. Maybe even a snowball fight in between."

He grinned. "I do like a good snowball fight."

"Well, you're invited, if you change your mind."

"Thanks," he said, but I knew in my gut he wouldn't come.

I looked down at my mug, rubbing the handle with my thumb. "You know, I wanted to tell you . . . I know what it's like to go through fertility treatments. I couldn't get pregnant either."

"I'm sorry."

I offered him a sad smile. "Thanks. I feel very grateful that IVF worked for me. I never did get an answer as to why I can't get pregnant—just stubborn, defiant eggs, I guess. Anyway, I didn't mention it the other night because I felt bad. I didn't want you to think I was comparing my situation to yours. Obviously, I got lucky, and—"

"You don't have to feel guilty, Sylvia. I'm happy for you. I'm sorry you had to go through what you did, because I know how hard it is, but there's no reason for you to feel bad that you have two perfect kids. I would never begrudge anyone a family just because I don't have one."

God, he was such a good guy. It really sucked that his wife had given up on the marriage. I was trying not to be judgmental—after all, I didn't have her side of things—but it was hard not to wonder how she could let a guy like Henry go.

Again I wondered if he'd like to get remarried someday, try again to have a family.

But it was really none of my business.

I took one last sip and set my mug down. "I should probably get back. Thanks for the coffee, and for the talk. I was feeling really bad about the way we left things last night."

"I was too." He stood up. "I'm glad you came by."

Rising to my feet, I nearly put a hand on his shoulder, but then I remembered—no touching. I quickly shoved my hands beneath my armpits. "Near rule infraction. Sorry. This might take some getting used to."

He laughed, following me to the front door. "Just don't wear the red dress again, and we'll be fine."

I tugged on my boots. "I shall banish it from my wardrobe forever."

"Good." He took my coat from the closet and held it out; I slipped my arms inside and zipped it up.

When I faced him again, he looked much more relaxed than he had when I'd arrived—maybe not totally at ease, but at least less tense. "Are we okay?" I asked softly.

"We're okay."

"Good." I grinned. "I'd hug you goodbye, but—"

"Don't you fucking dare." He moved around me and opened the door. "Now get out of here before I throw you out."

"I'm going, I'm going." But when I was halfway out, I looked at him over my shoulder. "Merry Christmas."

"Merry Christmas. Give my best to your family."

"I will. Bye."

"Bye."

I hurried to my dad's Cadillac and started it up, waving to him one last time as I backed out of the driveway.

By the time I got home fifteen minutes later, I felt both relieved and slightly let down, which I realized was totally unfair. I should be glad he hadn't tried anything, right? The whole point of going over there had been to reassure him we were still friends while firmly establishing the safe boundaries of that relationship.

We couldn't kiss again. We couldn't touch each other. I wasn't allowed to wear the red dress, and he wasn't allowed to call me beautiful. If we stayed inside those lines, eventually the burgeoning desire we felt for one another would ease up, right?

Of course it would. It had to. Last night had just been emotional for both of us—our first Christmas Eve alone—and we'd sought solace in each other.

But I had to admit there *was* a part of me that had been hoping we'd take one look at each other today and pick up right where we'd left off last night. It would have been reckless and wrong and irresponsible, but that little part of me was definitely alive and feisty and kicking at its cage.

After all this time, it would have felt good to set it free.

CHAPTER 8

Henry

I SHUT the door behind Sylvia and went back to the couch, where I'd been lying around feeling sorry for myself one minute and hating myself the next.

I still couldn't believe what I'd done last night.

Actually, that's not true—I could totally believe it. I'd been thinking about kissing her since she walked into the winery the other night. But how had I lost control that way? Was I a fucking animal?

Maybe I could blame Santa. If it wasn't for him, I wouldn't have been there so late at night, I wouldn't have fantasized about being married to her, I wouldn't have given in to that compulsion to know what it felt like to touch her, to pretend she was mine just for a moment.

But she wasn't mine—that was as much a fantasy as Kris Kringle.

Crossing my arms over my chest, I tried to decide if I felt better or worse now that she'd been here. Better, I guessed. It was nice to hear that not only was she not angry, she'd actually enjoyed that kiss. I'd made her feel sexy and beautiful, which—unbelievably—no one had made her feel in a long time.

But I felt frustrated too. I wanted more, and I couldn't have it.

My phone vibrated on the coffee table, and when I checked it, I saw it was my older brother, Anthony, calling from Indiana. He was probably just calling to say Merry Christmas and thank me for the gifts I'd sent—or at least his wife was. Alison had begged me to come celebrate Christmas with them and their four kids this year, but I'd told her I couldn't leave work for that long. My two younger brothers, also both married with kids, had invited me to come visit them for the holidays as well, but I'd given them the same excuse. It wasn't a total lie, but beneath the excuse was a disinclination to spend the holidays envying my brothers their happy families. Maybe it was shitty and selfish, but I just couldn't handle it right now. Next year would be different.

I hoped.

Feeling guilty, I answered the call from Anthony and talked to both him and Alison, thanking them for the gifts they'd sent and listening to the kids holler with excitement over their new toys in the background. I reached out to my other brothers, Mark and Kevin, and repeated the conversation two more times—expressing gratitude for their gifts, wishing them and their families Merry Christmas, assuring them I was fine and had plans to hang out with friends later. Alison asked if I was seeing anyone, and I said no. When she started in about how young I was and how I needed to get back out there, I cut her off by saying I wasn't ready, although now that Sylvia was in the picture, that wasn't exactly true.

While I was on the phone with Kevin, Mack texted and reminded me I was invited to come to their house for Christmas dinner, but again, I responded that I had other plans. Sitting across the table from Sylvia would not be helpful today.

And anyway, it wasn't a lie—a while back, I'd accepted an invitation from my friend Lucas Fournier, another winemaker in the area, to have Christmas dinner with his family. Lucas and his wife Mia ran Abelard Vineyards, a winery on Old Mission Peninsula, and he and I shared a lot of the same views on small-scale, responsible farming, and adapting old world techniques in new environments. His family owned a winery in southern France, and we'd met when I'd gone there one summer to work the harvest. In fact, he was the one who'd told me about the job opening at Cloverleigh Farms. Over the years, he and I had gotten to be pretty good friends, and Renee and I used to socialize quite a bit with them . . . until Renee could no longer handle being around their three kids.

Part of me wanted to cancel and spend the rest of Christmas Day drinking scotch, eating the chocolate-covered potato chips Mark's kids had sent me from Fargo, and watching old Jimmy Stewart movies, but I liked Lucas and Mia. I hadn't seen them in a while, and I'd always felt I owed him a debt of gratitude for recommending me to John Sawyer. Plus, lying around the house wasn't going to put me in a better mood, and going into work was out of the question. What if Sylvia saw my truck and came looking for me?

She trusted me to behave, and I'd said I would.

But it wasn't going to be easy.

"Hi, Henry! Merry Christmas!" Mia Fournier kissed both my cheeks before giving me a hug. She was short and slender, with shoulder-length brown hair and a bright, welcoming smile.

"Merry Christmas." I handed her a bottle of wine and a box of chocolate-covered cherries.

"Mmmm, thank you," she said, shutting the huge oak

door of their impressive home behind me. Their winery was similar to Cloverleigh Farms in that they grew many of the same grapes we did, held weddings and other events on the premises, and had an excellent reputation, but it was a little smaller and much different in style. While Cloverleigh retained the feeling of an American farm, Abelard was built in the image of a French château, a nod to Lucas's heritage and their history—they'd actually met in France. Their house, with its steeply pitched roofline, limestone facade, and corner turrets, would have fit perfectly in the French countryside.

Two kids—a boy and a girl—went racing by, shouting at the top of their lungs, followed by a boy several years younger, who clearly struggled to keep up with his big brother and sister. In fact, he tripped and fell flat on his face. But without missing a beat, the kid picked himself up and took off running again, making me laugh.

Mia sighed. "I'd make them all come back and greet you, but I don't have the energy to yell. They got up *so early* to open presents this morning and have been going like that ever since."

I squelched the pang of envy. "I bet."

"Come on in." She motioned for me to follow her. "Lucas is in the kitchen. We have some other people coming for dinner, but they're not here quite yet. I think you'll know them—my friends Coco and Nick Lupo and their kids; my assistant Skylar Pryce, her husband Sebastian and their kids."

"Sure, I know them. Sebastian Pryce is my lawyer, actually."

"Oh, is he?" Mia smiled at me over her shoulder. "Such a great guy."

"He is."

"My friend Coco is actually interviewing at Cloverleigh Farms after the holidays," Mia added.

"Oh, really? For what position?"

"Apparently, April is looking for some help with event

planning. Coco and I used to run an event planning business in Detroit together, and she took it over and ran it on her own before they moved up here. She's a total pro. She's only looking for part-time work, but when Chloe called and asked if I knew anyone, I thought of her right away."

"Sounds perfect," I said as we entered the kitchen, a large airy space full of natural stone and wood.

Lucas stood at the marble-topped island chopping carrots, but when he saw me, he put down the knife and came forward to shake my hand. "Hey, stranger. How are you?"

"Good."

"Thanks for coming. Can I get you something to drink? Beer? Glass of wine? Cocktail?" Lucas spoke perfect English, but still retained the slight accent of someone who'd grown up speaking two languages.

"Wine's good."

Mia reached for the knife. "Why don't you guys open a bottle, pour me a glass, and go sit in the library? I can handle things in here for a bit."

Lucas looked at me and wrapped an arm around his wife, getting her in a headlock. "She's trying to get rid of me. I'm probably not chopping the carrots to her precise specifications."

"Stop it," Mia protested, laughing and swatting at his arm. "I'm not trying to get rid of you. I just know you guys haven't seen each other in a while."

Lucas kissed the top of her head and let her go. "Thanks, love." To me, he said, "I've got a bottle of Burgundy I've been dying to open."

"Perfect," I said, tamping down another jolt of jealousy at the easy affection Lucas enjoyed with his wife. Had Renee and I ever had that? If so, I couldn't remember.

In the library, Lucas and I sat in leather chairs drinking Burgundy and discussing last season's harvest and what we thought we might see this winter.

Eventually, the other guests arrived, and we moved into the kitchen, everyone pitching in with the meal preparations, and then into the dining room, turning the kitchen over to the kids for eating.

Coco and Nick had four kids—three dark-haired, dark-eyed, school-age boys and one tiny, doe-eyed girl still unsteady on her feet. She stumbled once on the stone floor, and Nick picked her up and hugged her close, drying her tears.

Skylar and Sebastian had twins, a boy and a girl, that I guessed were around three. Add the Fourniers' three children to the mix, and the picnic-style table in the kitchen was pure chaos. One parent or another was always getting up from the dining room table to go cut someone's meat or wipe up a spill or put an end to an argument. Still, I envied that too. It was hard not to notice I was the only single, childless person at the adult table. At least nobody asked about Renee.

After dinner, the grownups sat around in the large great room with coffee and dessert while the kids played games on the floor near the Christmas tree. Around eight, the other two families packed up and said goodnight, but Lucas asked me to stick around. "Just let me help get the monkeys in bed, and I'll be right back down. Make yourself at home."

"No hurry," I said, watching him leave the room with his son on his back. Mia had already taken the other two upstairs.

While he was gone, I tortured myself by scrolling through social media on my phone, looking at everyone's joyful Christmas morning photos. It made me feel worse, of course, so I put away my phone and wondered if I should make up an excuse and leave. I was so sick of feeling like the odd man out everywhere I went—even the fucking internet.

But just as I was about to stand up, Lucas returned with a bottle in one hand and two glasses in the other. "Done," he said. "So how about some scotch?"

"Sounds good."

He poured and handed one glass to me. "I'm glad you came tonight. I wasn't sure you would."

I shrugged, tilting my scotch this way and that, watching the legs of the amber liquid coat the glass. "I thought about canceling. But I didn't want to be an asshole."

"Since when?"

I gave his grinning face the finger.

"Seriously," he went on. "Mia and I are glad you're here. You've been such a hermit lately."

"Yeah, well . . . I've been busy at work."

"Really? Or are you just working yourself into the ground to avoid dealing with your issues?"

I gave him an irritated look. Lucas had been a psychology major and had taught college psych for a few years. Sometimes he fell back into the habit of analyzing people.

"Look, you can tell me to fuck off, but if you want to talk or whatever, I'm here."

Instead of responding, I took another sip of my scotch.

"Is that '*fuck off, Lucas*'?

I managed a wry smile. "It's close."

"Okay, fine. If you tell me you're okay, I'll believe you and leave you the hell alone."

"I'm telling you, I'm okay. It's taking some effort to come to terms with everything, but with time and scotch and porn, I'm getting there."

He laughed and tipped up his glass. "Maybe you need to get laid."

"You're fucking telling me."

"So go get laid."

"It's not that easy."

He gave me a look of disbelief. "It's not? I mean, it's been a while since I've been out there, but I can't imagine *you* would have trouble."

"Maybe not if I just wanted to fuck the next willing woman." I stared into my glass. "But I don't."

Lucas was quiet a moment. "Is there someone you have in mind who's . . . *not* willing?"

"It's complicated."

He crossed an ankle over his knee. "Complicated is my favorite word. Go on."

I took another sip, debating the wisdom of talking about Sylvia with Lucas. On one hand, it felt dangerous—like I was making my attraction to her more real or giving it more strength by speaking of it. On the other, Lucas was a good friend, he was smart about this stuff, and it might feel good to just say shit out loud. "It's Sylvia Sawyer."

"Ah." Lucas took a drink. "Remind me. John's oldest daughter, right? Married? Lives in California?"

"Right. She *was* married, for fifteen years. She's recently divorced and is moving back here with her two kids. Her husband was a real dickhead. Left her for someone else, who's already pregnant."

"Fuck, that is shitty. She must have been devastated."

"Yeah." I finished what was in my glass. "She was really hurt, and coming home again is part of her effort to start over. I never knew her all that well before, but since she got home, we've been talking kind of a lot."

"You guys probably have a lot to talk about." Lucas reached for the bottle of scotch and poured me a couple more fingers.

"We do. That's part of the problem. She's really easy to talk to, and I find myself telling her things I don't tell anybody. Talking about my marriage and the breakup and how I *feel*." I shook my head. "She's been home less than a week. It's fucking ridiculous."

"It's not ridiculous. You're comfortable with her, because you know she understands. You're going through a similar—and difficult—life experience."

"But it's not just that." I leaned forward, elbows on my knees. "She's so damn beautiful. And sweet. And vulnerable.

I always thought she was nice, but now I can't stop thinking about her in ways that are . . . *not* nice. They are not nice at all. They're downright filthy."

Lucas chuckled. "It's okay. You're entitled to your own dirty thoughts."

"Yeah, except last night I did more than just think."

He paused. "What did you do?"

"I kissed her."

"Against her will?"

"No. It wasn't like that. But it was kind of . . . sudden. And even though we both wanted it, we know it's too soon. She said she's still healing, and she knows I am as well."

"She sounds very smart and self-aware."

"She is." I frowned. "But it's not her self-awareness I want to fuck."

Lucas laughed, and I set my glass on the coffee table to bury my face in my hands. "God, I'm such an asshole. Tell me to leave this poor woman alone."

"I can, but I don't think you need me to. You're not an asshole, Henry. You're a guy who's been really unhappy for a long time, and you're lonely and angry and frustrated, but you're not an asshole. You'd never do anything to hurt her."

"I know, but . . ." I sat back again in defeat. "It just really sucks that assholes like her ex-husband get everything handed to them—the perfect wife, awesome kids, dream life —and they can just abandon it and start again. It's so easy for them."

"Because they're narcissists. And they don't care about anyone but themselves. She deserves better, Henry."

"Yeah." I grabbed my glass and took a drink.

"But she also deserves the time she needs to figure out who she is now and what she wants—and so do you. I think it's smart to go slow in this situation. Be cautious. Maybe don't put yourself in situations where you're going to be tempted to do what you did last night."

"Yeah." I rubbed my chin. "She wants to work in the winery. She asked me to teach her."

Without saying anything, Lucas leaned over and poured a little more scotch in my glass. "Fortitude, my friend."

I lifted my glass. "Here's hoping I have some."

CHAPTER 9

Sylvia

"SO? WHAT HAPPENED?" As soon as she got her coat off, April cornered me in Mack and Frannie's living room, dropping down next to me on the couch.

"We talked," I said, glancing around to make sure no one else could hear us. It seemed like we were safe. Our parents were helping Mack and Frannie with dinner, and the kids had been charged with setting the table. Chloe was at Oliver's parents' place, and Meg was at Noah's mom's house.

"I'm going to need more details, please."

I lifted my shoulders. "He kept trying to apologize, but I told him it wasn't necessary. He said it wouldn't happen again, and I agreed that would be best. He stayed on his end of the couch, and I stayed on mine."

"That's it?" April looked a little disappointed. "Huh. I brought wine for nothing."

"Well, what were you expecting to happen?"

"Honestly? More ass-grabbing."

"I have to admit, I thought about it. I haven't felt very desirable in the last year or so. And now all of a sudden to have someone telling me I'm beautiful and sexy and he *wants* me . . . it's messing with my head. It feels so good to hear those things, I just want *more*. It's like a drug." I shrugged. "Maybe he feels that way too."

"Do you think it's just a surface-level attraction kind of thing?"

"Who knows?" I tossed my hands in the air. "I really like him. He's gorgeous and sensitive and smart, and the physical attraction is definitely strong. But I haven't even been here a week. And we agreed that it's not worth ruining what could be a nice friendship—not to mention that he works for our family. He feels totally weird about that, and I don't blame him."

April sighed. "Yeah. Me neither."

"Plus, he said something else that I keep thinking about." I played with the end of my loose French braid.

"What?"

"He said he doesn't know what he wants. To me, that means he recognizes that whatever we're feeling could just be a temporary physical thing and he might never want more than that." I shook my head. "I can't risk that. I can't put myself in a situation where I might develop feelings for someone, and then it turns out he doesn't want me that way. I just went through it, and it tore me apart."

April put a hand on my leg. "Be right back. Grabbing that wine."

I smiled, though I suddenly felt like crying. "Okay."

While she was in the kitchen, I wondered where Henry was tonight, if he was thinking about me. Would he come into work tomorrow? Would it be wise to stay away if he did? Or would we be perfectly fine, now that we'd gotten that kiss out of the way and openly discussed how we felt about it?

When April came back, I decided to ask her.

"I need some advice," I said, after she handed me a glass of something cold and white.

"I don't know if I'm the right person to ask, but I'll try." April settled next to me again.

"I'd like to learn more about the winemaking at Cloverleigh, maybe start working on a regular basis in the winery, and Henry agreed to sort of take me on as a student."

"Okay." April took a sip of wine.

"It would mean spending time together, sometimes alone. Do you think it's a bad idea? Should I just ask Chloe to train me if she can find the time?"

"Do you want the truth?"

"Please."

"I think you should be careful." She reached out and touched my wrist. "But only because I can see that you're really confused and torn about your feelings for him. And I know how lonely he's been. It's easy to sense the chemistry between you two, and I just feel like it would be really hard to toe the just-friends line if you had to spend all kinds of time alone together."

"It would be," I admitted.

"I know I encouraged you the other night to get to know him, and if I'm honest, I'd sort of hoped something might develop over time, but I didn't think it would happen so fast." She smiled. "I thought maybe you'd be more like Meg and Noah—what did it take them, fifteen years?"

I laughed a little. "Yeah, it definitely makes sense to be just friends first."

"And I'm not saying that you shouldn't learn everything you can from him—he's brilliant at what he does, and I'm sure he'd be a great teacher. But training under Chloe would probably be safer." She shrugged. "Maybe let a little time go by before spending time alone with Henry? A couple weeks? Let the flames die down a bit?"

"It was just a kiss," I said defensively. "There weren't exactly flames."

She tossed me a knowing look. "You don't grab a guy's ass while he's kissing you if you don't want to know what kind of heat he's packing, that's all I'm saying."

Now she had me laughing again. "There was some serious heat," I confessed.

"See?" She clucked her tongue. "Damn that old clock."

"It was probably a sign," I said with a sigh. "It was Grandma Sawyer telling me our timing is all wrong."

"Listen, if Grandma Sawyer can send us messages about our love lives from beyond the grave, I'm taking that clock home and asking it some questions."

"Like what?" Curious, I took a sip of wine. It reminded me of the riesling Henry and I had tasted the other night, and set butterflies loose in my belly.

"Like where is my soul mate and why is he avoiding me?"

"April, you're not even looking for your soul mate. You spend all your time at work—you're as bad as Henry."

"I know." She looked into her wine. "But I'm going to make some changes in the new year. I promised myself."

"Me too." I put a hand on her leg. "We can promise *each other* and keep ourselves accountable."

She nodded, her expression going surprisingly serious. After a moment, she said, "It'll be eighteen years soon."

I was shocked. April never brought up her past. "I know," I said softly. "Do you want to talk about it?"

She shook her head. "No."

While I was wondering if now was finally the time to insist she unpack what she'd gone through all those years ago, Frannie called everyone to the table. Before I could even remind April that I was here if she ever wanted to talk, she jumped off the couch and headed for the dining room.

Slowly, I rose to my feet and followed her, thinking that no matter how well you knew a person, you could never really know the depth of what they were feeling.

Everyone was so good at hiding things.

I took April's advice and stayed away from the winery for the next three days. It wasn't easy, especially because I saw Henry's truck in the lot every single one of those days from morning until night, but I told myself April was right. Why torture Henry or myself by spending time alone together? Maybe if we gave this thing a chance to cool down, it would.

I used the time to contact a real estate agent my mom recommended, discuss with her what I was looking for in a home and what my budget was, and upon receiving her list of available properties, drove by them all with my dad. Many I was able to cross off my list right away, but there were several I was interested in going through. I asked my agent to schedule appointments for the following week, after January first.

I also spoke with the realtor who had the listing for the Santa Barbara house, who said she'd put up the sign and had many interested clients already. Would it be okay to start showing it?

I said of course, hung up, and took my kids to a movie to prevent myself from curling up in a ball on my bed and crying over the thought of strangers traipsing through what had been my dream home, trampling over all my happy memories—as if Brett hadn't trampled them enough.

The kids had finally reached him on Christmas Day, and thankfully, the asshole had had the heart to spend time talking to both of them. Whitney was actually smiling when they hung up. "He said we can go to Aspen next week," she told me excitedly. "Without Kimmy—just the three of us!"

"That would be fun," I said, wondering how he had talked Kimmy into that.

Turns out, he hadn't.

On Saturday afternoon, the day before the kids were scheduled to fly out and stay with him for the last half of the break, he texted me.

Brett: Call me. Need to talk.

The last thing I wanted to do was talk to him, but in case it was something related to the kids' visit, I called back—from the privacy of my bedroom, in case I had to swear.

Which I did.

"Yes?" I said when he picked up.

"Listen, there's been a change in plans. The kids can't come here tomorrow."

My blood iced over, and then boiled. "Why not?"

"Because Kimmy is having a difficult pregnancy and she needs peace and quiet."

"So leave her alone while you take the kids to Aspen like you fucking promised."

"I can't leave her alone—she's pregnant, and she doesn't want to be alone."

"Do I need to remind you of all the times you traveled for work when *I* was pregnant?" I seethed.

"Look, I'm trying to be better this time. Do things differently."

I had *all* kinds of things to say about that, but I let it go. "So bring her along. She needs to learn to get along with your children."

"I suggested that, but she feels it would be too much. The last time Whitney was here, she was very disrespectful to Kimmy."

I snorted. "Says who? *Kimmy*?"

"Yes."

"Well, tough. Whitney's your daughter, Brett. If she's being needlessly disrespectful, discipline her."

"Look, Sylvia," he said in that arrogant, know-it-all tone that drove me nuts, "the kids need to stay with you for the rest of their break. That's all there is to it."

I inhaled through my nose and exhaled through my mouth, trying to gain control of my anger and not lose my shit that he was telling me how it was—again.

"Fine with me. So tell them," I said coolly. "Call Whitney's cell phone right now."

"Yeah, well, the thing is, I was kind of hoping you would tell them. I'm actually at work right now, and—"

I burst out laughing, but it wasn't funny. "You're fucking crazy. I'm not telling them."

"Sylvia, this isn't the time to be vengeful."

"Oh, I'm not vengeful," I told him, although my hands shook with fury. "I don't give a shit what happens to you, good or bad. But I'm not doing you any favors. You don't want them to come tomorrow, you tell them that. I'm not crushing their feelings as a favor to you. No fucking way."

"You know, I didn't have to let you take them out of the state," he spat. "I didn't fight you on anything so it would make this easier on you. Can't you do this one thing for me?"

"Gee, let me think—no. *Fuck no.* You're on your own, Brett. Just like you wanted." I hung up, threw my phone on my bed, and put my head in my hands. My entire body was trembling with rage. I wanted to vomit. I wanted to kick him in the balls. I wanted to scream so loud, he'd hear it. I wanted to crawl into my bed, hide beneath the covers, and not come out.

But I couldn't.

Even if Brett told the kids himself, I was the one here. I was the one who'd have to pick up the pieces of their broken hearts. I was the one who'd have to console them and make sure they knew they were loved and cherished and wanted.

I sank down onto my bed, wishing someone could please fucking do that for me.

An hour later, I was still lying on my bed when I got another text.

Brett: I told them. Maybe you should check on Whitney. She seemed upset.

"She seemed upset?" I yelled at my phone. "Of course she did, you dipshit asshole!"

Hating him all over again, I changed his name to Dipshit Asshole in my Contacts, got off my bed, and went to her bedroom door.

"Whit?" I knocked twice. "Can I come in?"

"Why?"

I swallowed hard. "I want to talk."

"Fine."

Slowly, I turned the knob and pushed the door open, entering the room. Whitney lay on the bed on her side, facing away from me, but I could tell she was crying.

"Did you talk to your dad?"

"Yes. He doesn't want us to visit. After he promised we could go skiing."

Shutting the door behind me, I went over and sat on the edge of the bed. "I know. He hasn't been awesome about keeping his promises, has he?"

"He doesn't love us anymore."

"Of course he does." I brushed her blond hair off her forehead.

"I hate him," she said, crying harder.

I leaned over, pressing my lips to her temple. "It's okay to feel angry, sweetheart. All the things you feel are okay."

"He cares more about *her* than he does about us. And now he'll care more about that *baby*," she sobbed. "He doesn't even want us anymore."

"No, honey. That's not true." Even if it felt true.

She rolled away from me and sat up, wiping her nose with the back of her hand. "It *is* true, Mom! And I hate him for it! And I hate that I still love him and miss him! I don't want to."

It was taking all my strength not to break down and cry too, but I wanted to be a rock for my daughter—one solid thing she could depend on. "I'm sorry, honey."

"No, you're not. You don't even care that he left," she wept. "You're not even sad."

"Of course I'm sad, Whitney. Why would you say that?"

"You don't even cry!" She jumped off the other side of the bed and faced me, mascara-streaked tears streaming down her face. "You act like it doesn't even matter that he left us! And you must have done something to make him want to go, because why else would he do it?"

I closed my eyes, willing myself to be strong and remember she was just a child, a hurt, scared child, whose world had been turned upside down. Everything she thought she'd known for certain was in question now. She didn't feel safe, and she needed someone to blame. Her dad wasn't here, but I was.

"I did cry, Whitney." I opened my eyes and looked at my daughter. "For a while, I cried every night. And I still cry sometimes. But I make sure never to let you hear me, because I don't want you to think I'm not okay, or that things won't be okay again. Because they will."

"How?" she cried, wiping her cheeks with both hands. "I feel like I'm just supposed to accept this new life with no dad, when I didn't get a say in it!"

I nodded, swallowing hard. "I get it. And I'm sorry. I wish things were different, honey. But they're not. And the truth is, I didn't do anything to make your dad leave. I know you're looking for something to point to, some reason he did what he did, some way to make it make sense, but . . . I can't really make sense of it either. I didn't want this, but I have to accept it and get through it just like you guys do."

She hurled herself back onto the bed and wailed into her pillow, but she didn't protest when I lay down beside her and rubbed her back. There was something to be said for a good stress relief cry. A few tears slipped silently down my cheeks too.

Eventually, her sobs quieted, and then stopped.

"We were really unhappy, Whitney," I said softly. "So unhappy that we couldn't go on like that."

"I know."

"It has nothing to do with how much we love you. Even though your dad is being selfish right now, he does love you."

She sniffled and turned her head toward me, speaking over her shoulder. "He's being an asshole. You can say it in front of me."

I had to laugh. "He's being an asshole."

She was silent a moment. "I'm sorry I said those things. I just get so mad sometimes."

"It's okay." Sitting up, I smoothed her hair back, my throat tight. "When we're angry, sometimes we say things we don't mean to people we love, and they forgive us."

"Do you forgive me?" She rolled to her back and looked up at me with tearful blue eyes that mirrored mine.

"Always. And I will always be here for you."

"Promise?"

"I promise."

"Should we go tell Keaton?" she asked, her face growing concerned. "He's going to be really upset."

My heart swelled with love for her. "Let's do it together. And then let's think of something fun to do tonight, okay?"

"Okay."

My baby sister came to the rescue. When I called Frannie and told her what happened, hoping she might bring the girls over as a distraction, she offered to have my kids at her house for a sleepover.

"Are you sure?" I asked. "Both of them?"

"Yeah, why not? We've got the room—Whit can sleep with Millie, Winnie can bunk in with Felicity for the night, and Keaton can have Winnie's room. Plus, it's movie night tonight, and Mack got to choose, so it'll be something Star Wars for sure. Doesn't Keaton love Star Wars?"

"He's obsessed," I told her. "You're the *best*. Should I feed them?"

"Nope, we're ordering in. Just bring them over any time."

The kids were excited about the sleepover and packed their bags right away. I was dismayed to see that Whitney came downstairs with a fresh application of makeup on, but I didn't say anything. Maybe she was trying to cover up the fact that she'd been crying.

I dropped them off around six, giving Frannie an extra-long hug at the door before I left.

"You okay?" she said, looking at me anxiously.

"Me? I'm fine," I told her, although it wasn't entirely the truth. "It's the kids I'm worried about. Did you see Whitney's face?"

She glanced over her shoulder toward the noise. "I wondered about that."

"I assume it's some kind of armor. Maybe she feels like it protects her or something. Or it makes her feel tough." I grimaced. "Hopefully she doesn't ask to give Mack's girls a makeover."

Frannie waved a hand in the air. "It's just makeup. I'm not worried."

"I am." I shook my head, fighting tears. "I feel like I don't know what I'm doing. Like the decisions I'm making right now are going to affect my kids forever. One minute I'm confident about them, and the next I'm doubting everything. Was it right to move them here? I don't know. Should I take the makeup away from Whitney? I don't know. Should I play nicer with Brett so he doesn't take it out on the kids to spite me? I don't know. I'm a fucking mess, Frannie."

"You're not. You're just worn out." She squeezed my arm. "Take the night off from being Mom and do some things for you. Drink wine in the tub. Read a romance novel. Watch porn."

That actually made me laugh. "I have never watched porn in my life."

"Maybe you should." Her eyes lit up. "Or play with toys —the adult kind."

"I don't own any."

She shook her head. "Jeez, I thought *I* was sheltered. Now I know what to get you for your birthday."

"Goodnight, Frannie." I turned around and headed out. Snow was just starting to fall, heavy and thick. "Thanks again. I'll pick them up in the morning."

"No rush!" she called. "Drive carefully. I think we're getting hit hard tonight. Like eight or nine inches."

I spun around and walked backward a few feet. "Maybe *you're* getting hit hard with nine inches tonight—I'm getting nothing!"

She burst out laughing. "Enjoy your evening anyway!"

When I got home, the house was empty. My parents had gone to have dinner with Oliver's mom and dad, who were old friends of theirs, and wouldn't be back until late. I puttered around the house, looking for things to do, but the kitchen was clean and the family room picked up and my mother liked to leave the Christmas decorations up at least through New Year's Eve.

If the inn had been open, I might have wandered down to the bar for a glass of wine, but it was closed until Monday to give the staff some time off. I thought about calling April, but then I remembered she was having dinner with a high school friend who was in town for the holidays. Chloe and Oliver were also at his parents' house, and Meg was surely with Noah tonight.

I thought about running a bath and relaxing in the tub with a book, but I felt too antsy. I didn't really want to sit still. I didn't really want time to think.

Laundry, I thought, getting pitifully excited at the idea of a Saturday night spent sorting and washing and folding. At least it would keep my hands busy. I grabbed a basket from the laundry room and brought it upstairs, collecting my dirty clothes before heading into Whitney's room. She was fairly neat, like I was, and everything that needed to be washed was piled on a chair in the corner.

Keaton was a different story. His clothes were tossed all over the room. I was gathering them up when I noticed a bunch of crumbs on his unmade bed. Frowning, I lifted up his pillow, but nothing was hidden there. Kneeling on the floor, I bent down and checked under the bed. Nothing there either. When I stood up again, I pulled open the nightstand drawer —and found a pile of chocolate candy, a stash of Christmas cookies, and a ton of empty wrappers.

My anger at Brett flared all over again. This was all his fault and I had no idea how to deal with it. I didn't want to have to deal with it. I didn't want to spend another Saturday evening feeling like a terrible mother. I didn't want to be living at my parents' house at my age. I didn't want to be alone tonight.

I wonder what Henry is doing.

Stop it, I told myself immediately. *It doesn't matter what he's doing.*

But what if he was still at work? If he was, would it be okay to go say hello? It had been three days. That was enough cooling time, right? Surely by now, we could have a conversation without being tempted to do stupid things. And that was all I needed—a conversation. Someone to talk to. Something to take my mind off things. Someone to reassure me I existed outside the realm of all my problems, to lift me out of this pit and make me forget.

Make me feel good. Make me feel beautiful. Make me feel sexy and desirable and feminine and alive.

Without giving myself any more time to think about it, I threw the laundry basket aside, raced downstairs, and put on my coat and boots. *Maybe his truck won't even be there,* I thought as I hurried away from the house. The snow was thick beneath my feet. *Maybe he's already home for the night because of the blizzard. Maybe he's even out with those other friends. It is Saturday night. Not everyone is sitting at home being lonely and miserable.* I followed the path toward the winery, but I could see before I got too far that the parking lot was empty, covered in a pristine layer of white.

I stopped walking. My shoulders sagged, and my heart ached. Any hope I had of salvaging this evening was gone.

Or was it?

Turning around, a plan began to take shape in my mind. A wicked, reckless, irresponsible plan.

But I was none of those things. I was a good person. I could always be counted on to make the right decisions. I put others before myself. I was not the sort of person who went around acting on foolish impulses for the wrong reasons. And what I was thinking of doing was very, very foolish—more foolish than eight mimosas at Breakfast with Santa. It was greedy too. And it came with a much greater risk.

But once the idea was in my head, I couldn't stop myself.

CHAPTER 10

Henry

WHEN I HEARD THE KNOCK, my gut told me it was her.

For the last three days, I'd been expecting her at the winery with a mixture of dread and anticipation. Each night, I'd come home feeling grateful that she hadn't shown up and yet still wishing she had. Because even though I knew nothing could happen, I liked being around her. I missed talking to her. I missed her face. I missed the way it felt to do nice things for a woman I was attracted to.

I was trying to do what Lucas had said, give both Sylvia and I some breathing room, but I hadn't stopped thinking of her for a minute.

My heartbeat quickened as I switched off the television and walked from the couch to the front door, my mind a jumble of questions. If it *was* Sylvia, what did it mean that she was knocking at my door at nine o'clock on a Saturday night? Did she still want to be just friends? If I invited her in, could I be trusted to keep my hands to myself? It seemed like a bad sign that I wasn't sure.

I unlocked the door and pulled it open.

"Hi," she said breathlessly. She wore a long wool coat

buttoned all the way up, and her legs were bare below the knee. On her feet she wore high heels, the same ones she'd worn on Christmas Eve. Her hair was done like it had been on Christmas Eve too, and she was wearing the perfume—the one I'd told her never to wear around me. Snowflakes clung to her coat and hair.

Right away I assumed she'd been out at a party or something, and jealousy kicked me in the gut. What I wouldn't give to see her across the room at some function and be able to walk over and introduce myself. Get to know her without so many fucking complications. Tell her she took my breath away and kiss her until she lost hers.

"Can I come in?" she asked.

I realized I had been standing there staring at her, and she was out in the cold. "Oh—sorry. Yes." I opened the door and stood back as she entered, then shut the door behind her.

"How are you?" she asked.

"Okay." I shoved my hands into my pockets. "You?"

"Terrible." She started to unbutton her coat.

"Terrible?" I frowned. "Where were you tonight?"

"Home alone. The kids are sleeping at Mack and Frannie's. My parents are out."

Confused, I glanced at her high heels. "You were home alone?"

"Yeah. And I couldn't stop thinking about you." She finished with the buttons and clutched the coat together at her chest.

My cock twitched. Was she fucking naked under there? "You couldn't?"

"No. And it made me realize something."

"What's that?"

"I want to break the rules." She opened the coat and let it fall to the floor.

My jaw dropped. She wasn't naked.

She was wearing the red dress.

"I want to touch you," she said, her eyes locked on mine. "I want to hear you tell me I'm beautiful. I want you to misbehave."

"Sylvia," I said, working very hard to keep my cool. "Do you know what you're saying?"

"Yes." She began slowly walking backward down the hall.

I followed her like a predator stalking its prey. "Have you been drinking?"

"Not a drop."

"Are you under the influence of drugs?"

She shook her head.

"Am I dreaming right now?"

She stopped moving, allowing me to get close enough for her to reach out and put a hand on my dick, which was thick and hard under my jeans. "Am I?"

I grabbed her by both wrists and pushed her up against the hallway wall, pinning her arms above her head. "I'm going to give you one chance to come to your senses, Sylvia."

"And if I don't?" She strained against me, pressing her breasts into my chest.

I put my lips at her ear. "Then I'm going to spend the rest of the night doing very bad things to your body."

"Do them," she whispered. "I'm begging you, Henry. Do them."

Hearing my name on her lips like that—hearing her beg—flipped a switch in me. I was done asking permission, done worrying about whether this was right or wrong, done trying to talk her out of something I so desperately wanted—no, *needed*—to do.

I crushed my lips to hers, plunging my tongue into her mouth. My hands moved down her body, along curves covered in red, and I wanted nothing more than to tear that dress from her skin with my teeth.

But first I had to taste her.

Dropping to my knees, I shoved her dress up her hips and reached for her underwear—except she wasn't wearing any.

"Jesus fucking Christ," I whispered, the bulge in my jeans growing even bigger. "You knew what you wanted when you came here tonight, didn't you?"

"Yes," she said, breathing hard. "So don't stop."

I lifted one high-heeled foot and kissed the inside of her ankle. Her calf. Her knee. I placed it over my shoulder and kissed my way up her inner thigh.

She flattened her hands on the wall beside her and gasped as I put my mouth on her pussy, stroking up the warm, slick center with my tongue, lingering at the top. I moaned at her sweet taste, at her velvet-and-satin texture, at the irresistible scent of her. I teased her clit with the tip of my tongue, and reveled in the way she moved her hips, and put her hands on my head, and tightened her leg against my back, pulling me in closer. She panted and sighed and murmured incomprehensible words of pleasure and disbelief. The leg she stood on trembled.

"I'm so close," she whispered, and I sensed something like fear in her voice, almost like she was afraid her orgasm wasn't going to happen. "Don't give up."

Give up? Was she fucking serious? Why would I give up? It made me wonder if her husband was an even bigger asshole than I'd previously thought.

But half a second later, he was out of my head.

I slipped one hand between her legs and slid one finger easily inside her, then two, searching for the spot that would put her over the edge. I knew I'd found it when her body tensed up and I felt her muscles contracting around my fingers.

"Henry," she said, almost frantically. "My God, it's going to happen. It's going to fucking happen, and it's been . . . *so* . . . *long*."

Beneath my tongue, her clit was firm and swollen and I

sucked it into my mouth, flicking it with quick, hard strokes. She cried out repeatedly, her fingers fisting tightly in my hair, her entire body going stiff except for the rhythmic pulse of her orgasm around my fingers.

Fuck, it felt good to make a woman come, to know that I was giving her that kind of pleasure, to hear her sounds and taste her desire and see her bare before me. To touch her and kiss her and fuck her with my tongue *just because I wanted to*. And because *she* wanted me to. She wanted it so badly she'd come here in high heels and a red dress with no panties underneath.

And that wasn't all she wanted.

"Come here," she panted when she could talk again, yanking on my shirt.

I rose to my feet and she reached for my belt. "I want to get my hands on you," she said against my lips. "I can't stop thinking about it."

I groaned as she undid my jeans and slid her hand inside, wrapping her fingers around my cock. Fuck, it had been too long—if she kept working me with her hand like that, I was going to lose control and come all over her fingers.

Not that I'd *mind* a hand job from someone other than myself for once, but that wasn't how I wanted this to go.

I took her hand off me and spun her around. She braced herself with two palms against the wall. I'd only intended to unzip her dress, but seeing her like that—the long, silky hair spilling down her back, that dress hiked up above her ass, her thighs bare, those high-heeled shoes—I couldn't help myself.

Pressing up against her back, I lowered my lips to her ear. "Spread your legs."

She stepped out slightly.

"More," I told her, pushing my jeans down enough to take out my cock.

When her legs were opened wide enough, I paused. "Do we need to be careful about—"

"No," she said breathlessly. "All good."

I slid inside her, slow and deep. A guttural sound escaped my throat—she was warm and wet and soft and tight. She gasped and whimpered as her body stretched to accommodate me, arching her back and sliding her hands up the wall.

God, I hoped she left handprints. I'd fucking frame them.

Gripping her hips with both hands, I began to move, rocking into her with deep, rhythmic thrusts that made her cry out every time I plunged inside her. It felt so good that I forced myself to slow down, breathe, take it all in—if I only had one night with her, I was going to make it one she never forgot. I buried myself as deep as I could, sliding one hand between her legs and rubbing circles over her clit with my fingertips.

Her head fell back as she moaned.

"Is this what you wanted?" I asked, kissing her throat. "My mouth on your skin? My hands on your body? My cock inside you?"

"Yes," she panted. "All of it. I wanted to be this close to you."

"God, Sylvia." I inhaled her perfume, and the room seemed to spin. "I've never wanted anyone the way I want you. You're so fucking beautiful. I don't even deserve this."

"Yes, you do," she whispered. "You make me feel so good. I want to make you come, Henry. I want to know I can make you come."

Jesus, how could she have any doubt? Strapping my other arm across her chest, filling my palm with her breast, I held her tight to me and worked my fingers faster between her legs. "Do you know how hard I'm trying not to come right now?"

"W-why?"

"Because I want you to come again first. Then it's my turn."

"I can't come twice in one night."

"You can and you will. Right here."

"It's never happened before."

"Even better." I slipped my hand inside the top of her dress and teased her nipple with my fingers. "God, I love your body. I took one look at you in this dress at the party and wanted to fuck you right there in the bar. You make me so goddamn hard."

"Yes." She took one hand off the wall and looped it around the back of my neck, gripping tight. "Tell me."

"Tell you what—how much I loved fucking you with my tongue? How good you taste? How badly I want to feel you come on my cock?" I pushed even deeper inside her and rubbed a little harder with my fingertips.

She moaned and arched and writhed against me, and in seconds, her pussy was clenching my shaft over and over again, my name falling softly from her lips. "Come for me, Henry. Now. *Please*."

I lost it—grabbing her by the hips, I drove into her hard and fast, forcing her to brace herself against the wall again. *Don't be so rough, asshole*, I told myself. *She didn't come over here so you could take out all your sexual frustration on her.*

But I couldn't help myself. I cursed and growled, my jaw clenched, my muscles flexing—arms, back, abs, legs. My body was hot and tight, desperate with the need to release all the tension and ache and frustration and anger that had been building inside me for so long and was now wrapped in uncontrollable desire for this woman begging me to come and asking nothing in return. She wanted me for *me*. She wanted my body because it turned her on. She wanted my cock inside her because it fucking felt *good* there—so good I exploded inside her with the force of a volcanic eruption. My world went black, and everything seemed to move in slow motion as the orgasm took over my body, making it billow and throb again and again and again.

Afterward, the first thing I was aware of was the scent of

her hair. Then the sound of her breath. I opened my eyes and saw her propped against the wall in front of me, palms flattened above her head.

I wrapped my arms around her, pressing my lips to her shoulder. "You okay?"

"Yes." She paused. "Wow. I can't believe I did that."

"Did what?"

"Um, all of it. Came over here wearing heels but not knickers. Had two orgasms. Demanded sexual things."

I laughed. "I'm not complaining. In fact, I would like to tell you right now that you are welcome to come to my house every night of the week wearing heels but not knickers and demand sexual things—as long as you don't expect me to behave like a gentleman once I let you in."

"I think I'd be offended if you did. Half the fun was just seeing your face when I took off that coat."

"*Half?*"

She giggled. "Maybe not half. But your reaction was perfect. And it made me feel so good. Almost as good as the two orgasms."

"I'm glad." Carefully, I pulled out of her. "Don't move, okay?"

"Okay."

Tucking myself back into my jeans and zipping them up, I hurried into the kitchen and grabbed a clean dish towel, wetting it with warm water from the sink before returning to the front hall.

"Thanks," she said, reaching for it. She'd tugged her dress back into place.

"Let me." I knelt in front of her, moved her dress again, and gently cleaned her up. When I got to my feet again, I saw that she was wiping tears from beneath her eyes. I tossed the towel aside and took her in my arms. "What's wrong? Did I hurt you? I was trying not to be rough, but—"

"No, no. It's not that." She threw her arms around me and

held on tight, weeping on my shoulder. "You're just such a good man, Henry."

"That's why you're crying?"

"Yes."

I rubbed her back. "I feel a little lost."

"Sorry." She laughed and sniffled. "I know I'm not making much sense. One day I'm here saying I just want to be friends and three days later I'm here trying to seduce you."

"It worked like a charm."

More muffled laughter, then she let me go. "I know. And it's not that I'm sorry, but I feel like I need to be honest with you about why I came here tonight."

I took her by the shoulders and held her at arm's length. "Sylvia, you can totally say it was for my massive dick. I won't be offended. In fact, I'll like it."

She smiled. "That was definitely part of it."

"Good. Confess the rest if you must, but whatever it is, I promise I'm okay with it."

"Even if it was selfish?"

"You're going to tell me you came for the orgasms? No pun intended."

She laughed. "Kind of. I had a really terrible day, and I wanted to feel better. Originally, I went to the winery only to talk to you, but you weren't there, and I was really sad. Because I feel like I can tell you anything and you understand. You always know what to say to make me feel better. So I decided to come find you."

"God, I'm glad I never gave you my phone number."

She smiled, shaking her head. "I wouldn't have used it. Because the more I thought about it, the more I wanted something beyond conversation. I've been so sad for so long, Henry. I've felt so unwanted and undesirable. Words are nice, but they can still be lies. I wanted to *feel* with my body—and with yours—the kind of desire that can't be faked. I needed *proof* that you find me beautiful and sexy. I wanted to be so tempting you couldn't resist. I wanted to have that kind of power over you and give you that kind of power over me. Does that make sense?"

"I think so." I paused, running a hand over my jaw. "Is it terrible that I just really wanted to fuck you?"

Her head fell back as she burst out laughing. "No," she said. "That is actually perfect."

"Is it terrible that I'm already thinking about doing it again?"

Her laughter died down, but a smile stayed on her lips. "No."

"Good." I swept her off her feet and started walking toward my bedroom. "Because I wasn't about to let you leave."

CHAPTER 11

Sylvia

HE CARRIED me to his bedroom. *Carried* me. Like I was a bride, or he was a caveman, or maybe like he was a fireman rescuing me from a burning building and taking me to safety —and I *did* feel safe in his arms.

But I felt other things too. Deliciously naughty. Unabashedly sexy. Fearlessly free to say and do and have everything I wanted.

And I wanted him in every possible way.

He was better than any fantasy I'd ever had, not that my fantasies had even gotten close to what I'd experienced in the hallway. The way he talked made my body turn molten. The way he kissed made me weak. The way he put my pleasure first—*twice!*—before he thought about his own was a revelation. I couldn't believe it.

And then once he'd given himself permission to let go . . . good God, I thought he'd tear me in two. I'd never been with anyone so strong or big or rough.

But he was gentle now, setting me on top of his sheets. The room was dark and smelled like him. I inhaled the scent, dizzy with lust and happiness and anticipation.

He switched on a bedside lamp. "I hope you don't mind the light."

I smiled, rolling onto one side, my head resting on my arm "I don't mind. I like seeing you. It gives me butterflies."

"I was hoping it would make you want to get naked." He pulled off one of my heels.

Giggling, I sat up and watched him remove the other. "That too. Want to unzip my dress?"

"That would be a *hell* yes." He took my hand and pulled me to my feet. "Turn around."

I turned, lifting my hair off my neck. Slowly, he pulled the zipper down my back, and the red dress fell to my feet. Stepping out of it, I suddenly felt self-conscious. I hadn't been fully naked in front of a man without the cover of darkness in a long time. I hadn't been fully naked in front of anyone but my ex since I was twenty—and I didn't have that body anymore. I'd had two children. Even though I knew it was stupid, that nagging little prickle of insecurity still stung . . . I'd been left for a younger woman. He'd told her I didn't excite him anymore. Was my body to blame? Before I could stop myself, I covered my chest with my arms, wrapping one fist inside the other and tucking them beneath my chin.

"Hey." Henry turned me by the shoulder so I was facing him again. "Don't do that."

"What?" I had trouble looking him in the eye.

He tipped my chin up. "Don't hide yourself from me."

"I'm not hiding," I said, but of course I was.

Taking me by the wrists, he forced my arms down to my sides, and looked at me.

I started to panic a little.

I was totally bare before him—stretch marks, C-section scar, less-than-perky breasts and all. Unlike many of my friends, I'd never had surgery to restore my post-baby body to its former tight, bouncy, unmarked state. Now I was kind of wishing I had.

I'd never felt so naked or vulnerable in my life.

"Sylvia, I'm going to say this once," Henry said seriously. "And then, since you've learned not to trust words entirely, I'm going to spend the rest of the night showing you that it's true—I think you are the most exquisite woman on the face of the earth, in every way. There is no part of your body, no inch of your skin, that isn't perfect, because it's *yours*." He took my head in his hands and kissed me, hard but sweet. "And all I want to do is make you mine, even if it's just for tonight."

"Yes," I whispered. I rose up on my toes, pressing my lips to his again while my hands went to work unbuttoning his shirt. "Make me yours tonight, Henry. That's all I want to be."

As our kiss grew more passionate, we managed to work off his clothes, although it wasn't easy since neither of us was willing to unlock our lips for very long. But soon we were skin to skin, wrapped in an embrace much like we'd been on Christmas Eve, only naked this time.

His body—lean and hard—made the flames in me jump higher. They burned beneath my skin, desperate to escape. My hands roamed over his broad shoulders, slid down his sculpted chest, brushed over the taut ridges of his stomach. I'd never been with a man like Henry, whose solid muscles were built by labor and honed by hours spent at the gym. I wanted to feel his weight on me, wrap my legs around him as he entered my body, see his face above mine as we moved together.

"Your body is incredible," I told him, letting my palms move down over his ass. "I had no idea."

"Generally, I try to wear clothes in public, so—oh, fuck."

I'd reached between us and taken his cock in my hand, and he groaned as his hot, thick flesh slipped through my fingers. I had forgotten how exhilarating and empowering it was to make a man this aroused, this needy, this hard. I loved the way he thrust inside my fist, the way his fingers dug into my hips, the way he cursed and growled, like he was trying to hold back but wasn't sure how long he could last. It made me feel sexy and confident.

"You're so hard," I whispered against his lips, tightening my grip. "How is that even possible? It hasn't been that long."

"It's only possible because it's you."

Again he scooped me into his arms and placed me on his bed. I felt feverish with need as he stretched out above me and opened my legs so he could settle his hips between my thighs. He reached low and touched me, easily slipping his fingers inside and rubbing the warm, slick wetness over my clit. I gasped, arching my back with my arms tossed above my head.

My eyes closed and I felt his lips close over one hard, tingling nipple, felt his tongue tease and stroke it. My belly hollowed and quivered, and gooseflesh rippled across my skin. I threaded my fingers in his hair as he moved to the other breast and sucked greedily, his fingers moving faster, rubbing harder.

Was it possible I could actually come a third time?

I would never have thought so, but as the sensations swirled deep within my core, as my legs began to thrum with pleasure, as I twisted languorously beneath him, I decided to stop thinking about it and just immerse myself in this vast, warm ocean of sensual bliss.

"Henry," I panted, "I want you inside me."

Immediately, he moved up my body and positioned the tip of his cock between my thighs. Both of us moaned as he slid inside me one hot, wet inch at a time. When he was buried so deep I'd have sworn I couldn't take any more, he crushed his lips to mine and kissed me savagely, his tongue lashing between my lips, his breathing quick and ragged as he set a rhythm above me.

Then he went deeper. Harder. Rougher.

My head fell back, and I knocked his jaw with my chin. I gasped and dug my nails into his biceps, tears springing unbidden to my eyes as my body reacted to the brutal, ceaseless motion of his driving hips. I cried out with every violent thrust, I saw stars explode behind my eyes, I was positive this man was going to bruise and break me.

But I loved it . . . because *I* was doing this to him.

Every vicious stroke meant he couldn't hold back. Every predatory growl meant he wanted more. Every rock-solid inch of his cock was hard *for me*—and I couldn't get enough.

As soon as I pushed past the shock and pain of being fucked so mercilessly, I let myself go and embraced it fully. I lifted my hips to match his rhythm. I clawed at his ass, pulling him deeper. I put my lips near his ear and said anything I felt, words I'd never even thought about uttering before.

God, I love the way you fuck me.

You make me so wet.

I want to come on your cock so hard you can feel it.

Each dirty word seemed to push him closer to the edge. He moved his hands beneath me to grab my ass, tilting my hips up toward his and driving even deeper, the base of his cock rubbing against my clit.

I couldn't talk anymore—my body was spiraling out of control, the tension pulling so tight I wasn't sure I could take it. I felt the muscles in my lower body begin to contract just as the buzzing heat from the friction between us sent me rocketing higher and higher through space. Then, with one glorious stroke of lightning, everything inside me burst wide open, shattering me into a million pieces that glittered and burned like shooting stars. My body clenched and pulsed around his, and his pounded and surged inside me. We flowed into each other as we clung and kissed and held on tight, riding the wave until it finally crashed onto the shore, leaving us damp and breathless in each other's arms.

"So what was it that made today so terrible?" Henry pressed both of my palms between his, like four hands steepled in prayer. We were in the bathtub, and I was lying back against him like he was a human recliner.

I sighed. "Today was terrible because once again, my fucking ex did something selfish and shitty that hurt the kids' feelings."

"What did he do now?"

"He told them they couldn't come visit him the last part of their vacation because J.Crew Kimmy needs peace and quiet."

"Who the hell is J.Crew Kimmy?"

"His pregnant girlfriend. She used to work at J.Crew, until she took over as trophy-wife-in-training. Apparently, she and Whitney are not getting along. But he'd promised Whitney they could go skiing at Aspen without Kimmy. My guess is that the idea did not go over well."

"What an asshole. Were the kids upset?"

"Extremely. I was worried enough about them before this happened—Whitney is painting her face with so much makeup you can hardly see her skin, and Keaton is sneaking junk food. I'm afraid this is going to push them off the deep end. I need to find them a therapist. I need to find *me* a therapist."

"I'm sorry." He wrapped his arms around me. "I'm here if you want to talk. I'm not a therapist, but I'm a good listener."

I hooked my hands over his muscular forearms. It did feel

good to talk to him, even if he wasn't a professional. "Whitney took some of her anger out on me, and even though I know she didn't mean the things she said, they pretty much gutted me."

"What did she say?"

I took a breath. "That I must have done something to make him leave."

"That must have hurt."

"It did. She apologized later, but the words stung. Because that's my deepest fear, you know? That I wasn't enough. That no matter how hard I tried, I failed because there's something wrong with me. It was my fault, and now the kids have to suffer for it."

"There is *nothing* wrong with you, and the divorce was not your fault." Henry's tone was fierce. "You were married to someone who didn't appreciate what he had."

"Thank you." I dropped a kiss on his thick, masculine wrist. I loved his hands, his long elegant fingers, the veins that ran up his arms. "Mentally, I know you're right, but my insecurity sometimes creeps up on me. I'm working on it, but there's a lot of bad stuff that's accumulated over the last few years to work through."

Henry was silent for a moment. And then, "Can I ask you something?"

"Sure."

"Earlier tonight, when we were in the hallway, you said something."

I smiled. "I said a lot of things."

"This was something you said, uh, *during*."

"During? I wasn't even aware I could talk during."

He chuckled, his chest rumbling beneath my back. "You said a few words here and there."

"I might have. But your words were better." I shivered recalling the hot, dirty things he'd said.

"Are you cold?" He sat up and reached for the faucet,

which was freestanding and placed to the right of the claw-foot tub. "I can add some more hot water. We've been in here a while."

"We have, but I'm not cold. I just like the memory of what you said." I looked at him over my shoulder. "It was an excited shiver, not a cold shiver. It was a *wiggle*."

He laughed, looking boyish and adorable with his spiky damp hair sticking up. It looked darker when it was wet, making his eyes look deeper green. "Okay."

"So what was it I said?"

"You said, 'Don't give up.' It was right before—"

"Oh." I felt heat in my cheeks. "I know when it was."

"What was that about?"

I hesitated, my eyes dropping to our legs beneath the water, his hairy ones outside my much paler, smooth ones. My red toenail polish popped against the white porcelain enamel finish. It was a beautiful cast iron tub, like something out of a Victorian movie set. I couldn't believe it when Henry told me no one had ever used it. When I asked why, he said he'd bought it to surprise Renee, an effort to help her relax, but she'd moved out before it had even been delivered. He'd installed it anyway, but since he was not a bath kind of guy, it had never gotten used. I'd been more than happy to christen it tonight.

"You don't have to tell me," Henry went on.

"No, it's okay." I looked at him again. "It can take me a long time to reach orgasm. My ex used to get impatient."

Henry's expression plainly conveyed his disgust. "You're fucking kidding me."

"No."

"I already knew he was a dick, but Jesus. That's a whole new level of assholery."

"Yeah." I bit my lip. "After a while, it made me really self-conscious about even trying for one. I used to fake them."

A smile ghosted his lips. "I hope you told him that eventually."

"I wish I had."

"I cannot believe the way he treated you. Or his kids." Henry gathered me in his arms and pulled me back against his chest again. "It makes me fucking furious."

"Me too."

He pressed his lips to my wet hair for a moment. Then he abruptly picked up his head. "Wait, you weren't faking tonight, were you?"

I had to laugh. "No, I assure you, I was not. Those were all real. I could hardly believe it when I felt the first one building. I haven't had one in so long—at least not one that I didn't give myself." It made me blush to admit it in front of Henry, but it also felt so good to be this open with him.

"Oh, believe me, I get it. Mine have all been self-service lately."

"For how long?" I asked, curious if there had been anyone since his wife left.

"Maybe six, eight months?"

I sat up again and looked back at him. "Eight months? Didn't your ex just leave you last fall?"

"Yeah, but things had been pretty terrible throughout spring and summer. Once that final round of IVF failed, she wanted nothing to do with me. And even before that, sex had become a chore for both of us."

"Oh." I settled back against him again.

"What about you? How long had it been?"

"God, I don't even remember. He lost interest in me sexually years ago. We'd go through the motions every once in a while, but like I said—it wasn't like I got any real pleasure out of it. I was always left feeling lonely and unsatisfied afterward. It was physical, but not emotional. We had no real connection."

He kissed my head again. "I get it."

"But tonight." I grinned, flipping over and bringing my knees astride his thighs. "Tonight was *very* different."

"Yeah?" He gave me a cocky half-grin that riled me up inside, even though we'd already had sex twice and it had to be nearly one in the morning.

I nodded, the strands of my wet hair dangling between us. "I've had more orgasms in one night with you than I've had in the last five years of marriage."

"Good." He looked smug. "Well, good for me, anyway."

"And good for me too." With my hands on his chest, I leaned forward and kissed him, soft and honey-sweet at first, gently plucking at his top lip, his bottom lip, caressing them both with my tongue. Between my legs, I felt his cock stir, and it made me smile.

"What's so funny?" he asked, sliding his hands over my ass.

I slid my hands up his neck and into his hair. "Nothing. I'm happy. I told you earlier that I came here tonight needing more than distraction—I needed validation. I needed assurance that I'm still sexy and alive. I needed to feel noticed and appreciated and desired. I never expected to feel this kind of . . . reawakening in myself. I didn't expect my own sexual drive to be so hungry and demanding—or so easy to indulge." I'd begun to rock my hips over his, sliding back and forth over his hard length. Already my stomach had that weightless feeling, and my blood was rushing faster. "But I'll come again for you. I'll come for you all night long."

"Jesus Christ," he said, his voice deep and gravelly. "Tell me this doesn't have to end in the morning, or I might actually have to tie you up in my bedroom just so I can give you orgasms every night."

I laughed, rubbing my lips against his. "But I might *want* you to tie me up in your bedroom."

His cock jumped beneath me, and he gripped my ass even

harder. "Fucking hell, Sylvia Sawyer, what are you trying to do to me?"

"Right now, I don't exactly know," I said, lifting myself up slightly, then reaching between us. A moment later I was sliding down his long, thick shaft, hearing him groan with pleasure, taking him deep. "But it sure feels good."

Later—much later, since we got hungry and foraged for snacks at two A.M.—we fell into his bed, and snuggled up close.

"I can't remember the last time I slept naked," I told him, resting my head on his chest.

"Me neither." He wrapped his arms around me. "Are you warm enough?"

"Yes." The temperature outside had dropped below zero, the snow continued to fall, and an icy wind whistled against the windowpanes, but I'd never felt so warm and safe and cozy. It had been years since I'd fallen asleep in someone's arms this way, knowing there was no place else he'd rather be and no one else he'd rather be with.

I had no idea what I was doing, whether Henry and I sleeping together was a terrible idea or the best idea in the world, or how this was going to play out. Nothing had really changed. We were still two people fresh from bad relationships that had damaged us in ways we might not even be aware of yet. Neither of us knew what the future would bring. And I had two children that needed me to love them enough for both parents. This wasn't the time for me to go looking for romance.

My judgmental voice, the one that loved to speak up just when I was enjoying an unexpected moment of bliss, threatened to lecture me, not only about parental responsibility, but believing the lies men told and trusting someone with my body, my secrets, my feelings.

To shut it up, I listened to Henry breathe as he slept, focused on the slow, rhythmic rise and fall of his chest.

It was deep and even and peaceful.

CHAPTER 12

Henry

IT WAS EARLY when I woke up, the silvery morning light barely starting to slant through the blinds. I knew if I looked out the window, I'd see at least half a foot of fresh snow, which meant my first order of business today would be shoveling the driveway so Sylvia wasn't stuck here.

Not that I'd mind so much if she were.

I propped my head on my hand and looked at her. She'd rolled away from me during the night and lay on her side, facing the opposite direction. Her golden hair fanned over the white pillowcase, and her body was curled into a ball. She had the sheet tucked against her chest, but her naked back was exposed, her skin luminous in the shadows.

I was tempted to do so many things at once—run a fingertip down her perfect spine. Lean over and bury my face in her sweet-smelling hair. Move closer and curve my body around hers like a comma. Kiss the back of her beautiful neck.

In the end, I waited too long and she stirred, rolling onto her back and blinking at me. "Hi."

"Hi."

Her smile was shy and seductive at the same time—an irresistible combination. "I stayed the night."

"You did."

"We broke all our rules, didn't we?"

"And then some. But wasn't that the point?"

Smiling, she turned onto her side and faced me, tucking her hands beneath her cheek. "It sort of feels like it might have been a dream."

I reached beneath the sheet and pinched her ass, making her yelp.

"Ouch! Guess it was real," she said, giggling as she rubbed the sore spot.

"It was real." I put my hand on her lower back and pulled her closer. "It was unexpected, and it was even better than my fantasies, but it was real."

Her eyebrows went up. "You fantasized about me?"

"Many times. But only since you've been back and we've been talking."

She smiled. "I like that—being your fantasy."

"I like the real you even better."

The smile widened. "Thank you." She tucked herself into my body, her head beneath my chin.

I held her like that for a few minutes, gently stroking her back. It had been a long time since I'd wanted to be this close to someone, since I'd felt this protective and possessive.

"Henry?" Her voice was soft and tentative.

"Yes?"

"So what happens now?"

"Well, first I have to shovel a fuck ton of snow. You probably have to pick up your kids, and I need to go into work at some point."

"No, I mean . . . what now for us?" She pulled back and looked up at me, her eyes uncertain, her expression concerned. "I didn't really think about that when I came here last night. Do we pretend this never happened?"

"That's up to you," I said. "Your situation is more complicated than mine. You've got children to think about."

She nodded, biting her lip. One of her hands crept up my chest, and her eyes dropped to where her fingertips brushed softly over my skin. "I think it's too soon to make anything . . . public."

"I agree."

She met my eyes again, her expression guileless and sweet. "But I don't want it to stop."

"Me neither."

"Henry, are we crazy?"

"It's possible." I kissed her forehead. "But let's not worry about it for now, okay? We've both been through a rough time, and I think we deserve something for ourselves that just feels good. The more we overthink this, the worse we make it for ourselves."

"Okay." She started to say something else, then stopped.

"What?" I prompted. "You can say it."

"I just want us to always be honest with each other. If at some point, things don't feel right and we need to take a step back, I want us to be able to say it. I don't want either one of us to be blindsided or hurt."

"You have my word—I will always be honest with you. I know trust isn't easy for you right now, but my word is all I can offer."

"Your word is good enough for me." She looked relieved and cuddled in closer to my chest once more. "And I promise to always be honest too."

Holding her that way felt so right, it was hard to imagine either of us wanting to walk away from the feeling. But I wasn't an idiot—the circumstances were complicated. The timing was rushed. There was a lot at stake.

It was impossible to know what the future would bring, and for now it would just feel good to simply take each day as it came and enjoy one another's company.

Naked.

As often as possible.

While I shoveled the front walk and driveway, Sylvia made coffee, scrambled some eggs, and sliced some fruit for us. Since she'd arrived wearing only that red dress and high heels, I'd loaned her a T-shirt. It was huge on her, hanging nearly to her knees, but she looked adorable in it, moving around in my kitchen in her bare feet, hair in a messy pile on top of her head.

I could get used to that so easily, I thought when I came in from the cold and saw her look up at me and smile. It was enough to keep me from going to her and tearing the shirt right off. Sylvia in my kitchen on a Sunday morning was not something I should get used to. In fact, it would probably be a really long time before it happened again—if it ever did.

After breakfast, she put the red dress and heels back on, buttoning her coat all the way up to the top. "I should have brought a change of clothes—and some boots," she said at the door, shaking her head as she looked out the front window. "What was I thinking?"

"You were thinking about fucking me," I reminded her, helping her with the top button.

"True story." She sighed. "Oh well. I'll live."

"I could carry you to your car," I offered, only half-joking.

That made her smile. "No, that's okay. The walkway is shoveled, and I can pull right into the attached garage at Cloverleigh. Hopefully no one is in the kitchen and I can sneak up to my room."

"Okay. Hey, I was thinking about something you said last night while I was outside—about your kids being disappointed about not skiing. What about taking them skiing here? It's not Aspen or anything, but the drive to Crystal Mountain or Boyne isn't bad."

Her face brightened. "You're right. I don't know why I didn't think of that before."

"You were thinking about fucking me, remember?"

She blushed and swatted my chest with her gloves. "You're making me sound like a fiend. But that's a great idea. Thank you."

"You're welcome." I planted one last kiss on her lips, resisting the urge to ask when I might next see her. "Drive carefully, okay? The roads are probably still a mess. Hey, will you let me know when you get home so I'm not worried?"

"Sure. But you're going to have to give me your number for that." She pulled her phone from her purse, opened up her contacts, and handed it to me.

I put my information in and gave it back to her. She glanced at what I'd entered and looked up with a smirk. "You really want to be in here as Big Dick DeSantis?"

"A hundred percent yes," I told her.

She was still laughing when she went out the door.

After she'd gone, I cleaned up the kitchen, took a quick shower, got dressed, and headed into work. Since it was Sunday and the roads were shitty, traffic wasn't bad at all. There were cars in the employee lot at Cloverleigh Farms since the inn would open up again today, but the winery wouldn't open again until tomorrow, so I had the place to myself.

My mood was the best it had been in a long time—go figure—and I went about my work feeling upbeat and optimistic. Normally when the temperatures dropped below zero, I lost sleep worrying about my vines, but last night I'd slept like a baby.

Around noon, I ran out for a quick lunch, and when I came back, I saw Sylvia's kids plus Mack's three girls out on the lawn between the inn and the winery playing in the snow. It made me smile—I remembered how much fun my brothers and I used to have outside during winter, until one of us took a hard-packed snowball in the face and went in crying to our mom. Since none of us would ever admit who had thrown it, we'd all get sent to our rooms. But then she wouldn't be able to stand the noise in the house, and she'd send us outside again.

After parking my truck, I walked by the kids and gave them a wave. Then I noticed they were having trouble pushing a massive snowball that would undoubtedly be used as the bottom third of a snowman.

"Mr. DeSantis!" cried Mack's oldest daughter, Millie. "Can you help us? We made the butt too big!"

I laughed. "Sure."

Once I managed to push the giant snowball where they wanted it, we went to work making the rest of the body. When all three snowballs were stacked, we went hunting for things to use for his face and clothing. On the ground we found two shriveled crab apples to use for his eyes. In the stables, someone found half an abandoned carrot. Mack's daughter Felicity thought of using small stones for the mouth, so we trudged through the snow toward the creek to find some. Whitney found sticks for the arms, and in the barn, Keaton spotted an old hat on a hook in the wall. I lifted Mack's little daughter Winnie up so she could place it on our snowman's head.

"But he's going to be cold," she said in dismay. "He needs a scarf."

"He's a snowman, dummy," Felicity scolded. "He doesn't get cold."

"Then why would he need a hat?" she said, giving her sister the stink-eye. Then she turned to me. "Mr. DeSantis, could we use your scarf? Then he won't be cold."

One look at her big eyes peering up at me, and there was no way I could refuse. "Of course."

"Yay!" The younger kids jumped up and down as I untied my scarf and tied it around his neck.

"Now let's make a snow *lady*," Winnie suggested. "We don't want the snowman to get lonely."

Everyone agreed, so we started rolling a large snowball for the bottom. I was helping to push it along when I heard Keaton yell, "Mom! Come see our snowman!"

I looked up to see Sylvia walking across the lawn toward us, all bundled up with her hands tucked into her pockets. My body warmed despite the cold.

She smiled at me. "Hey, guys. Hi, Henry. Playing hooky from work?"

"Mr. DeSantis gave us his scarf to use on the snowman," Whitney said excitedly. "Can we have yours for the snow lady?"

"Sure," she said, laughing as she unwound it from her neck. "That was very nice of him. Did you say thank you?"

"Thank you," Whitney said to me with a guilty smile. Her lips were neon pink, and she wore eye makeup too. I recalled what Sylvia had said about Whitney painting her face and felt sorry for them both. This was *exactly* the kind of parenting issue I wouldn't want to navigate as a single dad.

"You're welcome," I said, rising to my feet. "Is this where you guys want the bottom of the snow lady?"

"That's good," Millie decided. "Let's make the middle and top of her now."

"And then let's give them some kids!" Felicity shouted.

The kids got busy rolling more snowballs, and I moved closer to Sylvia. We stood elbow to elbow, but not near enough to touch. "Hey."

"Hey."

"Kids have fun at their sleepover?"

"Not as much fun as I had at mine," she murmured.

I laughed. "They seem like they're in good spirits today."

"I think they are. They loved the skiing idea."

"Good."

"I booked us a weekend at Boyne in January."

"Excellent. You'll have fun. Lots of snow this year."

She was quiet for a minute, and when she spoke it was nearly a whisper. "I can't stop thinking about last night."

"That makes two of us."

She laughed softly "I wish I knew when we could do it again."

"Again, that makes two of us."

She inched a little closer to me. "Maybe I could come by the winery later tonight. Since I'm working in the tasting room tomorrow, I thought maybe you could teach me some things."

Her sex-kitten tone told me she wasn't thinking about things like the body profile of our pinot noir. My cock twitched in my pants, and I cleared my throat. "You can come by the winery tonight."

"The inn is going to get busy with people checking in this afternoon, and I promised my mom I'd help. Then I have to get the kids fed. But after that, they're going to watch a movie with my dad. Maybe I could come then? Around eight, if that's not too late?"

"That's fine." She could have said midnight, and I wouldn't have cared.

"I won't be able to stay too long."

"I'm a good teacher. We'll work fast."

She smiled up at me. "I'll see you tonight."

CHAPTER 13

Sylvia

WHEN FRANNIE CAME to pick up the girls, she asked if she could talk to me alone.

"Sure," I said, glancing at the kitchen table, where all five kids were finishing up ice cream sundaes. "Want to go in the family room?"

"Um, let's go upstairs," she said, her expression concerned. She lowered her voice. "I really don't want them to hear us."

"Okay." My stomach twisted into knots as we made our way up to my bedroom. Once we were inside, I sat on the edge of my bed and Frannie shut the door, leaning back against it.

"I don't want you to freak out," she said, holding up both palms.

"Frannie, you're scaring me. What's going on?"

"So, you'd mentioned once before that your kids are not allowed on social media, right?"

"Right. I've told them they have to wait until high school."

"Well, Whitney has an Instagram account."

"No, she doesn't."

Frannie nodded. "She does. She showed it to Millie. And you need to see it."

My stomach churned. "Oh, God."

"It's not terrible—it's just . . . I think you should talk to her." Frannie came and sat next to me on the bed, pulling out her phone. It took her only a few seconds to find Whitney's account.

The profile name wasn't real, but the photos were—a series of selfies of her in full makeup, pouting for the camera. I scrolled through, relieved not to see anything too suggestive but sick to my stomach to think she'd done this and hidden it from me. I glanced up at the bio: *Just a girl who wants to feel beautiful.*

I squeezed my eyes shut, fighting back tears. "Shit."

"It's not that bad," Frannie said, taking the phone from my hand. "The account is set to private, and it's relatively new so she doesn't have many followers. But I thought you'd want to know."

"Thanks. Now tell me what to do about it."

She laughed gently. "Sorry, I haven't dealt with this one yet. But it's probably coming. Millie is all over Mack about social media, but he always refuses."

"What would he do if he found out she'd done it anyway?"

"Take her phone away. Ground her for life. Overreact and lecture her about all the creeps and weirdos out there on social media trying to prey on young girls. And then, because the lecture would involve a lot of cursing, he'd probably have to put like twenty dollars in the swear jar."

I sighed. "Yeah, that's not really my parenting style. But maybe my style is all wrong. Maybe if I'd been tougher, she'd have respected my rules more. Maybe I deserve this."

Frannie put an arm around me. "Stop it—you're a great mother. She's just been through a lot. And really, this isn't that big of a deal. Just talk to her."

"I will." I stared down at our shoes, swallowing hard. "It makes me so sad that she doesn't feel beautiful. Is it my fault somehow? Am I fucking up this whole single parenting thing already?"

"No," Frannie said emphatically, giving me a squeeze. "You're doing the best you can in a shitty situation. All girls her age go through this—Millie is right there with her. I cannot tell you how many tears she has shed over her hair before school in the morning. Her hair is ruining her life."

I shook my head, laughing a little because I remembered those days all too well. "I know they do. I certainly did. But she never acted this way before the divorce and I'm just worried some of it's coming from being deserted by her dad."

"That's why you have to talk to her. Or find a therapist for her. Mack's girls went to someone after his ex left. Want her number? They really liked her."

"Yes, *please*," I said.

"You got it. I'll get it from Mack and text it to you." She stood up and tucked her phone into her purse. "You gonna be okay?"

I nodded. "Yeah. It just seems like whenever I think I'm making progress at my fresh start, something sets me back."

"This isn't a setback, Syl. It's a little bump on the parenting road. You can handle it."

I smiled at her and took a deep breath. "Thanks. And thanks again for having them last night."

"My pleasure. We had fun. Did you enjoy your night alone?"

My face got hot. "Um, yes. I enjoyed it a lot."

"Sylvia . . ." Frannie's head tilted. "Why are your cheeks so red?"

"Because I wasn't exactly alone."

She gasped. "What?"

I covered my face with both hands. "I can't even believe I'm telling you this."

"Oh my God—you were with Henry, weren't you?"

I nodded, still hiding behind my palms.

"I knew it!" she crowed. "I *told* Mack something was up between you two on Christmas Eve. So what happened?"

I let my hands fall into my lap. "Everything."

"Like, *everything* everything?"

"Three times."

Frannie squealed and bounced around. "Oh my God, Sylvia! That's amazing!" She stopped moving. "Wait—*was* it amazing?"

I nodded. "It really was. I haven't been able to think about anything else all day."

"Wow. So you and Henry."

"There's not really a me and Henry. We're not exactly sure what we're doing," I admitted.

"Do you have to know right now? I mean, can't you guys just see where it goes?"

"That's sort of the plan," I told her. "So don't say anything to anyone, okay?"

"My lips are sealed," she said, pretending to zip them shut. "I won't even tell Mack if you don't want me to."

I didn't like asking my sister to keep a secret from her husband, but I felt like the fewer people who knew right now, the better. "Thanks. I don't think Henry would mind if Mack knew, but—"

Frannie held up her hands. "Do not worry. I totally get it. When Mack and I were first messing around, it was the same way—we had to keep it from everyone, especially the kids." She dropped her arms. "Although, as it turns out, we weren't really fooling them."

Frowning, I said, "Yeah, kids are smart. And mine have been through so much, I just don't want to add any complications."

"But you deserve to be happy too, Syl," Frannie said

softly. "And if spending time with Henry makes you happy, I say go for it."

"Thanks." I looked down at my hands in my lap, wishing it were that easy. "I'm supposed to go over to the winery and see him later tonight. Now I wonder if I shouldn't just stay here and be with the kids. Talk to Whitney."

"Can't you do both?"

"Maybe." That was really the question, wasn't it? Could I be the kind of mother I needed to be and also have this sexy thing with Henry on the side?

I wasn't sure I really wanted the answer to that question.

Downstairs, Whitney begged me to let Millie sleep over, and Frannie said it was okay with her. I said it was fine, relieved that at least I was off the hook tonight—I didn't want to have the Instagram conversation with anyone else around. Plus, I needed some time to think about how I was going to approach it. I didn't want to be angry and accusatory—that was not a tactic that worked well with preteen girls. And it wasn't like I didn't understand her desire to feel beautiful.

My God, wasn't that the reason I loved being around Henry? Because of the way he made me feel about myself? Because I'd felt ugly and worthless for so long? Were all the likes Whitney was hoping for akin to the attention Henry paid me? How could I judge her when I was guilty too? Was I a hypocrite?

It started to bother me so much that I decided to text Henry and tell him I couldn't come. I took out my phone and brought up his contact info—*Big Dick DeSantis*—and it made me laugh. Maybe I wouldn't cancel. A little wine and laughter with Henry sounded pretty damn good right now. It might not solve any of my problems, but they weren't going to get worse while I was gone, right?

And it's not like we had to have sex. We could just talk. He could start teaching me. I just liked being around him.

After getting the kids supplied with snacks and drinks

and blankets in the family room, I told my dad I was going over to the winery to help Henry with something.

"This late on a Sunday?" My dad's brow furrowed as he settled on one end of the couch, opposite Keaton. "What on earth is he still doing there?"

"I'm not sure," I said, hurrying away before he could ask any more questions. "But I won't be long."

I bundled up and walked over to the winery. Henry's truck was in the lot, but since it wasn't totally covered in snow I knew he must have left at some point and come back. I wondered if he'd eaten dinner out or at home alone.

When I reached the large glass door, I looked inside, but didn't see him right away. I pulled the handle, surprised to find he'd left it open. He appeared at the top of the cellar stairs as it closed behind me.

"Hey," he said, a smile on his face. "You made it."

"I made it." My heart tripped faster at the sight of him, and my insides tightened. I pulled off my hat and gloves, setting them on a high-top table.

He approached and glanced behind me. "Alone, right?"

"Alone."

"Good." He locked the door, switched off the overhead lights, and took me in his arms. When his lips met mine, rekindling the fire inside me, I knew I hadn't come here just to talk.

I'd come here to feel.

I wrapped my arms around his neck and kissed him back until we were both breathless and hot and frustrated by the bulky layers of clothing between us.

"Come here," he said, taking me by the hand. Making our way through the dark, he brought me to the steps and led me down into the cellar. He took me past the steel tanks and rows of oak barrels to his office door, shouldered it open, and tugged me inside the small, dark room.

"Lesson one," he said, shutting the door behind me. "Never let the winemaker get you in his office after hours."

I laughed as he unzipped my coat and tossed it aside.

"Lesson two," he went on, lifting my sweater over my head and unhooking my bra. "Do not, under any circumstances, allow him to undress you."

"I think I'm going to fail this course," I murmured as he knelt down and yanked my boots off.

"Lesson three." He unzipped my jeans and shimmied them down my legs. "If he tells you he can't stop thinking about the way you taste and needs to find out if it was really as good as he remembers, beware."

"Beware of what?" I asked as he took me by the hips and backed me up to his desk.

"His motives." Henry lifted me up and set me on the edge of the desk, pushing my thighs apart and dropping to his knees. "They are likely nefarious."

"Nefarious?" Then I gasped when his tongue swept across my clit.

"Yes." He did it again, one long, slow stroke that made my entire body shiver. "He just wants to fuck you with his tongue."

I fell back onto my elbows and moaned as he tantalized me. "He does?"

"Yes. But also with his cock."

"Good," I said, barely able to speak. "Because I heard he's got a big dick."

"He does. And it's getting bigger by the minute."

I laughed, my head falling back as he hooked his arms beneath my thighs and pulled me closer to his mouth. My toes curled as he plunged his tongue inside me. He devoured me like he'd been starving for me. He licked and stroked and sucked and caressed me with his tongue, moaning as if I was the most delicious thing he'd ever tasted. He told me he couldn't get enough. He made me believe it was true.

After he made me come with his mouth, he jumped to his feet and unbuckled his belt. "Let me," I panted, unbuttoning and then unzipping his jeans. I reached for his cock and it burst from his boxer briefs as if it had been freed from its cage. He groaned as I sheathed it with both hands, working them up and down his hot, hard length. "Take off your shirt," I demanded. "I want to feel your skin on mine."

A minute later, he was pushing inside me, my legs wrapped around him, his hands gripping my hips to hold me steady. I grabbed on to his thick, muscular shoulders, digging my fingers into his skin. He lifted me off the desk and put my back against the door, driving his cock deep inside me with quick, powerful thrusts. I winced as my head banged against the wood.

But it felt so good to be the object of this raging lust inside him—to inspire this aching need to *ravish* me so completely. He buried himself even deeper and stayed there, grinding against me, bringing me right back to the edge of another orgasm.

Breathing hard, he tipped his forehead to mine. "You feel too fucking good. I have to slow down."

"No, don't stop," I begged, circling my hips. "I want you to come."

A growl erupted from the back of his throat as he resumed his quick, hard rhythm, my back pounding against the door. All the muscles in my lower body clenched up tight as I reached the peak and stayed there for a moment, suspended, heart racing, eyes closed, breath stopped—until I felt his cock surge and throb inside me, pushing me past the breaking point. His lips hovered close to mine and we shared a breath as our bodies surrendered to one powerful, all-consuming pulse.

This, I thought to myself, as chills swept across my skin. *This is what it's supposed to feel like. This is what I've been missing. This is what I want.*

Was there any possible way I could have it for keeps?

After we got dressed, Henry did spend some time showing me around the winery, telling me what all the equipment was for, describing what wines were in each group of barrels or tanks, showing off the recently purchased bottling line. "But the most important thing coming up for me is the pruning," he said as we stood by the huge windows in the tasting room that overlooked the vineyard. "The quality of any vintage can be dictated by how well we prune, and we do it all by hand."

I hid a smile. "I've heard it's an art form."

He threw an arm around me, getting me in an affectionate headlock. "Are you making fun of the teacher?"

"I would never," I said, laughing as he squeezed me tight. "Not after such an enjoyable class, although I'm not sure I learned all my lessons. I might need a review session."

"That can definitely be arranged—maybe even tonight." He loosened his hold on me just enough for me to turn and face him.

"I wish I could," I said, running my hands up his chest, "but I have to head back. In fact, I wasn't even sure I should come tonight. I almost canceled."

"Why?"

I shook my head. "Just some stuff with Whitney."

"Do you want to talk about it?"

I played with one of the buttons on his shirt. "I don't want to bore you with my problems. I feel like I'm always complaining to you."

"Stop." He lifted my chin. "You never bore me. And it's not complaining—I *asked*. Is everything okay?"

"She's okay. She just broke a rule I have about social

media—she's not allowed to have it, but I found out that she created an Instagram account and posted a bunch of pictures of herself."

He looked slightly terrified. "What kind of pictures?"

"Nothing risqué. Mostly just her face in full makeup, lots of pouting selfies. And her bio said something like, 'I'm just a girl who wants to feel beautiful.'"

"Oh."

"But it won't help to have her mother scream at her that she *is* beautiful."

"Probably not."

"I know it's nothing a million other teenage girls aren't doing, but I don't like it. And I hate that she's hiding it from me. I want her to feel like she can talk to me about anything."

"Are you thinking this has something to do with the divorce? Like she's acting out to get your attention?"

"No, I don't think it's that. I think it's more like . . . like she's lacking something and she thinks likes on Instagram are going to deliver it. The divorce left this giant hole in all of us where our family used to be, and we're all trying to deal with it in different ways. Whitney's trying to cover it with makeup, Keaton is trying to stuff it with junk food, and I'm . . ." I groped for words.

"Trying to fill it with a big dick?" He frowned. "Sorry, that was totally inappropriate."

I laughed. "But not entirely inaccurate. I do think what we're doing is helping me get over some of my issues. But I'm an adult. Whitney is still a child. And she's in such a fragile state right now, one mean comment might destroy her. And people can be horrible on social media. I just want to protect her."

Henry pulled me in close and held me tight. "I know. And I shouldn't make jokes. You guys have been through so much."

I rested my cheek on his chest and wrapped my arms

around his waist, wishing I could take the warm strength of his embrace with me when I left here tonight. "Thanks for being here for me. I really appreciate it."

"You're welcome. You'll figure this out. Whitney doesn't strike me as the type to use defiance as a weapon."

"She isn't. She's a good girl. I think she's more . . . insecure than defiant." I took a breath. "And I get that. God, do I get that."

He rubbed my back but didn't say anything.

"In fact, one of the reasons I was going to cancel tonight was because I felt like a huge hypocrite—how can I judge her for wanting to do things that make her feel beautiful? I drove through a blizzard last night in a red dress and heels just so you'd look at me that way. And want me that way. And . . . like me."

He laughed a little. "I did like you, didn't I?"

I nodded and smiled up at him. "You liked me three whole times."

"And did those three likes make you feel better about yourself?"

"Immeasurably." I snuggled into his chest again.

"Then try not to be too hard on her." He kissed the top of my head. "Or on yourself. We're all just stumbling our way through life, hoping to arrive at the right destination. If something makes you feel good on the way, why not do it?"

I thought about his words as he walked me home, as he bid me farewell with a chaste hug in case anyone happened to be watching, as I shed my layers of winter clothing and joined the kids and my parents in the family room. The movie was over, and they were playing a board game now. They invited me to play too, and even offered to start the game over, so I couldn't say no.

But I kept thinking about Henry. I wished he were here. I could smell him on me. I heard his voice in my head . . . *If something makes you feel good, why not do it?*

It seemed like such a fearless attitude to have, and it made me think about the opposite too—if something makes you feel bad, why not stop it? For so long, I'd lived in fear of being abandoned, of being alone and having to start over, of failing. And I let that fear prevent me from leaving a marriage that not only didn't fulfill me, but robbed me of joy, of confidence, of self-worth.

But those days were over.

We could bloom here, all of us. I could feel it.

In the back of my mind, that voice reminded me that part of the new start I'd envisioned for myself meant learning to be happy on my own, and this thing with Henry did not exactly mesh with that plan. Becoming dependent on Henry to validate my own self-worth wasn't any better than what I was doing before, was it? And what made me think I could trust him?

But being with him made me feel *so damn good*.

And if something made you feel good, why not do it?

CHAPTER 14

Henry

THE NEXT DAY, it was back to business as usual. I hit the gym early and got into work by nine, calling hello to Chloe at the tasting counter as I made my way down to the cellar. Now that the inn was open again, and I knew we'd be busy with tastings and tours all day—all week, actually.

My assistant, Mariela, was already in the lab, and I waved to her as I headed for my office. When I opened the door and saw my desk, all I could think of was Sylvia naked on it with my head between her legs. When I shut the door behind me, all I could think of was fucking her against it. When I tried to focus on the day ahead and what I had to get done, she refused to get out of my head. When I closed my eyes, I swore I could smell her skin.

I was sitting there in a stupor, staring at the surface of my desk and trying not to get an erection, when someone knocked on the door.

"Yeah?" I called, shifting in my seat.

Sylvia poked her head in and grinned. "Hi. I'm officially here working upstairs but I wanted to say good morning."

"Good morning." Her smile made it hard to breathe for a second. "You'll be busy up there today."

"Chloe says we're totally booked. I'm a little nervous."

"You'll be great."

"Thanks." She gave me one last smile before disappearing, and a moment later, Mariela knocked on the open door.

"Hey. How was your Christmas?" she asked, leaning against the frame.

"Good. How about yours?"

"Great. Ready to get started filtering the riesling?"

I nodded, glad for the distraction. "Let's do it."

As predicted, the day was hectic in the winery—tons of guests coming in and out all day to look around, taste wine, purchase bottles to take home. Many of them wanted to chat with me, and I spent a good amount of time answering questions and explaining our process. Chloe and Sylvia were swamped at the counter, but every time I stole a glimpse of her, Sylvia had a huge smile on her beautiful face and was chatting away easily with customers, telling them about growing up on the farm, and talking about our wines. I couldn't imagine how many bottles she'd sell by the end of the day.

At one point in the afternoon, I noticed Chloe was alone at the counter and wondered where Sylvia had gone. A little later, I checked my phone and found a text from her apologizing for leaving so fast and explaining that she had to check on the kids and take care of dinner at the house. At seven o'clock, I was back at my desk trying to clear out my email inbox when she appeared in my office doorway, a smile on her face. "Hi."

My blood warmed. "Hey, you. Come on in."

She wandered in, carrying her jacket in her arms. "Still working, huh?"

"Finishing up. How was your first day in the tasting room?"

"Chaotic, as promised—but good, I think. Chloe says we sold a ton of wine."

"I believe it. I saw you working your magic up there. Who could resist you?"

She blushed at the compliment. "Stop it. I don't have any magic."

"I beg to differ."

"And I'm sure I screwed up the notes Chloe gave me for each wine a million times. I need to memorize the whole fruit-forward versus savory, and full-bodied versus light-bodied, and tart finish versus bitter . . ." She shook her head. "I don't know how you guys have so much information in your heads!"

I smiled. "You'll be a pro in no time."

"Thanks. You were busy in the cellar too, huh?"

"We were." I pinched the bridge of my nose with my thumb and forefinger. "It was a lot of talking to people for a guy who mostly deals with grapes. My head is pounding."

"I bet you probably haven't eaten anything today."

Had I? I couldn't even recall. "Maybe you're right. I don't think I did."

"Henry," she scolded. "You need to eat."

I shut my laptop. "I will. But first, shut the door and come talk to me. What were the kids up to today? The inn must have been slammed."

She closed my office door and leaned back against it. "It was. My mom was crazy busy at reception. And we put the kids to work helping April set up for the New Year's Eve party."

"Hard to believe that's tomorrow night already."

"Yeah." She stared at my desk for a moment, and lowered her voice to a whisper. "It's sort of insane that I was naked on your desk last night."

"It is." Swiveling in my chair to face her, I leaned back and put my hands behind my head. "But also awesome."

She blushed, dropping her gaze to the coat in her arms. "Have you ever . . . done that before? On your desk, I mean?"

"Nope."

"Me neither." She met my eyes. "But I liked it."

"Me too. I'd say we should give it another go right now, but I'm not sure the other employees here would appreciate the noise, even with the door shut."

She laughed and shook her head. "Yeah, let's save that for another day. I actually just came to invite you over to the house for dinner."

I paused. "Are you sure that's a good idea?"

"Why wouldn't it be?"

I crossed my arms over my chest. "I don't know. Are people going to think it's strange?"

"What's so strange about my inviting you for dinner? We're friends, aren't we? And if you happen to feel like helping Keaton set up his telescope, even better."

"Aha." I grinned at her. "So dinner is just a bribe, huh?"

She batted her thick, dark lashes at me. "Maybe."

"I don't mind helping with the telescope. You don't have to feed me."

"I like feeding you. And I've seen your fridge. It's sad." She wrinkled her nose. "I bet you were just going to eat takeout for dinner, right?"

"You know me too well."

"It's also an excuse to be with you again." Her cheeks went a little more pink and her lips curved into a soft, sexy smile. "I think I've got a crush on my teacher."

Our eyes met, and the small room crackled with electricity. "Then come sit on his lap."

She came toward me, laying her coat on the desk. I took her by the hips and pulled her onto my lap so she straddled my legs, her arms around my neck.

"If I come to dinner, can we sit like this at the table?" I asked, sliding my hands over her ass. My dick perked up at the unexpected proximity to its new favorite place.

She laughed. "No."

I pulled her close and whispered in her ear. "Then fuck dinner." Then I moved my mouth down the warm curve of her neck. "Let's go back to my house and get naked."

"Mmm, that is very tempting. But I think I'd be missed."

"Damn it." I stroked her throat with my tongue, tasting her skin. "I suppose I could try to behave during dinner."

"Does that mean you'll come?" she asked hopefully.

I exhaled and sat up straight again, knowing there was no way I could say no to her. And I really didn't mind helping her son with the telescope. "Okay. I'll come."

"Are you ready now? Or do you need more time to finish up?"

"I need about ten minutes to send a couple emails and get rid of my erection."

Laughing, she got to her feet. "Then I better get off your lap. Chloe is still closing up the tasting room, so I'll give her a hand. Meet me up there?"

"Perfect."

She gave me one last smile and moved toward the doorway, where she stopped and stared at the door I'd had her up against last night. "I'm surprised this thing isn't dented. I've got a bruise on my back, you know."

"I'm sorry."

Peeking back at me over one shoulder, she asked, "Are you really?"

Unable to suppress a grin, I shook my head. "No. But I'll take it easier on you next time."

Her eyes narrowed. "Don't you dare."

When I came upstairs, Chloe and Sylvia were chatting as they placed freshly washed and dried tasting glasses back on the shelves behind the counter.

"Are you coming to the party tomorrow night, Henry?" Chloe asked.

"I was planning on it," I answered, pulling my coat on.

"You better," Sylvia said. "I asked April to make sure we're all at one table."

"Is April bringing anyone?" Chloe asked, holding one last glass up to the light to make sure it was spotless.

"Not that I know of," Sylvia answered. "She claims she'll be too busy working to even sit down anyway."

"That girl needs time *off*." Chloe came out from behind the counter and headed for the employee room to grab her stuff. "She has no life."

"I heard she's interviewing someone after the holidays," Sylvia said, picking up her coat from the back of a counter stool.

"I heard that too," I said, taking the coat from her and holding it up so she could slip her arms in the sleeves. "It's a friend of the owners at Abelard."

Chloe came out of the break room, zipping her jacket, then slinging her bag over her shoulder. "Yes. Her name is Coco, and I've met her before. She's perfect for the job. Let's hope April realizes it." When she looked up at us, she stopped short, as if surprised.

I took my hands off Sylvia's coat.

"You sure you don't want to come to Mom and Dad's for dinner?" Sylvia asked, freeing her hair from her collar. "I convinced Henry to join us. And April's coming over too."

"Um, yeah. I'm sure. Oliver says he has dinner for us at home." She was still looking at us a little strangely as she moved toward the door and switched off all the lights. "But I'll see you guys in the morning. Have a good night."

We went outside, and I locked the doors as Chloe trudged through the snowy parking lot toward her car. After making sure it started, Sylvia and I continued walking toward the house. Flurries fell slowly around us, and the night air was cold and silent.

"Did you have a chance to talk to Whitney yet?" I asked.

"No. I'm totally avoiding it." She sighed, sticking her hands in her pockets. "I'm so bad. But I feel like as long as she's spending time with the family and enjoying herself, that's healthy, right? She had a smile on her face today—without the heavy makeup."

"Sounds healthy to me."

"Frannie gave me the name of a therapist Mack's girls went to after their mom left. The office was closed by the time I called this afternoon, but I left a message, so hopefully she gets back to me fast." She dragged her boots through the snow. "But still, I know I need to address the Instagram thing. Maybe I can do it later tonight."

We went in the back door to the house, and as soon as we stepped into the mudroom off the kitchen, my mouth watered. "Wow, something smells good," I said, shrugging off my jacket.

"Thanks. Hope you like Italian."

"It's my favorite."

"Is it?" She took my coat and hung it on a hook before sitting on a bench to pull off her boots. "Good to know."

"My parents were both Italian." I took my boots off too, so I wouldn't get the floor wet or dirty, and gave a quick prayer of thanks I was wearing new socks without any holes. "Neither was a hundred percent, but I'm more than half. I grew up eating a lot of Italian food."

"Aha—so it's in your blood." She straightened my boots into a row along with everyone else's. It was oddly touching somehow. "Sorry, it's a mom thing. My kids just throw their stuff everywhere, and it drives me nuts. I'm surprised you didn't learn to cook, having two Italian parents," she said as we walked into the kitchen.

"Yeah, my mom tried to teach us. Didn't work." My eyes nearly bugged out at the sight of all the food on the island. "Is that lasagna?"

"Yes. One is vegetarian and one has meat. And there's antipasto and Caesar salad and garlic bread, and it looks like my parents opened a bottle of red wine. Can I get you a glass?"

I stared at her. "Did you make all this today?"

She shrugged. "It's not a big deal. I didn't want my mom to have to cook after working such a long day, so I snuck over here this afternoon to put things together. Plus, I enjoy it. I really haven't gotten to cook for a large group in a while. I'd forgotten how much I like doing it. Help yourself."

"Thanks." I picked up an empty plate from the island and began to fill it. "And yes, a glass of wine sounds great."

"It's been nice to be home, but I'm actually getting a little antsy to have my own space. My own kitchen." She took two glasses down and filled them from the bottle of nebbiolo on the island. "I'm going to look at a few places next week."

"Oh yeah? Where are they?"

As she described the houses she was interested in, we finished filling our plates and took them into the dining room, where her kids and parents were already eating, along with April. I greeted everyone and took the seat Sylvia indicated for me, which was next to her and across from Whitney. While we ate, her parents and sister weighed in on which homes and locations they thought might be best for her, and the kids pleaded for the one with the most land so they could have animals.

"My dad never let us have pets," Keaton told me.

"Do you have a dog?" Whitney asked.

"I don't," I told her. "My, uh, wife was allergic."

"You have a *wife*?" She looked surprised.

"I did. But we're not together anymore. I mean, we're divorced."

"Oh." Whitney's eyes moved back and forth between Sylvia and me, and I suddenly felt uncomfortable.

"Then you should totally get a dog now," Keaton said.

"Do you have kids?" Whitney asked.

I shook my head. "Just nieces and nephews, but they all live in other states."

"Do you see them a lot?" Keaton asked.

"Not as much as I'd like," I admitted, tugging my collar away from my neck. I was suddenly warm beneath my clothing. Whitney was staring at me pretty hard.

Not that I blamed her. She was old enough to wonder who the hell this guy was that her mother kept bringing home to dinner. I had to remind myself that we weren't really doing anything wrong . . . were we?

"All ready for tomorrow night, April?" Sylvia asked.

"Almost." April took a sip of wine. "As long as the head chef doesn't throw a tantrum and none of my servers call in sick, I think we're good. The kids were a huge help today."

"Good." Sylvia beamed at her children. "They're ready and willing to work tomorrow too. Oh, Mom, will you be okay at reception without me tomorrow? Chloe needs my help again in the tasting room."

"Sure, sweetheart. That's fine."

"Henry has been teaching me about the winemaking process here," Sylvia went on as she lifted her glass. "It's so fascinating."

"Is that what you do?" Whitney asked. "Make the wine here?"

"Yes," I told her.

"Do you live close?"

"I live in Hadley Harbor. Not too far."

"Did you go to high school with my mom?" Her questions

were coming faster now. My leg had a nervous twitch beneath the table.

"No, I grew up on a farm in Iowa."

"Henry originally went away to school to be a doctor," said Sylvia. "He likes science just like you do, Keaton."

"Really?" Her son looked at me with interest.

I nodded, grateful for the opportunity to shift the conversation away from me. "I hear you got a telescope for Christmas."

"Yeah, but I can't figure out how to set it up."

"How about I take a look after dinner and see if I can help?"

He pushed his glasses up his nose and grinned. "That would be great."

After that, conversation centered mostly on the New Year's Eve party, their upcoming ski trip and what the conditions on the mountain would be like, and plans for a big retirement party for John in the spring, which would coincide with Cloverleigh's fortieth anniversary. Whitney stopped studying me and mostly stared at her plate, but every now and again I couldn't help noticing her watching the way Sylvia smiled at me, or put her hand on my arm, or paid me a compliment. Despite how delicious I found all the food, it was a little hard to eat under such intense scrutiny. I could practically hear the wheels turning in Whitney's head.

Eventually, I set down my fork. "Everything was delicious. Thanks so much for inviting me to eat with you guys."

"You're always welcome here, Henry." Daphne smiled at me, and then at her daughter. "But this was all Sylvia."

"It was nothing." Sylvia rose to her feet and started collecting plates. "I'll get the dishes if you guys want to get started on the telescope."

"Yes!" Keaton threw his napkin onto the table. "I'll show him where it is."

Although the directions that came with the telescope were terrible, I managed to get it set up in under an hour. Keaton was desperate to take it outside and test it out, and since it had stopped snowing, we piled on our winter stuff and brought it out onto the patio, which was blanketed in white.

My knowledge of astronomy was decent because my grandfather had always been interested, and he had taught my brothers and me about the major constellations when we were young. Later, I'd studied it a little at Cornell. I'd forgotten much of it, but Keaton didn't seem to care—he was eager to hunt for anything I suggested might be visible tonight, and asked a ton of smart, curious questions about each star or planet I pointed out.

Sylvia joined us a couple minutes later.

"Is it working?" she asked, sliding the glass door shut behind her before shuffling through the snow in her unlaced boots.

"Yes!" Keaton shouted. "And Henry says I might be able to see an interstellar comet!"

"Wow." She laughed, her breath escaping in little white puffs, and looked at me. "Is this true?"

"It's true. Some guy discovered it in August and it's supposed to be closest to Earth this month. They call it the Christmas Comet."

"And how do you know this?" she asked.

I shrugged. "I'm part science nerd, remember?"

"And he showed me where to find . . ." Keaton looked at me for guidance. "Pegasus?"

"Perseus," I corrected.

"Perseus," he repeated. "Come and look, Mom. I'll tell you where it is."

Sylvia bent forward and looked through the lens. "Okay, what am I looking for?"

"First, you find the stars that make the W," he told her, repeating what I'd said. "Can you see them?"

"Yes," she said after a moment.

"That's . . ." Again Keaton looked at me.

"Cassiopeia," I said.

"Cassiopeia," he echoed, his breath thick and white in the frigid night air. "Now look below the left part of the zig-zag. Can you see a cluster of stars there?"

"I think so. Is that Perseus?"

"Yes. Henry was just telling me the story. Did you know that constellations have stories?"

"Yes, but I don't know many of them." Sylvia straightened up and let her son look through the telescope again. Shivering in the cold, she turned to me. "What's the story of Perseus?"

I wanted so badly to put my arms around her and warm her up, but I stayed a respectable three feet away. "Well, I'm probably not remembering every detail exactly right, but Perseus was the grandson of a Greek king who'd been told his grandson was going to kill him. So to prevent a grandson from even being born, he locked his own daughter up in a tower."

"Always the tower," she said with a sigh.

"Don't worry. Zeus fell in love with her and visited her in the form of, um"—I glanced at Keaton—"golden rain. Which falls into her lap and causes her to get pregnant."

Sylvia laughed. "Go on."

"So the king is really mad about the baby and locks them both in a trunk, then throws the trunk out to sea."

Sylvia gave Keaton a swat on the behind. "Remember this when you think *I'm* being too harsh."

I grinned. "Then Zeus rescues them and they end up on this island for years, where someone—and I can't even remember who or why—tells teenage Perseus he has to go bring back Medusa's head."

"Is she the one with snakes for hair?" Keaton asked.

"That's right. So no one actually thinks Perseus will be able to do it, but he does, and along the way he also falls in love with this beautiful girl named Andromeda. She was chained to a rock and left to die by her parents."

"Sheesh, this story is making me feel infinitely better about my parenting skills." Sylvia smiled at me. "Tell me there's a happy ending."

"There is. Perseus brings Andromeda home and they get married and have lots of children. Her constellation is next to his in the sky."

"Awww, I like that." Sylvia glanced up at the star-studded winter sky. "So he didn't kill his grandfather?"

"Oh yeah, he did. But that was more of an accident."

She laughed and shook her head. "I'll focus on the happily ever after part. But I'm freezing out here. Are you guys coming in?"

"Can I have a few more minutes?" Keaton begged. "I want to try to find the comet."

"I'll stay out here for a few more minutes with him," I told her. "You can go in and warm up."

"Thanks," she said, smiling at me. She glanced at her son. "I really appreciate this."

"It's my pleasure." I watched her go back into the house, feeling anxious beneath my skin.

"So how many stars are actually visible?" Keaton asked.

I tried to remember. "To the naked eye, I think a few thousand. But with your telescope, maybe more like a hundred thousand."

"Wow." He moved the telescope slightly to the right. "And how many are there total in the sky?"

"In our galaxy? Oh, maybe a hundred billion or so."

"A hundred billion in our galaxy alone?" Keaton's voice

was full of awe. "And then more in other galaxies beyond that?"

"Yeah. Amazing, isn't it?"

I tilted my head and looked up at the sky, wondering which star was the right one to wish on, the one with the most luck, the most magic, the most power to deliver on its promise.

But if my chances of finding it were one in a hundred billion, what hope could I have that Sylvia might one day really be mine?

CHAPTER 15

Sylvia

AFTER LEAVING Keaton and Henry on the patio, I came in and made some hot chocolate—on the stove top, like my mom used to make it when we were kids, with milk and cocoa powder sweetened with Cloverleigh Farms maple syrup, a little vanilla, and bits of crushed chocolate bar stirred in.

April wandered in while I was putting it together and leaned back against the sink. "So," she said, her expression amused.

"So?" I focused on stirring the cocoa into the hot milk in the pan.

"So is this what *going slow* looks like?" She made little air quotes with her fingers.

"Um . . ." I flashed her a guilty grin.

Her eyes lit up. "Spill the tea, sis."

"Ah, well, we sort of, uh . . ." Heat rose to my face.

"Banged?"

"Shh." I looked over my shoulder toward the family room, where my parents were sitting. "Yes."

"I knew it!" she whispered fiercely.

"How did you know?"

"Well, first of all, it was kind of obvious just from looking at you guys tonight. The way you were touching him. The way he looks at you. Also, Chloe texted me a little bit ago and said . . ." She pulled her phone from her back pocket and read aloud. "'What the fuck is going on between Sylvia and Henry?'" Grinning, she tucked her phone away again. "So it's not like I'm reading minds."

"Oh." I whisked in the vanilla. "I thought maybe Frannie told you."

April's mouth fell open. "*Frannie* knows?"

"It sort of slipped out on Sunday when she was here. But she claimed she could tell something was up between us on Christmas Eve."

"That's what I said too! But then you told me the next day you weren't going to let it go anywhere. You were going to stay away from him for a while."

"Yeah, I was going to." I turned off the heat beneath the pan. "But then somehow I didn't."

"When did this happen anyway?"

"Saturday night at his house when the kids slept at Frannie's," I said, whisking in the chopped-up chocolate bar. "And Sunday evening in the winery."

"Oh my God!" April clapped both hands over her mouth. "Where in the winery?"

"His office." Just the thought of it made my body ache for him again.

"Like on his *desk*?"

"Yes."

"I can't believe it." She shook her head. "So was it good?"

"It was incredible." I took seven mugs out of the cupboard. "You know how we were wondering last week about where to find a good guy who's kind of dominant in the bedroom but sweet to you too?"

"Yeah?"

"Well, I found one."

"He handcuffed you?" she squeaked.

"Will you keep your voice down?" I glanced into the family room again to make sure my parents weren't listening, and shook my head. "No handcuffs, he was just . . . surprisingly rough and demanding at times. But then he was gentle too. He was exactly what I needed."

Through the window over the sink, I could see Henry and Keaton, and it warmed my heart and soul to see Henry so patiently pointing things out to my son, answering his questions, teaching him.

"Wow." April leaned back against the sink again. "So now what? Are you guys a thing?"

"No. So don't say anything," I told her as I poured chocolate into the mugs and placed them on a tray. "We're just friends for now."

She snorted. "Now you really *do* sound like Meg."

"I'm serious." I added a can of whipped cream and a bowl of mini-marshmallows to the tray. "It's too soon to be anything more. Neither of us is in a position to offer the other anything but some fun right now. We agree on that."

"Well, you guys deserve some fun." She sighed. "But it's too bad you couldn't have met each other at a different time in your lives. Maybe you could have made it work for real."

"I can't start wondering what if," I told her, picking up the tray. "I've got enough regrets. The past is past, and I've got to concentrate on moving forward."

April folded her arms across her chest. "Yeah. I hear that."

I set the tray down again. "I'm sorry, April. We're always talking about my issues. How are *you* feeling about . . . everything?"

"I don't know. Okay, I guess."

"The other night, you mentioned eighteen years was coming up."

She nodded, and I briefly saw tears in her eyes before she

looked away. "Yeah. It's hitting me kind of hard. But the milestone birthdays always do. And the holidays."

"I bet."

"It's kind of crazy that I was only eighteen when I had him."

"You were *very* young."

"I was. And in no way ready to parent a child." She tugged at the hem of her hoodie. "But I've been thinking lately about . . . reaching out. Maybe meeting him."

I was shocked. "Really?"

She took a deep breath. "Yes. I think I'm about ready. And the couple who adopted him always said that if and when I decided I'd like to meet him, they'd be okay with it as long as he was."

"Wow." I tried to wrap my brain around meeting a child I'd given birth to for the first time in eighteen years but couldn't. "That's . . . that's a lot to think about."

"I know, but in all honesty, I think I need some closure—some certainty that I did the right thing."

I put a hand on her arm. "You did the right thing, April."

Her lips tipped up, but it wasn't exactly a happy smile. "In my head, I know you're right, but my heart often wonders. I've struggled with it."

"Have you ever talked about this with anyone?"

"Not until now. I never even told anyone else I was pregnant. Tyler knew, Mom knew, Grandma Russell knew—because I went and stayed with her the last three months—and *you* knew. That's it. I think Mom probably told Dad, even though I begged her not to, but he's never mentioned it to me."

"Me neither." I paused. "Have you considered getting a therapist?"

"I'm thinking about it."

"Will you contact Tyler and tell him what you're doing?"

April shook her head vehemently. "No. I haven't spoken

to him in years, and he was one hundred percent in favor of the adoption. He never even signed the birth certificate. I mean, he wasn't a jerk about it," she said quickly. "He was apologetic, and he offered to pay for anything I needed, but he didn't want his name involved."

I nodded. The father of April's son had been a legend in our small town, a left-handed pitching phenom drafted to the major leagues right after graduation. "So you didn't stay in touch? You guys were such good friends."

"We were, but . . . I don't know." April's shoulders rose. "The random one-night stand made things kind of awkward between us *before* we knew it resulted in a baby. Afterward, it was just plain weird. Neither of us knew what to say to the other."

"Right."

"And anyway, I'm still thinking about it. I haven't made up my mind yet." She pushed off the counter and put on a blank face. "Ready with the hot chocolate?"

"Yes. But I just want to say that I'm always here if you do want to talk more about it, okay?"

"Okay."

I picked up the tray and carried it into the family room, April following behind me.

"Mmm, something smells good," my mom said.

"Hot chocolate?" I offered, setting everything on the coffee table.

"Looks delicious." My dad reached for a mug and settled back into his favorite recliner.

"I'll have some too." My mom set her paperback aside. "Good idea. Those boys are going to be chilled to the bone when they get in here."

"I know." I picked up a mug and let it warm both hands as I looked out the glass door onto the patio. I could just make out Henry pointing toward the sky and Keaton following the line of his arm.

"Where's Whitney? Does she want hot chocolate?" April asked, sitting cross-legged on one end of the couch.

"I think she went up to her room," I said. "I'll go see."

Upstairs, I knocked on Whitney's bedroom door. "Whit? I made hot chocolate. Want to come down?"

"No, thanks."

I frowned at the wood. "Are you sure?"

"I'm sure."

"Well, what are you doing in there?" I tried to open the door but it was locked.

"Nothing." A few seconds later, she opened the door. Her face was full of makeup, her expression dour. She looked like a very unhappy clown. "Just playing with the new palette."

"Oh. Well, if you want to come down and join us, feel free. Just wash your face first, please."

"Is Mr. DeSantis still here?"

I paused. Was there something accusatory in her voice? Or was I imagining it? "Yes. He's outside with Keaton showing him how to use the telescope. Want to come down and look through it?"

"No, thanks."

"Okay. I'll be up in a bit to say goodnight. Don't get any makeup on the bedding please."

"I won't." She shut the door with no further comment.

On my way back downstairs, I wondered if Whitney suspected something was going on with Henry or if I was just being paranoid. All we'd done was sit next to each other at the table. I decided I must have imagined the suspicious tone of her question—probably just my own mixed-up feelings about what Henry and I were doing.

When I got back downstairs, Henry and Keaton were just coming into the family room, their cheeks and noses red from the cold.

"Guess what, Mom?" Keaton asked excitedly. "Henry goes to a boxing gym and he said he'd take me there sometime!"

"That's awesome, buddy." I smiled at him.

"They have classes for kids," Henry said, setting the telescope in a corner where it wouldn't get knocked over. "They look like fun."

"I've always wanted to learn how to box, but my dad said team sports were way better." Keaton inhaled deeply. "I smell chocolate."

I laughed. "It's on the table. Help yourself."

While Keaton grabbed a mug from the tray, I turned to Henry. "Can you stay for something hot to drink?"

He hesitated, rubbing the back of his neck. "I should get back."

"Come on. You have to try some hot chocolate—I made it from scratch." I brought him a mug and he took it from me, his hands closing around mine all too briefly.

"Okay. But I can't stay long."

He lowered himself onto the couch opposite April, and I sat in between them. Keaton took the other end of the couch my mother was on and babbled excitedly about all the things he'd seen in the sky. The entire time, Henry seemed stiff and uncomfortable, and he barely touched his hot chocolate. If someone spoke to him directly, he replied, but other than that, he was silent.

After about ten minutes, he set his mug back on the tray and stood. "I really do need to get back. Thanks again for dinner."

I rose to my feet and set my cup down too. "I'll walk you out."

"That's not necessary," he said.

"Goodnight, Henry," called my mother from the couch. My father and April gave him a wave.

"Night." Henry gave a wave to everyone. "See you all tomorrow."

Despite what he'd said, I followed him to the mudroom, where we piled on all our cold-weather apparel in silence. I caught his eye once, and he shook his head like I was a hopeless case. The moment we stepped outside, he pulled me around the side of the house and wrapped me in his arms, crushing his lips to mine in the shadowy dark. Relief mingled with desire—I'd been a little worried that being around my family had made him too skittish. Like maybe he'd decided this was too much of a risk where his job was concerned and I wasn't worth it.

His kiss tasted like chocolate, and he smelled like leather and winter and maybe a little like the oak barrels in the cellar. We stood in nearly a foot of snow, but I'd have stripped us both naked in a heartbeat just to feel his bare skin on mine. Our winter coats were cumbersome, our gloves annoying as we tried and failed to get close enough to satisfy the urge within us.

"Christ," he muttered against my lips. "I've been telling myself all night I wouldn't do this."

"Why?" I asked.

"Because it's not right. Your family is right inside. Your dad is my boss. And your daughter knows something is up."

"You think?"

"Did you hear her asking me all those questions? And she was definitely giving me the side eye across the table."

"She's thirteen. Her face is always like that."

"Still." He took my face in his hands. "We need to be careful, Sylvia."

"April knows," I confessed. "And Frannie. Also, Chloe might have guessed."

"Okay," he said slowly, as if he were trying to process what that meant.

"I didn't mean to betray your confidence," I said quickly, "but I was just so excited, I had to tell someone. So I sort of told Frannie, but I made her promise not to tell Mack."

"So how did April—"

"April just sort of guessed after seeing us together tonight.

And Chloe must have gotten the idea after being around us at work."

He was silent for a moment, but his jaw was set.

"Are you mad?" I asked. "I'm sorry. I know we said we were not going to take this public."

He shook his head. "I'm not *mad*, Sylvia. I just don't want your family thinking I'm taking advantage of you."

"They don't," I protested. "My sisters are happy for me. And they know I'm not a child, Henry. I can take care of myself. I came to *you*, remember?"

"But you've said it yourself—you're vulnerable right now, and from the outside, I'm worried this looks shady on my part."

"Listen to me." I put my hands on his chest. "I know what I said. But being with you is helping me get stronger. It's making me happy. It's nobody's business but ours, right?"

He exhaled. "I'd like to think that. And I'm glad your sisters are happy, but what about your kids? I don't like the idea of having to lie to them. And I'm not good at pretending to feel one way when I feel another. I wish . . . fuck. I don't know what I wish." He slid his arms around me again and rested his chin on the top of my head. "I wish we'd met sooner. Or later. I want things to be different."

"I know." Wrapping my arms around his waist, I pressed my cheek against his chest. "Our timing feels all wrong, doesn't it?"

"It's the *only* thing that feels wrong."

We stood that way for another minute, until I began to shiver.

"Go on inside," he said with gruff affection. "It's freezing out here."

I pulled back and looked at him. "I'm sorry about all this."

"Don't be sorry. Nothing is your fault."

"But I made you come here tonight, and you felt uncomfortable."

He didn't deny it. "Maybe we just have to see each other in private from now on."

I almost laughed. "Privacy is in short supply when you're a single mom living with two kids and two parents."

"Yeah. But at least you've got them. And family is what matters most." He rubbed my arms and dropped a quick kiss on my lips. "I'll see you tomorrow."

After going inside, I made myself go up and knock on Whitney's door. I couldn't put off this conversation any longer, as much as I was dreading it. Henry was right—family was what mattered most, and my kids needed me to be the parent with her head on straight. Or at least straight*ish*.

"Yeah?" Whitney called, her voice muffled.

"Can I come in?"

"I guess." She opened the door a moment later. "What?"

"I need to talk to you." I entered the room and shut the door behind me.

"About what?"

I sat on the edge of the bed and looked at her heavily made-up eyes, penciled-in brows, and bright pink lips. Beneath it all I saw my baby-faced girl, and my heart ached for her. "About Instagram."

Immediately I could tell she knew what I meant. She crossed her arms defensively. Stuck out her chin. "What about it?"

"I saw your profile."

"So take my phone away. Is that what you came up here to do?"

I sighed, leaning back on my hands. "I don't know, Whit. It doesn't seem like that would solve the real problem."

"What's the real problem?"

"That you lied to me. You hid this from me. I wish you would have come to me and just been honest."

"Why? You'd have said no. You always say no when I ask about that. You say no without even listening to my reasons."

I hesitated. Was that true? Had I ever given her a chance to make a case, or had I just refused to consider it because I didn't trust the rest of the world to treat my child with respect? Was that a parenting success, or was it a fail, because I wasn't teaching her anything about the world or the way it views girls? Was I protecting her . . . or me?

"And *you* had an account," she reminded me. "You posted all the time."

"Okay, but I am an adult," I reminded her, "and I've stopped posting because I realized how fake it all is. It was making me sad."

"Well, it makes me happy," she insisted. "I create a version of me I like better than the real thing."

"But that's the whole problem," I said, realizing that I'd been doing for *years* exactly what she was doing now—creating a public version of myself that came along with a whole I'm-just-so-happy story that was pure fiction. "Why use it if you're just going to pretend to be someone you're not?"

"I'm not pretending anything," she said hotly. "It's still me. It's just a different me. And I don't get what the big deal is. It's just my face with makeup on."

"Why don't you ever post a photo without all the makeup on?"

"Did *you* ever post a photo of yourself without makeup on?"

I stared at her, annoyed by her keen understanding of things as well as her sassy tone. "You're making this really difficult."

"So ground me."

I sat up straight. "I don't want to just *ground* you, Whitney. I want to figure this out, so can you please drop the attitude? I realize you're angry at your dad and probably at me, and I'm trying to figure out if this is an act of defiance on your part to get back at us, or if you're just a girl who really likes Urban Decay, all right? Help me out here!"

"Sorry," she said, but she rolled her eyes afterward.

I took a deep breath. "Look, I understand wanting to feel beautiful. What woman doesn't? And I remember what it's like to be thirteen and feel weird in your own skin. Add to that all the drama you've had to deal with over the last few months . . . I'd want to pretend to be another me too sometimes."

She was silent for a moment. "Does that mean I can keep the account?"

I regarded my daughter, telling myself not to react out of fear but out of love and understanding. "As long as you are using these photos to *express* something about yourself and not"—I struggled for the right words—"not *prove* something to someone, or even to yourself, I suppose you can keep the account."

She allowed me a tiny smile. "Thanks."

"But I'm going to follow you."

The smile disappeared and she rolled her eyes again.

"And you have to keep it private and never, ever answer anyone you don't know who tries to message you. To monitor that, I'll need your login."

A scowl formed. "Maybe I don't even want it anymore."

"That's fine too," I said. "Now come here."

Grudgingly, she came and sat next to me on the bed, and I put an arm around her. "You know I love you, and I want you to be happy and safe."

She was silent.

"Is there anything else you want to talk about?"

She didn't say anything right away.

And then.

"Is Henry your boyfriend now or something?"

I stiffened, but tried not to let her notice. "Of course not. We're just friends. Why do you ask?"

She shrugged. "He's around a lot since we've been back. I see you talking to him all the time."

"Oh. Well, he's been here for many years. You probably just never noticed." I paused. "We're getting to know each other better, that's all. We've got a lot in common."

"I didn't know he had a wife." She played with a loose thread on the comforter. "Did he cheat on her like Dad cheated on you?"

"No! Their divorce was nothing like your dad's and mine. They just sort of . . . grew apart."

"When?"

"I think earlier this year."

She took that in. "So you're not dating him?"

"No, Whitney. I'm not dating him. We're just friends." In the back of my mind, I could still hear my words hanging in the air . . . *You lied to me. You hid this from me. I wish you would have come to me and just been honest.*

But I wasn't lying to her, was I? I *wasn't* dating Henry. Dating was when you went places together, like movies or restaurants or concerts. Henry and I stuck to hallways and bathtubs and subterranean offices. Those were definitely not dates. They were two people helping one another through a hard time, making life a little less lonely, reassuring each other that their deepest insecurities weren't the truth.

But as I hugged Whitney goodnight and left her room, a knot began forming in my stomach.

The knot continued to tighten, growing ever more complicated while I loaded the mugs in the dishwasher, said goodnight to my parents, and coaxed Keaton up to bed. After he'd put his pajamas on and brushed his teeth, I turned off his light and went and sat on the edge of his bed.

"Did you have fun tonight?" I asked, brushing his hair off his face.

"Yeah. Mr. DeSantis is cool. Can I really go to his boxing gym?"

"Sure." I glanced at the nightstand, which I'd emptied the other night without saying anything to Keaton. If I opened it right now, what would I find? "I think some physical activity will be good for you. Especially after the holidays. We're all eating so much junk food."

He didn't say anything.

I forced myself to be brave. "It's been really hard, hasn't it, this first Christmas without your dad. It feels strange."

"Yeah."

"Sometimes when things feel hard or strange, we do things to try to make ourselves feel better, like eat cookies or chips. But it doesn't really work, because we can't . . . eat away our bad feelings."

"Do you do that? Eat when you feel bad?"

"Sometimes."

"Like when?"

"Like when I'm sad."

He paused. "I do it when I'm mad at Dad."

Relieved that it was finally out, I took a deep breath and continued stroking his hair. "I understand."

"But it doesn't help."

My throat got tight, and I swallowed hard. "No, it doesn't, does it? But you know what?"

"What?"

"I bet boxing will. And when you start school, making new friends will. And I'm definitely going to need your help picking out a house."

"And a dog?" he asked hopefully.

Sniffing, I laughed. "Maybe a dog. We'll have to see, okay?"

"Okay."

"You know what else will help?"

"What?"

"Talking to someone about how you feel. Aunt Frannie gave me the name of a counselor, and I'm going to make appointments for you and your sister after we get back from skiing."

"Okay."

I leaned over and kissed his head. "See you in the morning."

"Night."

Inside my room, I shut my door and flopped face down on my bed, wanting to believe I'd earned at least a B+ in parenting tonight, but feeling like shit for lying so blatantly to Whitney. It's not like I didn't understand her fears.

But being with Henry was the *one thing* I was doing for myself. Was it too much to ask to start the new year with something I was excited about? A little promise of hope that maybe I wouldn't be so fucking lonely all the time?

Hope is something you can't afford, scoffed that bitchy inner voice. *Just where do you think this thing with Henry can go, anyway? How long do you think you'll be able to hold his interest? You should put the brakes on now while you still can. For your sake, and for the kids'.*

"Shut up," I said into my pillow. "Just shut up."

Maybe the voice was right and I should put the brakes on, but like a child, I didn't wanna.

I just didn't fucking wanna.

CHAPTER 16

Henry

BELIEVE IT OR NOT, I'd planned to keep my hands off her on New Year's Eve.

Not because I felt any less attracted to her—if anything, I wanted her more every day—but because her entire family was going to be there, I still felt anxious about what her daughter suspected, and I didn't want Sylvia to think all I wanted from her was physical gratification.

The first night she'd come to my house, it *had* been a lot about the sex, but over the last few days, things had shifted somewhat, at least for me. I wanted to *know* her more deeply. I wanted to spend time with her doing everyday things and making her laugh. I wanted to learn her expressions and smiles and sighs. And as ridiculous and juvenile as it sounded, I wanted to take her somewhere and hold her hand. Buy her dinner. Be the guy who got to put his arm around the back of her chair.

Be the guy who made her happy.

I knew that would take time, and it surprised me that I even believed myself capable of it after my marriage had disintegrated so spectacularly, but something about her wouldn't let me be.

I was ready to move on, and I wanted it to be with her. But what if she wasn't?

If we got a chance to talk quietly during the party, I was hoping to tell her how I felt—that I wanted more than just no-strings sex on the side. And I wanted to deliver the message while we were fully clothed and—at least mostly—sober, so that there wouldn't be any confusion. I could keep my hands to myself for the night, couldn't I?

Of course I could. If I was the kind of guy who was worthy of her, I could be a respectable gentleman for one night.

And then I saw her in that skirt.

It was short. And tight. And mesmerizing.

It was the color of champagne and sparkled as she moved, almost like a disco ball. Sylvia wasn't tall, but her bare legs looked endless beneath that glittering little skirt. On top she wore a loose-fitting white blouse with long sleeves that draped into a V at her chest, barely hinting at the curves I knew were underneath. I saw her standing near the appetizer table, sipping a glass of something bubbly and talking with Chloe, and the sight of her stopped me in my tracks. My confidence in my ability to behave respectably wavered.

She saw me, and her lips curved into that slow, secret smile that made my ears feel like they were burning and my neck feel like the knot in my tie was too tight. Eventually someone bumped into me, and I realized I hadn't started walking again yet. Trying not to tug at my shirt collar, I moved toward her.

"Hi, Henry. Happy New Year!" she said, opening her arm as if to embrace me. She wasn't wearing the bright red lipstick tonight, but her lips shimmered with something that made them look like sugar-coated peaches.

Respectable gentleman. Respectable gentleman. Respectable gentleman.

"Happy New Year." I leaned forward and kissed her cheek, then did the same to Chloe. "Where's Oliver?"

"Around here somewhere." Chloe waved a hand in the air. "He's trying to convince my dad to let him shoot off fireworks at midnight. I told him it's never going to happen. Sparklers are about as crazy as my father has ever let us get."

"Oh, shoot!" Sylvia snapped her fingers. "I forgot the bag with the sparklers in it for the kids! I left it on the counter at home. Think I have time to go get them?"

"Dinner is about to be served," said Chloe, "but you'll have time before midnight for sure."

"Okay. Don't let me forget."

Her ass in that skirt sort of reminded me of sparklers. Dazzling. Fiery hot. Slightly dangerous. I glanced at the bar. "I'm going to grab something to drink. Can I get either of you anything?"

"I'm good." Chloe touched Sylvia's arm. "I'm going to find April and make sure everything is running smoothly."

"Sounds good," Sylvia said. "Let me know if she needs anything." Once Chloe had wandered into the crowd, she turned to me. "I'll come with you. I could use a refill."

"Okay." I wished I could take her arm as we walked toward the bar at the back of the room, but even though the party was in full swing and the room was packed with guests of the inn who had no idea who we were, I still didn't feel right about it.

At the bar, I ordered a whiskey on the rocks and she ordered a glass of sparkling white. While we waited for the bartender to pour, she moved closer to me and spoke softly. "You look amazing."

"So do you. I like your outfit."

She blushed and looked down at her legs. "Thanks. I was a little hesitant to wear this skirt because it's so short, but I decided to go for it."

"I'm glad you did."

"My ex hated this skirt. He said it was trashy."

My hands flexed. "Your ex was a fucking idiot."

"He was. But lucky for me, he's gone, and I no longer care what he thinks about my clothes. *I* like this skirt, so I'm going to wear it."

"My ex hated all my shirts with holes. I think that's why I still wear them."

She laughed. "I will love it even more every time I see a hole in your shirt."

When our drinks had been poured, she picked up her glass and tugged at my elbow. "Let's go sit with Mack and Frannie. They're at our table."

I walked behind her, admiring her pert little ass in that glittering skirt and trying not to drool. The crotch of my pants was already growing tight.

Respectable gentleman. Respectable gentleman. Respectable gentleman, I repeated in my head.

So far, it was not going well.

At the table designated for the family, Mack and Frannie sat chatting with Meg and Noah. "I saved these for us," Sylvia said, indicating two empty chairs. "And those are for Chloe and Oliver and April, if she ever gets a break."

"Thanks." I sat down, and she slid onto the chair beside me. It was obvious Frannie knew what was going on with us, because she was giving her sister a look that was like winking without the actual wink.

I took a pretty big swallow of whiskey. "Where are the kids sitting tonight?"

"They have their own table by the band," Frannie said, glancing in that direction. "The girls are insisting they can make it to midnight, but I've got my doubts."

"If Winnie falls asleep, we can just stick her on the couch in the office, like we used to do with you," Sylvia said with a laugh.

That led to a discussion about what it had been like to

grow up at Cloverleigh, all the changes over the years, and what the future might bring. Chloe and Oliver joined us eventually, and Chloe generously praised Sylvia's performance in the tasting room the last two days.

"She's a natural," Chloe said, clinking her glass to Sylvia's. "A couple weeks, and she'll know as much as I do."

"No way." Sylvia shook her head. "I have so much to learn. I really want to understand the whole process, from the planting to the harvest to the aging. I feel like what I'm describing to guests will make so much more sense. It's like what you were saying, Henry." She looked at me, leaning in my direction. "What people taste here is totally unique to our vineyard, to the way *we* make wine. And what they're tasting this year will be different than what they might taste next year, because every vintage tells a different story. I want to make them come back year after year to learn a new story."

Chloe laughed. "Sounds like someone has been reading the gospel of Henry DeSantis."

"Hey, she *asked*," I said, putting one palm up. "I didn't force it on her."

"No, I love it," Sylvia gushed, putting her hand on my fucking thigh. "I find it fascinating."

"I'm sure." The smirk on Chloe's face, paired with the look she exchanged with Frannie, told me we were not fooling the Sawyer sisters. Only Meg seemed a little clueless, but then, she and Noah were pretty wrapped up in each other.

My first drink went down easy and fast, so I had another. The whiskey eased my nerves and relaxed the tension in my shoulders, but it did nothing to take the edge off the desire I felt for the woman next to me. During dinner, I laughed and talked with everyone at the table, but every time she looked in my direction or gave me a smile or put a hand on my leg, I felt like I was coming out of my skin.

After dessert, the band switched from big band dinner

music to more upbeat oldies, and people swarmed the dance floor. After some coaxing, Mack agreed to dance with Frannie but slammed the rest of his beer first. Chloe convinced Oliver to get out there too, but Noah said there was no way in hell he was dancing until his current beer was empty, so Sylvia and I sat talking to them for a while.

I'm not sure when I put my arm around the back of Sylvia's chair, but I suddenly realized it was there when I noticed Meg staring at it. If I hadn't been halfway through my third whiskey, I might have removed it.

The band began to play a classic Elvis Presley ballad, and Sylvia turned to me with a hopeful look in her eye. "You wouldn't want to dance with me by any chance, would you? I love this song."

"Uh, I'm not much of a dancer."

"I don't mind."

The idea of holding her close, even on a crowded dance floor, was too tempting to resist. "Okay."

We walked onto the floor and found a spot among the slow-moving couples. She came into my arms as naturally as if we'd been dancing together for years. I could smell her perfume, and inhaled deeply. The scent stirred up memories of her bare skin on mine, and provoked a response in my body that I couldn't exactly hide. I glanced over her shoulder at the table where the kids were sitting and saw Whitney watching us, transfixed.

"Thanks for this," Sylvia said, looking up at me. "I know it's probably not comfortable."

"Your daughter is looking a little unsettled."

Sylvia shook her head. "I'm not even turning around to look at her. We are *dancing*, that's all."

"Okay." But I adjusted my hold on her, putting a little more space between our bodies.

Sylvia laughed. "Are you trying to leave room for the Holy Ghost?"

"I'm trying to be a good person, and you make it hard."

She nestled in closer, pressing her breasts against my chest. "How hard?" she whispered.

"Oh, Jesus." I shook my head. "You need to stop. My mind is going to some dangerous places right now."

"Tell me about it." Then she went up on tiptoe to whisper in my ear. "And use all the dirty words. You know how I like them."

I groaned, closing my eyes for a second. "Sylvia. We're in a room full of people and we're being watched."

She giggled and backed off—a little. "Okay, okay. Sorry. Misbehaving is new to me, and I'm a little addicted to it."

For the rest of the song, I told myself not to worry so much and just enjoy the feel of her in my arms. This was as much of her as I would get tonight, so I might as well savor it. When the song ended, we walked back to our table hand in hand.

"Hey, Syl," Meg said brightly, picking her purse up from the floor. "Come to the ladies' room with me."

"Okay." Sylvia reached beneath her chair for her purse before turning to me. "Be right back."

"No problem." I watched her walk away with her sister and knew in my gut Meg was going to ask her what was going on with us. It still didn't stop me from staring at Sylvia's butt and the way that skirt clung and shimmered as she moved.

"So," Noah said, tipping up his beer. "How long have you been in love with Sylvia?"

I made a sound somewhere between a choke and a laugh. "Uh, since I saw her in that skirt?"

Noah nodded and touched his beer bottle to my glass. "Good answer."

CHAPTER 17

Sylvia

MEG DASHED PAST THE LADIES' room at the pace of an Olympic sprinter. "There could be people in there. Come in here."

I felt myself being dragged into the catering office at the end of the hall. "Meg, what on earth?"

"We need to talk." She shut the door, snapped on the overhead light, and turned to face me, her eyes gleaming. "What's going on with you and Henry?"

"Um . . ."

"Don't even bother lying to me. I can see that there's a *thing* between you. You're all over him."

"What? I am not."

She rolled her eyes. "Syl, you've practically been in his lap all night. And he's been looking at you with that look in his eye."

"What look?"

Her brows peaked. "The *I've got ideas* look. Now tell the truth." She folded her arms. "Did you sleep with him?"

I sighed, giving up the pretense. "Yes."

She squealed and clapped her hands. "Yay! Once?"

"Yes." Then I grinned. "Once in the hallway, once in his bed, once in his bathtub, and once in his office."

The smile slid off Meg's face, her expression morphing from delight to shock. "Are you fucking kidding me? You've done it that many times since you've been home?"

"Well, most of that happened last Saturday night. But yeah, things did move kind of quickly." I lifted my shoulders. "I'm a little scared how quickly, actually."

"Why? He seems like such a great guy."

"Because he *is* a great guy. Because I like him so much. Because if my life were different and not so fucked up, he'd be exactly the kind of guy I was looking for." I swallowed hard. "I could fall for him so easily, Meg."

"But your life *isn't* fucked up anymore, Syl—that's the beautiful thing." She took me by the shoulders. "Don't scare yourself out of giving him a chance."

"I'm not, I swear." I shook my head. "In fact, I'd probably be wise to be *more* cautious, not less. But I can't seem to stay away from him."

"And that's a bad thing?"

"There's this voice," I blurted.

"Voice?"

"In my head," I explained. "And it makes me doubt myself. It makes me feel like I can't trust what I'm feeling."

"Don't listen to it," she said, as if it were that easy.

"But—"

"But nothing. I know how unhappy you were last fall—how unhappy you've been for years. If the thought of being with Henry makes you happy, you should give him a chance."

"It's not just me I have to think about," I reminded her. "I have two children."

"Oh yeah, I forgot about them." She sighed. "Children do make things more complicated. But I'm sure yours want you to be happy, right? You just have to talk to them."

I decided not to mention Whitney's suspicious questions last night—mostly because I just didn't want to think about them. "This whole discussion could be for nothing," I said. "I mean, Henry might not have any interest in dating me for real. He could have anyone—someone younger and prettier and without kids."

She smirked. "Trust me. He has interest. Even Noah asked me if you two were fucking."

"Jeez," I said, rolling my eyes. "Are we the two least chill people on the planet?"

She laughed. "It's possible, but hey. Good chemistry is good chemistry. And it's not easy to find, so don't waste it. Come on, we should get back to the party."

The overhead lights in the barn had been dimmed, and the room was lit only by strings of party lights hung from the rafters. Before I went back to my table, I checked on the kids, who seemed to be having a great time. Even little Winnie was still going strong.

"But Mom, what about the sparklers?" Whitney asked, out of breath from dancing. "I think we forgot them." She had quite a bit of makeup on, including some pretty garish teal eyeshadow, but I hadn't felt like arguing with her tonight. And she was clearly having fun—I felt a little more optimistic.

"Oh, that's right! I need to run home and get them." I patted her shoulder. "I'll be right back, okay?"

"Okay."

I walked back toward my table, where Henry was sitting alone. One ankle was crossed over his knee, and he leaned back in his chair, sipping his drink as he watched me approach, his eyes on fire. It struck me like a punch in the gut how handsome he was. How sexy. How strong. How *good*. Something in me ignited.

"Hey," he said, rising to his feet to pull out my chair. "I was beginning to wonder if you found someone better to sit next to."

"Impossible," I said, tossing my purse onto the table. Then I rose on tiptoe to whisper in his ear. "Want to sneak away with me for a minute or two?"

He closed his eyes. "Sylvia. Don't do this to me."

"Do what?"

"Tempt me." His eyes opened and seared into mine. "I promised myself I'd be good tonight because we're in public."

"So let's go somewhere private and be bad."

"Respectable   gentleman.   Respectable   gentleman. Respectable gentleman," he mumbled.

"What?"

"You're killing me, Sylvia. Everyone will see us leave. Our entire table knows we're screwing around. Probably because I can't stop staring at your ass in that skirt."

"I don't care who sees us. I want you. Now." I gave him my most seductive smile and spoke low. "I'll leave the skirt on for you."

"Fuck." He struggled with it for less than three seconds, and then gave in. "Where are we sneaking to?"

I grinned. "My house. I'll go first."

"I'll be two minutes behind—if I can wait that long."

Turning on my heel, I dashed into the coatroom by the exit, slipped on the wool dress coat I'd borrowed from my mom, and hurried out the doors. The air was icy cold, but it wasn't snowing and the walkway between the barn and the inn was freshly plowed. Still, I had to force myself to slow down so I wouldn't catch a heel and stumble.

If I was going to put marks on my knees, it wasn't going to be because of a slippery sidewalk.

The kick of doing something sexy and subversive coursed through me. I couldn't ever remember a time in my life when I'd behaved so wantonly or heedlessly. But I didn't care—at this moment, nothing else mattered to me except how I wanted to feel, and it was so fucking fantastic to have power over that again. I was taking my life back. What better way to say goodbye to the old me and hello to the new?

I turned off the pathway at my parents' driveway and used the code to open the garage. From there I slipped into the house via the back door, which led right into the mudroom. I left the garage door open, thinking that Henry would come in that way also, but I'd only been inside the kitchen long enough to spot the forgotten bag of sparklers on a kitchen chair when I heard a knock on the front door.

So much for waiting five minutes.

Shrugging off my coat and tossing it on top of the bag, I hurried into the front hall to pull it open. He stood on the porch in his formal clothes like an old-fashioned suitor coming to call, or maybe even my prom date coming to fetch me for the dance.

"Come on in," I said, moving back so he could step inside.

He shoved the door closed behind him. The hallway was dark and silent. "All alone, little girl?"

I nodded, taking his hand and leading him up the stairs. "My parents aren't home."

"Is it wise to invite the teacher into your house at night when your parents aren't home?"

"Well, I just thought you might want to give me a little private tutoring session. I'm so anxious to be your best student." I pulled him inside my room and he shut the door. My shades were lowered, but the bedside lamp was on. The light wasn't bright, but it was enough to see the hungry look in his eyes.

"A private tutoring session, huh?" He doffed his suit coat, tossing it onto my bed. Then he undid the knot in his tie and pulled it loose. "And what is it you want to learn?"

I lifted my shoulders and assumed an expression of innocence as I sauntered toward him, hands clasped behind my back. "How to please you, of course."

He yanked the tie from his collar. "Turn around."

I presented my back to him and saw our reflections in the full-length mirror on the back of my closet door. I half expected him to yank up the sequined skirt he liked so much and fuck me right there on my feet—while both of us watched. But instead, he pulled my hands behind my back and bound my wrists with his necktie.

Tight.

A little gasp escaped me. My heart was pounding. I'd never been tied up before.

"You wanted to learn how to please me." Henry locked eyes with me in the mirror.

"Yes."

"Sometimes I like to have all the control."

He stood there for one second longer, and I briefly wondered if he was debating how far to take this little game. I wanted to show him he didn't have to be afraid of hurting me, of offending me. I *wanted* to play—hadn't I started it? How could I let him know?

Facing him again, I dropped to my knees on the rug and looked up at him with wide eyes. "Tell me what to do." I licked my lips. "Please."

"Jesus." Henry put two fingers beneath my chin and ran his thumb across my bottom lip. "Your mouth is so fucking beautiful."

I parted my lips slightly, and he slipped his thumb between them. I stroked it with my tongue, circled it, sucked on it, all the while keeping my eyes locked on his.

His breathing grew heavier. "Do you know what you're asking for, little girl?"

I almost nodded—but then thought it might be *more* fun if I answered no. So I shook my head, pulled my lips from his thumb. "Show me."

He unbuckled.

Unbuttoned.

Unzipped.

Then he reached inside his pants and pulled out his cock, which was huge and thick and hard. He stroked himself a few times, and I felt myself growing wetter.

"Let me," I whispered.

He positioned the tip at my lips and I licked it like an ice cream cone with my tongue. One side then the other. Around in a circle. This way and that, while he gripped his shaft in his fist and worked his hand slowly up and down.

"Like that?" I asked coyly, batting my lashes at him.

"Fuck yes. Now open your mouth."

I did as he asked, and he pushed his cock between my lips, slowly, inch by inch, until he hit the back of my throat. For a second, I was scared I might choke, but then he pulled out. When he slid in the next time, it was only halfway, allowing me to play and tease and suck as he gently flexed his hips. His hands moved to my head, and he groaned as he adopted a quicker rhythm, a harder drive, a deeper thrust.

"You make me so fucking hard," he rasped. "Even when I have all the control, I don't. Every fucking second is a struggle around you."

Without the use of my hands, I had no control whatsoever, and the fear of choking or suffocating was real in my mind. But I loved his guttural sounds of ecstasy, the way his fingers tightened in my hair, the salty-sweet taste of him on my tongue. The animal noises I made were instinctive, helpless, throaty, frantic. Part of me was embarrassed by them, but another part thrilled at letting go of caring what I looked like or sounded like—I didn't have to conform to a manufactured version of myself anymore. I didn't have to be perfect all the time. I could be dirty, I could be real. I could be me.

"My God, your ass in that skirt," Henry growled, and I realized he was watching this in the mirror. Somehow, that made it even hotter. "I have to fuck you while you're wearing it."

Suddenly, he pulled his cock out of my mouth and yanked me to my feet. With my hands still tied, I felt myself being pushed toward the mirror, then spun around to face it. Henry dropped down and reached beneath my skirt to tug my barely-there red lace panties down my legs and help me step out with one foot. When he stood, he braced himself against the mirror with one arm, wrapped the other around my waist and slipped his hand under my skirt, between my thighs.

I moaned, my legs nearly buckling as he played with my clit—stroking it softly while he whispered in my ear. "Did sucking my cock make you this wet? Did it?"

"Yes," I managed. I could feel his cock pushing against my bound hands and I tried to rub it. Catching my reflection in the mirror, I could scarcely believe the woman in the glass was me. My hair was a wild mess. My lipstick was smeared all over my chin. My skin was flushed. My eyes were hooded and my mouth hung open.

"I love how greedy you are for me," he said, his voice gravelly with lust as he moved his fingers faster. Christ, he knew exactly how to touch me. "I tell myself you've never been this way for anyone else."

"I haven't. Oh God, Henry," I panted, that familiar panic setting in, the one I always felt when an orgasm hovered and I worried it would shimmer in front of me and then disappear, a mirage. "Don't stop, please don't stop."

Of course, he didn't stop, because this was my new life, not my old, and I was with someone now who put value on my pleasure and not just his own. I nearly wept as the orgasm rocked my body above his hand, turning my legs to jelly.

I was barely steady on my heels again before I felt my hands being freed, and I caught myself against the mirror with both palms just as his cock pushed inside me. My skirt rode up as he drove inside me again and again, his hands gripping my hips. I watched myself in the mirror, took in my hiked-up skirt and wide-spread heels, my red knees and wild hair. And I watched Henry fucking me savagely from behind, heard his ragged breathing and clenched-teeth cursing, felt his fingers digging mercilessly into my skin.

When he looked over my shoulder, our eyes met in the mirror, and two seconds later, he exploded inside me, his body going still, an arm hooking around my waist, his chest heavy against my back as his cock throbbed inside me. When the spasms subsided, we were still for a moment. He laid his forehead on my shoulder.

Chills broke out across my skin, and I shivered. But it was a good shiver—one of anticipation for the future, of the promise of being happy again, of all the possibilities that lay ahead.

Henry picked up his head. "You okay?"

"Yes."

"You sure? Was I too rough on you?"

"No. I might have some explaining to do about the rug burns on my knees, but I am more than okay."

"Good." He planted a kiss on my shoulder. "Because there's something I want to talk to you about."

"Sounds serious." I was teasing him a little—my sweet, sexy, serious Henry—but he nodded.

"It is, kind of."

"Oh, okay. Give me a minute?"

"Of course."

Henry waited in my bedroom while I went into the bathroom to clean up a little. When I came out, he was standing by my dresser, looking at a framed photo of my kids when they were little.

"Did you take this one?" he asked.

"Yes." I pulled a new pair of underwear from a drawer and slipped them on beneath my skirt. My feet were bare—I'd kicked my heels off on the way to the bathroom.

"Cute."

"They are. And hopefully I'm not messing them up too much."

He turned toward me, his hands in his pockets. His top shirt buttons were undone, and he hadn't put his tie back on yet. His hair was adorably mussed. "Did you ever talk to Whitney last night?"

"Yeah. I think we understand each other." I hesitated before adding, "She asked if we were dating."

He was quiet a second. "What did you say?"

"I said no." I ran my thumb along a nick on the wooden dresser top. Probably I'd put it there with my hairbrush on a bad morning. "Isn't . . . isn't that the truth?"

"Is that how you want it?"

I looked up at him. "What do you mean?"

"I mean, I don't want to rush you, and I know we've been saying we don't really know what we're doing, and we don't want to make this public yet, but . . . I *feel* something for you, Sylvia. And I don't want to hide it."

My heart swelled with hope, and I rose up on my bare toes as if buoyed by the feeling. "I feel something for you too."

His arms came around me. "I was up all last night

thinking about you. I know this isn't what you planned. I know people might say we're moving on too fast. A fucking boyfriend is the last thing you need and the last thing I ever thought I'd want to be at this point. But I want more than sneaking around with you. I mean, I want the sex, don't get me wrong, but I want to take you on real dates too. I want to be good to you."

I smiled. "You are good to me."

"I want to be good to you *out loud*. I want to help you settle into your new life here—I want to be part of it. I want to take you back to that party and kiss you at midnight." He kissed my lips. "I want you to be mine for real."

I shook my head, feeling my throat get tight. "You're crazy, you know that? You could have anybody you want."

"I just want you, Sylvia." He brushed my hair back. "Tell me there's a way."

I was overwhelmed by the way my heart was thumping. We could be so good together—I could feel it way down deep. But my fears wouldn't dissipate just like that. "Henry . . . being with me won't be easy."

"Nothing good comes easy."

"I have to make sure the kids are going to be okay with us. They've been through so much."

"Absolutely," he said firmly. "I know they come first."

"And I'm still a little wary of . . . of letting myself fall. It's not that I don't trust you," I went on quickly. "I know what kind of man you are. But it might take time for me to really feel safe turning over my heart. It's just starting to feel whole again."

"It's okay," he said, pressing his lips to my forehead. "Your whole heart is worth the wait."

I moved in closer to him, pressing my cheek to his chest and closing my eyes, wishing I could silence those doubts inside me forever. "This feels too good to be true, Henry. Too much, too soon. Is it?"

"You're safe with me, Sylvia." His voice was deep, calm, and reassuring. "I promise. Everything is going to be okay."

For the moment, I believed him.

We put ourselves back together, retrieved the bag of sparklers from the kitchen, and started down the path toward the barn, our breath visible in the icy dark. When we reached the door, through which the loud music blared, Henry turned to me. "Wait a second."

"What?"

He put his hands on my shoulders. "It's almost midnight, but I'm not going to be able to do this in there."

I smiled. "You mean kiss me?"

"Yes."

"So do it now—I'll have the memory at midnight."

He slanted his head over mine, and our lips met fully and openly. When he would have pulled away, I put a hand on the back of his neck and drew out the length of the kiss, my body warming as his arms moved from my shoulders to wrap around my back. We kissed deeply and intimately, but less impatiently than in my bedroom—this kiss was the beginning of something. A new year, a new life, a new hope. I felt the ropes of doubt and distrust that had been strapped so tight around my heart begin to loosen.

Suddenly the music got louder, and a voice rang out. *"Mom?"*

Henry and I jumped apart, and I opened my eyes to see Whitney standing in front of the open barn door, Keaton and Mack's girls filing out behind her.

"Whitney!" I exclaimed, exchanging a frantic glance with Henry. "What are you guys doing out here?"

"We were coming to look for you. You said you'd be right back with the sparklers, and it's been like an hour." Her face registered shock and dismay as she looked back and forth from me to Henry to me again. "What's going on?"

"Oh, well, we went to get them, uh, Henry and I did, and —and I couldn't remember where I put them. We had to find them." I could hardly think. My heart was hammering in my chest. Had they seen us kissing?

I had my answer a second later, when Whitney shook her head and said. "Just friends, huh?" Then she swept past me and took off running toward the house.

I whirled around and watched her moving farther away. "Whitney, come back! It's freezing and you don't have a coat on!"

"I don't care!" I heard her yell.

I faced the confused, shivering kids again and shoved the bag at Keaton. "Here are the sparklers. Take them inside and divide them up, okay? I need to go talk to your sister."

"Okay." He took the bag from me and scratched his head. "Is she coming back?"

"I hope so. Go on in now." When they'd all gone back inside, I turned to Henry, who looked as shell-shocked as Keaton. "I have to go."

"Of course. I'm sorry, Sylvia," he added resolutely. "It's my fault."

"It's not." I shook my head, fighting tears. "It's mine. I should have known this would happen." For a moment, I rested my forehead on my fingertips. "God, what was I thinking?"

"Sylvia—" Henry reached for me, but I pulled my arm away.

"Let me go," I said, starting toward the house. "I have to find her."

CHAPTER 18

Sylvia

THE GARAGE DOOR was open when I reached the house. As soon as I let myself in the back door, I could hear crying upstairs.

I hurried up the steps, her sobs growing louder as I approached her door. If possible, my heart grew even sicker. I tried the handle, but it was locked. I knocked a few times.

"Whit? Can I come in please?"

"No!"

"Honey, please. Let's talk about this."

"No! You'll just lie to me again!"

I put both palms on the door. "I promise you, I will tell you the complete truth, Whitney. Just let me in."

"I don't want to live here anymore!"

I took a deep breath. "Okay. Can we talk about it?"

"I'm going to live with Grandma and Grandpa Baxter in Arizona!"

If the situation hadn't been so serious, I might have laughed. Brett's mother and father were completely hands-off grandparents, other than sending a check on birthdays and Christmas. "Have you spoken to them?"

"Not yet. But I'm packing right now!"

I rested my forehead against the door and closed my eyes, reminding myself what it felt like to be thirteen on a *good* day—all the confusing emotions, the conflicting thoughts, the yearning to grow up paired with the strange ache to stay a child forever, the unwavering certainty that *no one* understood you. Whitney was dealing with all that plus the fear of abandonment the divorce had caused. I didn't blame her for wanting to leave before she could be left. I wanted to reassure her she was never going to lose me. I wanted her to know I was on her side, and I understood her fears.

But first, I needed her to let me in.

"Maybe I could help you pack," I called through the door.

She didn't say anything, and a moment later, the door opened. "Fine," she said, swiping her nose on the back of her hand. Then she spun around and went back to throwing clothes in her suitcase.

I sat on the bed and took her favorite stuffed animal onto my lap—a raggedy bear she'd slept with since she was a baby. I hadn't seen it in a while. "You don't like it here anymore?"

"No." She began shoving cosmetics into a makeup case on her dresser.

I sighed. "Then I guess I'll have to pack too."

"Where are you going?"

"Wherever you go. I can't live without my Whitney. And we'll have to bring Keaton too—I need both my babies."

"Why? You don't love us."

Even though I knew it was her anger and fear talking, the words hurt. I forced myself to see beyond them. "Of course I do."

She whirled around, fresh tears running down her face. "Then why are you doing this to us?"

"Doing what, honey?"

"Just what Daddy did!"

"Whitney, I'm not. I promise."

"Why should I believe a word you say?" she asked,

wiping beneath her eyes, smearing the dark eye makeup so that it looked like tire tracks across her face. "I asked you if you were dating him and you said *no*."

"Because we aren't dating, not exactly," I said, heat rushing my face.

"Please, Mom. I *saw* you dancing with him. I saw you *kissing* him. You're not just friends."

"Well, sometimes friends—"

She put her hands over her ears. "Stop lying to me! That's just what Daddy did!"

"Okay, okay." I held up my hands. "I'll be honest. Henry and I have feelings for each other. We'd . . . we'd like to be more than friends."

"I knew it!" she yelled, shaking her head. "You think I'm stupid, but I'm not. I know how this works. You fall in love with Henry, and then he'll take you away from us. You'll want to get married and have his baby, and then you'll realize you don't need us anymore."

"Oh, honey, that's not true." I stood up and moved toward her, but she ducked out of the way—to my recollection, the first time she'd ever rejected my attempt at affection. A lump of sadness and self-loathing lodged in my throat. "Please, sweetheart. Come here."

"No!" she cried. "You'll just hug me and tell me you understand, but you don't. *Your* parents are still together. Your house is still your house. You can come back here any time you want and everything is the same. You and Daddy took all that away from me. My entire life was just gone one day, and I can never get it back!"

I began to cry too. "Oh, Whitney, I'm sorry. I know I can never understand exactly what you're going through. You're right. I grew up here in this wonderful, warm home with two adoring parents, and it's a place I feel safe and loved. I guess I was hoping it could be that for you too, because honey, you *are* safe and loved. I'm here for you. I'll always be here for you."

"You don't mean that," she bawled. "You say it and say it and say it, but if you meant it, you wouldn't be with anyone else. You're no better than Daddy."

"Whitney, that's not—" But I stopped. I'd been about to say *fair*, but I realized at that moment that fairness was beside the point. Reason played no role in the emotional storm raging inside her head. And when I looked at her, I knew in my heart and soul I would do anything to make her feel safe, no matter what it took. I was a mother first and foremost, and the needs of my children would always come before my own.

That was the difference between me and their father.

"Okay, Whitney. If you're not ready for me to be more than Henry's friend, I won't."

"Just get out and leave me alone," she whimpered, throwing herself face down on her bed and wailing into her pillow.

Wiping my own tears, I sat beside her, relieved when she let me. "I'm afraid I can't do that. You're stuck with me, love." I rubbed her back the way she'd always liked as a child. "That's what being family means."

She cried hard for a few minutes—huge, racking sobs that made her shoulders shudder and soaked her pillow. Finally, they subsided, replaced with less violent weeping, but the sight and sound of it still broke what was left of my heart.

"W-wasn't D-Daddy family?" she sputtered. "He st-still left."

"That's true," I said. "But I was raised to believe that family sticks around. Family shows up. Family has your back. At least mine does."

She flipped around so that her head was in my lap, and I brushed the hair off her forehead. I was dying to mop up her face, but didn't want to wreck whatever accord we might've arrived at. Her tears slowed, and her breathing returned to normal, except for the occasional hiccup. "I don't really want to move to Arizona," she confessed.

"I don't blame you."

Her arms circled my waist. "I want to stay here with you and Keaton and have our new house. I want it to be *just us*."

I swallowed hard. I knew what she meant. "Okay."

She closed her eyes, and eventually even her hiccups ceased. "Mommy?"

The name brought the lump back to my throat. "Yes?"

"How do you even know if someone means it when they say they love you? How do you know they're not going to leave you and break your heart?"

Honestly, I didn't feel qualified to give the answer. The truth was, there were guys like Brett in the world who said they loved you for fifteen years and then up and left you for J.Crew Kimmy one day. How could I explain that to her without giving her trust issues for the rest of her life? Weren't my own issues enough? Did her father's actions have to scar us both for life?

"I don't know, Whit. I could make something up and tell you that you just know, but the truth is, sometimes you don't. Sometimes what looks like real love turns out to be infatuation. Sometimes real love exists, but people drift apart. Sometimes love is real, but the circumstances are all wrong. Love is tricky. And messy. And hard to explain."

She shivered and held me tighter. "I hope I never fall in love. It sounds scary and horrible. I'd rather be alone."

"Give it some time, okay? Maybe you'll change your mind."

She shook her head vehemently. "Never."

Part of me wanted to argue with her, but another part agreed with her one hundred percent. Love *was* terrifying. It put you completely at the mercy of someone else. You basically handed over your breakable heart and hoped that someone wouldn't shatter it. Whitney was right—there was never any *real* assurance you wouldn't get hurt.

Maybe I *was* better off alone.

At that moment, we heard shouts coming from outside. I checked the clock on her night table, and realized it was midnight. "I think we missed sparklers," I told her gently.

"I don't care."

"Do you want to go back to the party?"

She shook her head.

"Okay, honey. You don't have to. But I should go back and get your brother." I started to get up, but she gripped me tighter.

"No! Just . . . just stay for a few more minutes, okay?"

"Okay." Fighting tears, I began stroking her hair again. This wasn't the fresh start I'd envisioned. "It's going to be okay, baby. You'll see."

She squeezed her eyes shut and didn't answer, and I sat there with her for a little while longer, drying my tears with the sleeve of my blouse so they wouldn't fall into her hair. Within minutes, she fell asleep, and I carefully removed her shoes from her feet before pulling her comforter over her legs.

After leaving her room, I stopped in mine to trade my party clothes for a pair of jeans, a sweater, and some boots. In the bathroom, I tamed my hair into a ponytail and took off my ruined eye makeup. Then I went downstairs, put my coat on, and dragged myself back to the party, more miserable with every step.

An hour ago, I'd been so happy, so starry-eyed, my heart so full of hope.

How had everything gone so wrong?

CHAPTER 19

Henry

WAITING for Sylvia to come back to the party was torture.

I didn't feel like drinking, listening to music, or talking to people, but there wasn't really anywhere I could hide. I thought about leaving, but in case Sylvia needed me tonight, I wanted to be somewhere she'd be able to find me.

How the fuck had this night gone so wrong so fast?

I returned to our dinner table, where Mack and Frannie were sitting, and dropped disconsolately into my chair, where I proceeded to brood and fret.

"Everything okay?" Mack asked over the music.

"Fine." Out of the corner of my eye, I saw them exchange a look. It just made me scowl harder.

"Do you know where Sylvia is? I haven't seen her in a while," Frannie remarked, false brightness in her voice.

"She's at the house with Whitney."

"Why? What happened to Whitney?" Frannie asked.

I struggled with it for a moment, then realized their own kids were probably going to tell them what they'd seen. "She saw us kissing outside. She got upset and took off."

Frannie gasped. "Yikes!" She looked toward the door. "Do you think I should go over there?"

"I have no idea," I said, feeling like the least qualified person to give advice on doing the right thing. "But I might as well warn you, your girls saw the whole thing too. They might say something to you about it."

"Oh, our girls have caught us kissing a million times." Frannie reached over to pat Mack's arm. "They're used to it, right, babe?"

"Right." But Mack, who'd been a single father of three young girls, understood what the issue was. "Whitney doesn't like the idea of her mom with someone else?"

"Apparently not."

"But that's ridiculous," said Frannie. "Wouldn't she want her mom to be happy? The girls were thrilled when we stopped sneaking around and finally admitted what was going on between us."

"But that didn't happen right away," Mack reminded her. "My guess is that Whitney is upset because she lost her dad and thinks she's going to lose her mom too. My girls didn't want to let me out of their sight after Carla left. They used to cry when I dropped them off at school. They thought I might not come back."

"Oh, I remember that." Frannie shook her head. "That was so sad."

"It takes time," Mack said with a shrug. "I'm sure if you give it a while, things will calm down."

I nodded, but I didn't fucking want to give it time. I wanted to be with her *now*, and I was furious that somehow we'd already fucked this up before we'd even given ourselves a chance.

"You look so miserable, Henry. You really care about her, don't you?" Frannie gave me a sympathetic look.

I slumped down lower in my chair. "Yeah."

Just then, a server came by with a tray of champagne glasses. "Almost midnight," she said, setting a glass down for each place at the table. "Enjoy!"

But the occasion had lost all its appeal.

Just before twelve, I watched the kids light up their sparklers and listened to the crowd count down the last ten seconds of the year, but I couldn't even lift my glass as the band kicked off Auld Lang Syne. I didn't drink the champagne or even pretend to sing along. I just kept looking at the door hoping to see Sylvia come through it, and checking my phone in case she tried to send me a message. Each time, I was disappointed, and finally I gave up. Without even saying goodbye to anyone, I headed for the coatroom.

That's when I saw her come through the door.

She stopped short at the sight of me, about ten feet away, and crossed her arms over her chest. She'd changed her clothes, her hair was pulled back, and her face was bare. She looked young and vulnerable and sad.

I approached slowly. "Hey."

"Hey."

"How's Whitney?"

"Asleep. All cried out."

My heart ached. "I'm really sorry, Sylvia."

She shook her head. "It's not your fault. Whitney's feelings have nothing to do with you and everything to do with her dad and me."

"I'm still sorry you're going through it."

She tried to smile, but looked like she might burst into tears at any moment. "Thank you."

I wanted to ask what this meant for *us*, but knew it wasn't the time. I could tell from the way she was standing and the tremble of her lower lip that this Sylvia was a different one than the one I'd been next to at dinner and alone with in her room. Even the tone of her voice was different. That Sylvia had been confident and audacious and strong. This Sylvia looked shaken and fragile, like she would bruise if you looked at her wrong.

"Can I call you?" I asked, keeping my arms pinned to my sides. I wanted to hold her so badly it hurt.

Her eyes filled. "I need some time to think, okay? Things have been moving so fast, and I feel . . . off-kilter. I think I need a few days to find my balance."

"Okay . . . well." My chest was uncomfortably tight. "You know where to find me."

"Yes." She closed her eyes for a second and composed herself. "I need to get Keaton home."

"Of course."

"Goodnight, Henry."

"Goodnight."

She skirted around me and headed for the kids' table, and I hurried out of the building without even bothering with my coat. I'd get it another time.

When I got home, I felt like putting my fist through a wall, or taking a sledgehammer and smashing that bathtub to bits. It didn't even make sense how upset I was—Sylvia and I had only slept together a handful of times. It's not like I was in love with her. This shouldn't be so painful. So what the fuck was my problem?

I undressed in agitated, jerky movements, viciously scrubbed my teeth, and thumped myself into bed, punching my pillow several times before burying my head in it. But I couldn't sleep.

After a while, it came to me, in Sylvia's own voice—something she'd once said.

I missed the life I thought I would have.

Being with Sylvia had given me hope for a second chance.

And right now, it felt like that hope was gone.

CHAPTER 20
Sylvia

I GOT Keaton home and into bed, wondering if I should bring up what he'd seen earlier tonight or just let it go. In the end, he was the one who braved the topic.

"Mom?" he asked as I was tucking him in.

"Yes?"

"Are you and Mr. DeSantis . . ." he started, clearly uncertain how to end the question.

"No," I said. "We talked about it, and we do like each other a lot, but we're just going to be friends. I'm sorry if what you saw upset you."

"Okay."

"Did it?" I ventured. "Upset you?"

"Kind of. I don't know."

I nodded. "I understand."

"It's not that I don't like him. I do."

"I know, honey. And it's okay." I struggled to hold back the sob attempting to tear out of my chest. "Goodnight."

"Night."

Inside my room, I undressed, crawled into bed, and proceeded to soak my pillow with tears.

I felt like I'd let down everyone I cared about. I felt like I'd screwed up my fresh start. I felt like I couldn't do anything right no matter how hard I tried. Was I just destined to make mistake after mistake? I'd confused and upset my children, who were depending on me. I'd gone after Henry knowing full well I had nothing to offer him. I'd allowed myself to believe something more between us was possible—and I'd allowed him to believe it too.

How was I going to face him again?

I tried to list all the reasons why he would be better off without me . . .

I was an emotional wreck. I was a single mother. I had trust issues.

I was scared. Scarred. Damaged in places that couldn't be seen.

I would never feel completely safe in a relationship again. I would always doubt the promises he made. I would never be able to put him first, the way he deserved.

Then there were all the things about me that Brett hated.

I cried easily. I liked sappy movies. I listened to Christmas music starting on November first. I wore short skirts. I liked Michigan more than California. I preferred hugs to diamond bracelets. It sometimes took me a long time to reach orgasm—although that hadn't really been an issue for Henry.

But maybe the strongest case against me where Henry was concerned was my infertility. Granted, the issue of having children together should probably not matter until two people have had at least one actual date, but we weren't twenty-five and flippant about the future. The reality was that Henry wanted children, and that would never happen with me. It couldn't.

How could I have thought we made sense?

Because it felt so good with him. So easy. So right.

But in the end, it didn't matter—I had to give him up.

After a sleepless night, I came downstairs so early, my

mother was the only one up. She took one look at the bags beneath my bloodshot eyes and asked me what was going on.

I broke down and told her the whole story—minus the dirty sex stuff—over cups of coffee at the kitchen table. How I'd felt so drawn to Henry as soon as I'd moved back. How we spent so much time just talking and opening up to each other. How easily we understood one another and how good it felt to be wanted that way again. She listened, nodding in sympathy, and fetched me a box of tissues when I couldn't hold back the tears.

"Oh, darling, I'm so sorry," she said, rubbing my arm. "How terrible for you."

"Tell me I'm doing the right thing, Mom," I begged, blowing my nose.

"You're doing the right thing, Sylvia." Her eyes filled too. "Being a mother is the hardest job there is. I can't imagine doing it on my own. And there will be many times in your life where your own needs have to be put aside for those of your children."

"I know," I blubbered.

"But it's the most rewarding job too," she went on. "Raising you girls gave my life such beautiful purpose. Seeing you grow up has been the most fulfilling experience of my life. When you're happy, I feel it in my soul." She took my hand. "And when you're sad and struggling, it breaks my heart. So I know how you feel when you look at Whitney."

"I just never know if I'm making the right choices for them," I confessed. "Or for me. Everything I thought I knew turned out to be false. Everything I thought I had didn't really exist. Everything I thought I wanted seemed so close—and yet I could never fully grasp it no matter how hard I tried. And I did try, Mom. I tried so hard."

"I know you did, honey. I know you did."

I wiped away my tears. "In the end, I didn't even recognize myself anymore. Growing up, I felt so confident, so full of hopes and dreams, so sure that if I just followed my heart, good things would happen. Somehow I've lost that girl along the way. I thought if I moved back here, I might be able to find her, but now I'm afraid she's gone for good. What's the use of hopes and dreams anyway? They always get crushed."

"I don't believe that for one second," my mother said fiercely, taking my chin in her hand and forcing me to look at her. "That girl you were, the one full of hopes and dreams, she's still in there somewhere. Your father and I raised our girls to follow their hearts because *that* is where true happiness lies. I've never said it won't lead you through some dark woods, but you'll come out the other side. Give yourself time to find your way, Sylvia. And *never* stop following your heart —your daughter will learn from you. Remember that."

I swallowed the thick lump in my throat and gave my mother a frail smile, although her words had made me feel a little stronger. "Thanks. I needed to hear that."

She got up from her chair and came to stand behind me, wrapping her arms around my shoulders. "You're tougher than you know, my darling."

"I hope so."

"And I love you."

I placed my hands on her forearms and breathed in her familiar gardenia scent. "I love you too."

Later we took the kids over to Mack and Frannie's for football and chili. The moment I walked into the kitchen, my sister grabbed my hand and pulled me upstairs to her bedroom. Shutting the door behind us, she sat on the end of the bed and patted the spot in front of her. "Sit. And talk to me. I heard what happened."

"From who?"

"Last night from Henry, and then this morning from Millie. She's worried about Whit."

Promising myself I wouldn't break down, I lowered myself onto the bed. "Whitney's okay, I think. But I might not be." I caught her up on everything that had happened—how Henry and I had only grown closer over the last week, how I'd assured Whitney we were only friends, how he'd asked me for more last night and I'd been so excited, how we'd been kissing outside the barn when the kids discovered us because we wouldn't be able to kiss at midnight.

"Wow," she said. "So it was just really bad timing, huh?"

"Yes." I fit my thumbnails together. "But maybe it was meant to happen like that."

"What do you mean?"

"I mean, it was probably crazy to think about a new relationship so fast anyway. I need to focus on getting the kids in school, finding a house, getting a job . . ."

"I thought you were going to work in the winery. That's what Chloe said last night, that she was going to start training you to take over as manager."

I shrugged. "I mean, maybe. I'd like that, but I'm not sure if Henry will want me around."

Frannie was silent for a moment, and I couldn't bring myself to look her in the eye.

"Does that mean you're completely breaking things off with him?"

"I have to."

"Because of Whitney?"

"Yes." I felt her stare burning into me. "And because in the long run, big picture, I'm not right for Henry."

"Sylvia. Look at me."

Reluctantly, I dragged my eyes up to hers. "What?"

"I fully understand that Whitney needs time to get used to the idea of moving here, and feeling like she belongs, and seeing you with a man that's not her dad. Mack said as much to Henry last night as well, since he's gone through it with his girls. But why on earth would you think you couldn't be right for Henry? He's seriously crazy about you—you're crazy about each other. I could see it last night. Everyone could."

"Because we're at different places in our lives," I said, going with the strongest reason I'd come up with last night. "He wants children. I've already had mine."

She crossed her arms. "Yeah, Mack tried that excuse with me too, and I called bullshit. So try again."

"You're not even thirty yet, Frannie. I'm going on forty. And . . . I've never really talked about this before, but I've got infertility problems. My eggs are bad quality. I had to have IVF twice to get pregnant."

Her face registered surprise, but she quickly recovered. "I'm sorry to hear that. But I still don't get why it's a reason you can't give Henry a chance. He doesn't want to date your eggs. He wants to date *you*."

I stood up and went over to the dresser, catching my reflection in the mirror. I'd tried to disguise the evidence of my sleepless night with makeup, but I still looked pale and puffy-eyed. My hands trembled. "I just can't handle it, Frannie. I'm not ready."

She sighed. "Okay. I'm not going to pressure you. I'm only going to say this once, then I'll shut up. If you're going to push Henry away for the sake of your kids, I get it. Single parents have to do that sometimes. But if you're using the kids as an excuse to push him away because you're scared to let someone in—"

"I'm not doing that." I spun around and faced her. Gulped. "Much."

She shook her head. "Right."

"Put yourself in my position, Frannie," I pleaded. "If you had to walk a mile in my shoes, you wouldn't do things any differently. You would protect your kids . . . and yourself."

"It's hard to argue with you when you put it like that. I just want you to be happy, Sylvia."

"I know." I swallowed hard. "I'm working on it."

Rising to her feet, she came over and hugged me. Then she took my arm and tugged me toward the door. "Come on. Let's go have some nachos and a margarita."

The next few days passed by in a blur. The house in Santa Barbara sold for over asking price, and I made arrangements to return to California to pack it all up and ship things here within thirty days. The kids and I looked at eight different houses for sale and ended up making an offer on one—a refurbished farmhouse on two and a half acres about ten miles from Cloverleigh. I purchased an SUV, scheduled appointments for Whitney and Keaton at the therapist's, and took them school supply shopping.

And I didn't stop thinking about Henry for one second.

But I still hadn't been able to face the idea of seeing him yet. I knew I was putting off a conversation I didn't want to have. And part of me was scared that once I laid eyes on him, I wouldn't be strong enough to give him up. My feelings for him hadn't changed—I *wanted* to be with him.

On the final Saturday night of winter break, Frannie brought the girls over for one final vacation sleepover. "How are you?" she asked as she was leaving. "Lots going on, huh?"

"I can't even tell you. My brain is fried." I stuck a bag of popcorn in the microwave.

"I can't wait to see the house."

"I really do love it. Needs work, of course, but it's perfect for us."

"Are the kids nervous about starting school?"

"A little. But excited. We drove by both schools today. They seem okay."

"You got them appointments with that therapist yet?"

I nodded, pulling a container of lemonade from the fridge. "Yes. Week after next. That was the soonest she could get them in."

"Good." She paused a moment. "Have you talked to Henry?"

Guilt tightened my stomach. "Not yet. I needed some time."

"No pressure. I was just asking." She zipped up her coat and pulled her keys from her pocket. "Thanks for having the girls tonight. See you tomorrow."

That night I sat with the kids and watched a movie, but my mind wasn't on the action onscreen. It was on Henry and how much I missed him. How badly I wished things could be different. How heartsick I was that when I saw him next, I wouldn't get to touch him or kiss him or hear him say any of the things that always made me feel so good.

But it was for the best, I kept telling myself. My mother might have raised me to follow my heart, but right now that was a luxury I couldn't afford.

CHAPTER 21

Henry

I **SPENT** the first few days of the new year in the vineyard, brooding in the cold as I hand-selected the buds to start the next season's growth with. Normally, I loved the work—the first steps in the creative journey of the next vintage—but this year I was surly, gruff, and short-tempered. Mariela eventually stopped asking me how things were going, and the few hired hands I trusted to assist with pruning got the hint pretty fast that something was off with me this year. They took orders from me but kept to themselves, and they didn't invite me to go for beers after work like they had in the past.

Every day I hoped Sylvia might show up or even just send me a text telling me how she was doing, but she never did. Whenever Chloe stopped by the winery, I resisted the urge to ask about her, but the questions in my head were making me crazy.

Was she okay? Were the kids okay? Did they hate me? Did she still think I was a good man? Had we ruined everything, or was there any chance for us? I thought about her constantly and missed her with pangs like hunger.

And then five days into January, on a snowy Sunday afternoon, she came to find me in the vineyard.

I saw her coming up the row, bundled up in her winter jacket, hat pulled low over her head, hands tucked into her pockets. She walked toward me slowly, but she smiled when she got close, like she couldn't help it. "Hi."

"Hi." I felt like I couldn't breathe, and I didn't know what to do with my arms. They hung inert at my sides, shears clutched in one hand.

"Cold out here."

"Yeah." I scrambled for words. All I could think was, *She's so damn beautiful.* "How are you?"

"I'm okay. We've been busy."

"Yeah?"

She nodded. "I bought a car. Our house in California sold. And I put in an offer on a house here."

"Really? That fast, huh?"

"It's perfect for us, and the kids love it. It's not really even officially on the market yet, but our agent knew it was coming on and had a feeling it would be the right one. We went to see it a few days ago and offered this morning."

"Wow." I adjusted my hat. "Where is it?"

"Not far from here. Outside of town on about two and a half acres. So not a ton of land to manage, but enough for a couple horses and some animals. And it already has a barn."

"The kids must be happy."

"They are. They are." She looked down at her boots. The snow fell slowly and softly around us.

"What about you?" I asked. "Are *you* happy?"

She smiled at me, but her eyes were glossy with tears. "I'm . . . I'm hopeful about the house. I'm glad my kids are excited. And I'm looking forward to moving out of my parents' house, as much as I love them. But no, Henry. I'm not happy. I miss you."

"I miss you too."

She closed her eyes a second, took a breath. "But I have to

put the kids first. And right now, they're not ready for me to be in a relationship."

"I understand." I stared at the ground for a moment, letting the disappointment sink in. "So Whitney was that upset, huh?"

"Yes. A lot of it is my fault. The night she asked if we were dating, I could tell she was troubled by the idea of it. I could have spoken to her about it right then, been more open with her, but instead I lied to her to avoid a difficult conversation." She shrugged and smiled sadly, a tear slipping down one cheek. "I didn't want to face that what I was doing was wrong, because it felt too good. I was selfish."

"That's not being selfish, Sylvia. And you weren't doing anything wrong."

It was obvious she didn't believe me. "Anyway, seeing us dancing and kissing made all her fears real, and she was very angry with me. She told me I was just like Brett."

"You're not," I said firmly. "You know you're not."

She shook her head, fresh tears forming. "It doesn't matter what the truth is, Henry. Her feelings are real. And scary. And she's . . . she's struggling to trust people right now."

How could it not matter what the truth was? I didn't fully understand what she meant by that. And there was something else . . . I wasn't convinced Sylvia was talking only about Whitney here. *She* was scared too. Maybe hearing all of her daughter's fears out loud had opened up the wound on her heart.

But I couldn't help her heal if she wouldn't let me.

"Tell me what to do, Sylvia. I feel terrible."

She shook her head. "You shouldn't. None of this was your fault. I should apologize to you—I led you to believe something more between us was possible, but . . . it isn't, Henry. And I'm sorry." A sob escaped her. Then another, and another. "I'm so sorry."

I couldn't stand it. Dropping the shears at my feet, I gathered her in my arms and held her, letting her cry on my shoulder. Feeling her body shudder with sadness was agony, but at least I didn't feel so helpless. Comforting her gave me a purpose. "It's okay. Shhh, it's okay."

"It's not," she wept. "I behaved terribly, coming after you like that. And I promised myself I wouldn't embarrass myself by breaking down this way, yet here I am."

"You didn't behave terribly—I was a very willing participant. I won't lie and say I'm not upset, but your kids are more important, Sylvia. If I had children, you bet your ass in a sequined skirt I'd put them first too." I forced myself to make a joke, hoping it might make her smile.

She laughed a little, pulling back from me and wiping her eyes with her sleeve. "Thanks."

"Are you okay?"

"Yeah. God, I'm so sick of crying. It feels like that's all I've done for a year."

"So let's do something else," I blurted, thinking fast. "Want me to put you to work?"

She gave me a shaky smile and sniffed. "Here? In the vineyard?"

"Sure. Or in the tasting room. Whatever you want."

"I didn't think you'd want me around anymore."

"Well, you were wrong. I offered to teach you about the way we make wine, and the offer stands." I knew it would only make it harder to shut down my feelings for her if she was around all the time, but if it cheered her up, it was worth it.

"It does? Even though we can't—" She stopped talking and pounded one mitten into the other.

I had to laugh. "Well, I'm not going to argue with you if you ever want to take your clothes off, but yes. Even though we're only going to be friends, I'll still teach you what you want to know. I'm not a total asshole."

She stood taller, her eyes and nose still red, but her grin genuine. "I'd love that, Henry. When can I start?"

"How about right now? Want to learn how to prune these vines?"

"Yes! Show me!"

"Okay, so watch and listen carefully." Turning toward the plants, I gave her a look over my shoulder. "This is an art form, you know."

She actually laughed. "Go on."

"So the vines are dormant right now. The buds are alive, but they're basically sleeping, so now is when we want to go through and choose the ones we think have the best shot."

"Why not leave them all?" she wondered. "Wouldn't that give you the most fruit?"

I shook my head. "The vine will be more productive if you prune it the right way than if you just leave everything. We want to concentrate the energy of the vines into the buds we select."

"Got it."

I forced myself to focus on teaching her the task at hand, rather than on her nearness, the scent of her hair, the adorable way she held the tip of her tongue between her teeth in concentration when she was clipping a shoot.

"Like that?" she'd ask, her brow furrowed with concern.

"Perfect. Try this one now."

We spent almost two perfect hours working side by side that afternoon. She listened attentively, asked smart questions, and learned fast. I was in heaven—no one had ever been so interested in what I did out here. And each time she smiled or laughed, my heart would quicken in my chest.

But eventually, she said she should probably head back home to start Sunday dinner. "The kids start school tomorrow," she told me, handing the shears back. "I want to make sure they get a good meal and a good night's rest."

"Of course. That's a big day for them." I hesitated. "I'm

not sure I want to know the answer to this, but do they hate me?"

"Of course not." She put a hand on my arm. "They both like you, Henry—that's not the problem."

I nodded. "Tell them I said to have a great first day."

"I will, thanks." She glanced around. "It's starting to get dark. How much longer will you work?"

"I'm about done. I'll walk back with you."

We headed down the row in the direction of the winery. "Keaton is still really interested in that boxing gym," she said as she walked close beside me. "Do you think you could text me the name and location?"

"Of course."

"Thanks. I want to get him involved in something physical right away. Did I tell you the therapist Frannie recommended called back? I was able to get appointments for the kids in two weeks, right before our ski trip. Then right after that I leave for California to pack up the house."

"You've got a lot going on."

"Yes, but all good things." We reached the winery, and she turned toward me. "Thanks for the lesson. Can I do it again sometime?"

"Sure. I'll be out here for the next three months."

"I asked Chloe about helping in the tasting room again too. She said the winter months are pretty slow, so she doesn't necessarily need help with tastings, but she could use the time to train me."

"That's a great idea. By the time business picks up again toward spring, I bet you'll be ready to take over managing completely."

"You think so?" she asked hopefully.

"Definitely. You're a perfect fit."

Her smile lit up her face, and when she spoke, her voice was soft. "Thank you, Henry. For everything."

"You're welcome." I was praying she'd leave quickly

before I did something stupid like kiss her. Already I was doubting my sanity for inviting her back again. And yet my next question was, "Can I walk you home?"

"No, that's okay. I think it's better if I head back alone."

"Okay."

But she didn't move a muscle in that direction. "I wish more than anything that things were different," she said.

"Maybe they will be someday."

Her expression changed to one of concern. "I don't expect you to wait for me, Henry. In fact, you shouldn't. I'll feel worse."

"Goodnight, Sylvia."

For a second, she looked like she might argue the point, but she didn't. "Goodnight."

I watched her turn around and walk toward the house until I couldn't see her anymore, my hand gripping the shears like a vise, my jaw clenched tight, my legs aching to run after her.

But for what? She'd made her position clear, and I couldn't argue with it. Nothing I said or did was going to change the fact that she couldn't choose me, and I'd never ask her to.

Every time I thought about all the days and nights her dumb fuck of an ex had her and neglected or betrayed her, I wanted to go back in time and fucking punch his smug face at Mack's wedding, maybe even flip the table first.

It wasn't fair that an asshole like that won her heart, and I never even had a chance.

Would I ever?

Sylvia came to the winery almost every day, even if it was just for a few hours at a time. Sometimes she spent the time with me in the vineyard, or if we got too cold outside we'd go down to the cellar, where I'd teach her about the aging and blending processes. She also spent a good amount of time in the tasting room, where Chloe would coach her in tasting.

My favorite mornings were those we spent alone among the vines. We worked side by side in the cold, but she never once complained about the temperature. Sometimes she brought a thermos of hot chocolate, and we'd share it as we moved along the rows. She grew more confident with the shears, and while she worked, I'd make her repeat back to me the lessons she'd learned.

"We want to look for straight, clean wood starting low on the trunk," she'd say. "We need to think three years ahead."

"You know, you're going to be better than me at this pretty soon," I teased her.

"Hardly," she said, laughing. "But thank you."

Her offer on the new house had been accepted, and as we worked, she described it in more detail—a refurbished nineteenth-century farmhouse with four bedrooms, three baths, beautiful pine floors, a wood-burning fireplace, a big old gray barn, and her favorite, a weathered white picket fence. "It needs some updating," she said, "especially in the kitchen and baths, but the bones of the house are strong and beautiful."

"That's all that matters," I told her.

"Oh, I wanted to ask you where you found that bathtub at your house. I'd like to order one for the master bath."

"Sure. I'll get you the name of the site," I said, trying not to picture her in the bathtub at my house. It was a struggle whenever I was with her to keep my hands to myself, but after that first day, I refrained from even hugging her. One, I wanted her to know I respected her boundaries, and two, knowing the way I felt about her, I was sure one thing would lead to another. If I hugged her, I'd want to kiss her. If I kissed her, I'd want to touch her. If I touched her, I'd want to get her naked.

I'd want to hear those sounds she made. I'd want to feel her hands on my skin and her tongue in my mouth and her warm, soft body arching beneath mine as I made her come again and again . . .

So no hugs.

But the hours we spent together were the best parts of my day. I loved getting to know her better, hearing about her childhood at Cloverleigh Farms, learning about her sisters as kids—who got in the most trouble (Chloe), who was the most spoiled (baby Frannie), who got the best grades (Meg).

"What about April?" I asked. "What was her thing?"

"April was always the caretaker," Sylvia said. "So good with kids, always had the best babysitting jobs, always the first to jump up and help out someone in need. She really loves making people happy—that's why I think she's so good at weddings. She bends over backward to make sure brides get exactly what they want and takes care of every little detail."

"And what about you?"

"Me?" She grinned. "I was a typical oldest child, I think. A bossy perfectionist. But also vain and boy-crazy as a teenager. I cared a *lot* about my hair and my eyeliner."

I laughed. "At least you're honest."

She talked about her children too—how happy they were at their new school, the clubs they were joining (Keaton joined a science club, Whitney the ski club), the new friends they'd made. I hadn't seen them since New Year's Eve, but I knew Keaton had joined a youth boxing class at my gym because I saw his photo with a group of kids on the wall. It made me smile. I hoped he loved it like he thought he would.

"The kids had their first appointments with the new therapist last night," she said one Thursday morning in mid-

January. "And they *loved* her. I think she's going to be really good for them."

"That's awesome," I said, happy to see the genuine relief in her eyes.

I missed her like crazy when she took the kids skiing, but it was even worse when she flew back to California at the end of the month to pack up her old house.

She called me the third night she was there. It was so late I was already in bed, but I picked up right away when I saw it was her. "Hello?"

"Hi."

I smiled and settled back against my pillow. "This is a nice surprise."

"I'm sorry it's so late. Did I wake you?"

"No, I was up," I said aloud. *Longing for you to be next to me in this bed again*, I added in my head. "How's it going?"

"It's going okay. There's a lot to do, and my ex is being a total dick, of course."

"What's he doing?"

"Nothing to help out, that's for sure. I decided anything he doesn't come to claim by tomorrow, I'm having hauled off to the Salvation Army along with my wedding dress, our good china, and his grandmother's silver. Let him go try to find it and buy it back."

God, I'd have loved to see that. "Atta girl."

"The kids are flying out with my mom to pack up their rooms this weekend."

"They doing okay?"

"I think so. They're looking forward to seeing their dad, which has me worried he's going to disappoint them."

"Maybe he'll step up for once." I didn't believe that for a second.

"Maybe." Her tone said she didn't either.

"But either way, you can't control him, Sylvia."

"I know. And I don't have to make excuses for him either.

I'm so over that." She took a breath. "So how are you? How are my baby buds doing without me?"

I laughed. "They miss you. When do you come home?"

"If all goes smoothly here, maybe a week from today."

"I'll take good care of them until you're back."

"Thanks." She was silent a moment. "It's so nice to hear your voice, Henry. This house is so lonely and quiet."

Does she wish I was there as much as I do? I wondered. But I asked a different question instead. "Is it hard packing it all up and saying goodbye?"

"You know, not really. I think if I wasn't so excited about our new house and anxious to get back home, it might be. But I know where I belong now."

You belong with me, I wanted to tell her. The words were right there, I could feel them on the tip of my tongue—but I couldn't say them. It would only make things worse.

But the more time we spent together, the more I was convinced it was the truth.

She sighed. "Well, I should probably let you go. I know it's late there . . . I just wanted to hear your voice. Is that terrible of me?"

"Of course not. You can always call me."

She called two nights later, joyfully describing how angry Kimmy had been at the discovery of the missing silver. "It was hilarious," she said, giggling. "Brett was apologizing up and down for not showing up yesterday to get it, and she was tearing him a new asshole about how she'd told him over and over again that she really wanted it and he never listens to her. I was in the other room laughing my head off."

I laughed. "And the kids arrive tomorrow?"

"Yes. We should have everything cleared out of here by Monday, they leave that morning, the closing is Tuesday, and I'm on the first flight out of here Wednesday. I can't wait to get home."

"You sound really good, Sylvia."

"I feel pretty good. I'm a little worried how the kids are going to react to saying goodbye to the house—this is the only home they've ever known, and I think the concept of selling it has been mostly abstract until now."

"Yeah, that could be hard. I remember being surprised when my parents sold their farm how emotional it was leaving it for the last time, and I was already in my twenties. But I'd grown up there, and it felt like leaving a piece of my childhood behind."

"Tell me more about your childhood," she said. "I feel like we're always talking about mine."

We spent hours that night on the phone trading stories about our youths—favorite memories, broken bones, best friends, playground dramas, awards won, sports played, high school proms.

"Wait—*how* many guys asked you to the prom?" I asked in disbelief. "Did you say *four*?"

She laughed. "Yes."

"How did you choose?"

"Truth? I picked a name out of a hat." She giggled. "I let Frannie pick it."

"And was it fun? Did she pick the right one?"

"Yes. He was a perfect gentleman. What about you?"

"Um, I was not exactly a perfect gentleman."

"What? I don't believe it. Who was your date?"

"My girlfriend at the time. We'd been together for like a year by then."

"What was her name?"

"Michelle."

"Was she your first . . . you know."

I imagined her pounding a fist into the other palm and laughed. "Hell no. Michelle was a good girl from the Bible Belt, and never let me do anything beneath the clothes. But actually, on prom night, she did finally put her hand down my pants. First girl who ever did."

She snickered. "Was it everything you dreamed it would be?"

"Yes and no. First of all, I came almost immediately, all over her hand and my rented tuxedo pants, after which she burst into tears. Second, she felt so guilty about it, she told her *mom*, who then told *my* mom, who told my *dad*, and he had to come give me a talk about how to respect girls."

By that point Sylvia was gasping with laughter. "Oh no!"

"It was horrible. And my brothers were outside my room laughing their asses off."

"I bet. So whatever happened with Michelle?"

"I think we broke up right after that. She had trouble looking me in the eye after I jizzed all over her fingers. Frankly, I think she was surprised by the whole episode. I'm not sure she knew that was going to happen."

"Poor Michelle. Traumatized for life."

"It's possible."

She sighed. "I should let you go." Silence. "But I don't want to."

I wasn't sure what to say.

"Are you in bed?" she asked, her voice a little softer, more seductive.

"Yes. Are you?"

"Yes."

I waited, holding my breath.

"If I put my hand in your pants, would you immediately come all over my fingers?" she asked, which could have been sexy if she hadn't burst out laughing right afterward.

I groaned. "That's just mean."

"I'm sorry," she said, her giggles subsiding. "I couldn't resist."

"I've learned to control myself—somewhat—since then, thank you very much."

"I know you have." She'd stopped laughing entirely. "And I think about it all the time."

My throat was dry. "I do too."

"And now I really need to let you go, or else I'm going to say things I shouldn't."

"Me too." With the space of more than half the country between us, it seemed safe to admit it. "God, Sylvia. It just doesn't get any easier. I keep waiting and waiting for it to ease up, but . . . I still want you. Maybe even more than before."

"I know. I want you too."

But what we wanted didn't matter, and saying it out loud wasn't going to help.

"Maybe I shouldn't work at the winery," she said. "Maybe that's just making it harder for us."

"No—no, don't stay away." Then I'd never see her—a thought I couldn't bear. "I'm sorry I said anything."

"Okay."

I heard a sniffle. Was she crying? My chest felt ready to break open at the thought that I'd made her sad. What the fuck was wrong with me?

"Goodnight, Henry," she said, her voice shaky.

"Goodnight." I ended the call and tossed my phone aside, frustrated at the way the universe was fucking with me.

At the thought of going to bed alone every night for the rest of my life and wishing she was beside me.

At the gut feeling, deep in my bones, that I'd fallen in love with Sylvia without even trying.

And there was nothing I could do about it.

CHAPTER 22

Sylvia

ON THURSDAY MORNING, as soon as I'd gotten the kids to school, I threw on all my warmest winter gear and raced over to the winery. It was a sunny day, but freezing cold, with air that stung the inside of your nose and bit at your lungs when you inhaled. Still, my body warmed with anticipation as I counted down the last few minutes before I'd see Henry again.

His truck was in the lot, and my heart pounded harder at the sight of it. I'd missed him so much when I was away. I'd struggled with the decision to call him while I was gone—part of me knew I should just let the guy be—but in the end, I'd so longed to hear the sound of his voice that I'd broken down and reached out. He had this way of calming even the worst chaos in my head, of helping me keep things in perspective, of reminding me what really mattered. He knew how to make me laugh too, even at the most difficult times. I always felt understood with Henry. Accepted for who I was, faults and all. I never would have gotten through the last six weeks without his friendship.

When I'd gone to see him in the vineyard that first time after New Year's, I'd been stunned when he told me he was still willing to coach me. I thought once I told him there couldn't be anything romantic between us, he might get angry. Resentful. Bitter.

But he hadn't. He'd been sweet and understanding. Undeniably disappointed, but without making me feel bad about things I couldn't change. He'd comforted me. He'd taken me in his arms and reassured me that I wasn't a terrible person—I was human, I was doing the right thing, and I was forgiven.

Still, I promised myself that I wouldn't take advantage of his kindness. I wouldn't be a bother to him. I wouldn't show up there every day expecting him to pay attention to me.

But of course, that's exactly how it happened.

No matter how little or how much time I had to spend with him, he made it feel like a gift. He was patient and funny and kind. He answered all my ignorant questions thoroughly and never once got irritated when I asked him to repeat things. We laughed often. We told each other stories. We confessed our guilty pleasures—his were cheerleading competitions on ESPN, Krispy Kremes, and Restoration Hardware. I giggled every time I thought about him secretly surfing the RH website and holding himself back from purchasing a reclaimed oak table or Italian leather chair.

He made fun of my list too.

"I'm sorry," he said. "I have to disqualify your food item. A salad is not a guilty pleasure."

"Have you ever *had* a Greek salad at National Coney Island?" I demanded. "It's drowning in feta cheese! The beets are canned!"

"Canned beets? My God, the horror!" He reached over and pulled my hair, making me giggle.

But other than that, he never laid a finger on me. Not once.

Sometimes I caught him looking at me—and he would catch me looking at him, but we never said a word about what had gone on between us . . . or what was happening still. Somehow, in my mind, if we just didn't give it a name or put a label on it, we were safe.

But we weren't. Of course we weren't.

I burst through the tasting room doors and saw Chloe behind the counter, unpacking new glasses from shipping boxes.

"Hey," she said, "how did it go with the house?"

"Good," I answered breathlessly. "Is Henry around?"

"Downstairs. Too cold to work in the vineyard today. Do you want to—"

But I was already rushing across the cement floor toward the cellar steps. I spotted him right away, standing over a barrel with a long glass tube I now knew was called a "wine thief."

He heard me bounding down the stairs and looked up, a grin breaking out on his face. "Hey, you."

When I reached him, I was breathing heavy and I thought my heart was going to burst right through my chest, but it wasn't just from exertion. "Hi."

"How was the rest of your trip?"

"It was good." I was dying for him to hug me and couldn't help feeling disappointed when he kept his arms to himself. My entire body was like one huge live wire being so close to him.

"Kids do okay?"

"Yes. It was tough, and Whitney cried a lot, but I was expecting it." My hopes began to wither . . . He wasn't going to touch me. Not even an informal, good-to-see-you elbow nudge.

"Poor thing." He took a sample of the wine from the barrel. "You glad to be back?"

"Yeah." God, I missed the feeling of his arms around me. Would I never feel it again? "I feel like . . . like we can really move forward now."

"When do you close on your house?"

"I'm still waiting for the exact date, but I'm hopeful we'll have keys within the week." I tried to smile, but suddenly felt like crying for some stupid reason. What the hell was the matter with me? Of course he wasn't going to touch me—he was respecting my wishes like a good man would. Had I expected anything less from him?

"Optimism is a good thing," he said. "So what would you like to work on today? It's too cold to be outside, but you're welcome to hang out with Mariela and me down here or ask Chloe what she could use help with upstairs."

I swallowed the lump in my throat. "Maybe I'll head upstairs and see what Chloe needs."

"Okay."

I turned around and started to walk away.

"Sylvia," he called softly.

"Yes?" I looked back at him, my heart splintering in my chest. Every bone in my body was aching to run at him, jump into his arms, beg for another ending to this reunion scene.

"I'm glad you're back."

I smiled, although tears threatened. Were we doomed to this forever? Missing each other all the time, even when we were *standing right next to one another*? This was agony, and I saw no way out of it. "Me too."

Upstairs, I told Chloe I felt sick, which was true—my stomach was suddenly roiling.

My sister looked at me. "Yeah, your color doesn't look good. Why don't you go back home and get some rest? You've probably been going nonstop for days."

"Okay."

I bundled up again and walked home quickly, unshed tears burning my eyes, sobs trapped inside my chest. I didn't stop moving until I was inside my bedroom with the door closed, then I threw myself onto my bed, curled into a ball, and let it all out. I hadn't cried so much since Brett left me.

But this was my own fault.

I'd moved here to find peace and security, to feel grounded and safe and strong, to create a haven for myself and for my children, to piece my heart back together again and keep it better protected.

Instead, I'd fallen in love. I felt exposed and raw and vulnerable, and I hated myself for it.

Suddenly I knew I was going to be sick, and I rocketed from my bed into the adjoining bathroom, barely making it before losing the contents of my stomach.

Things couldn't go on like this.

Eventually I had to drag myself out of my bedroom and attempt to be a functioning adult. The kids would be home from school just after three, Keaton had boxing, Whitney needed to bake something for a ski club fundraiser, and I had to run to the bank and the realtor's office before they closed at five. I scrubbed my teeth, rinsed my mouth, and repaired my face as well as I could, but there was no way to disguise the fact that I'd been a blubbering mess for hours, and Chloe was right—my color was not good. My complexion had kind of a gray-green hue to it. Hopefully, sunglasses would help. At least my stomach felt a little better.

I managed to get my errands in before the bus brought the kids home, although everyone in the realtor's office and bank probably thought I was nuts for wearing my sunglasses inside.

Back at home, I made the kids a healthy snack and prayed they wouldn't notice my puffy eyes. Keaton seemed oblivious while he ate his celery sticks and peanut butter, chattering excitedly about a project he wanted to do for the upcoming science fair, but Whitney eyeballed me steadily over her plate of carrots and hummus and hardly touched her food.

"Aren't you hungry?" I asked her, avoiding eye contact.

"A little," she replied, pushing a few baby carrots around on her plate. "Are you okay?"

Keaton stopped eating and looked at me too.

"Of course." I tried to fake a smile, but it felt sort of ghoulish. "Finish your snacks so we can get to the gym on time. While Keaton is boxing, Whit, we'll hit the grocery store for whatever you need to bake. What was it you wanted to make?"

"Mississippi Mud brownies."

"Ooh, those are good. Let me pull up the recipe to make a grocery list."

She continued to study me while I checked the recipe on my phone, looked in my mother's pantry to see what was there already, and scribbled a quick list of what we'd need to purchase. We'd been getting along really well since New Year's Eve, although never again did we discuss Henry or what had happened that night. She knew I'd been working at the winery, but if it bothered her, she never said anything about it.

She'd been pretty sad and clingy while in California, but I hadn't blamed her. That was an emotional weekend for us all, and it didn't help that Brett was preoccupied with soothing Kimmy's ruffled pregnant feathers the whole time. He did manage to spend *some* time with the kids, but I knew it wasn't the kind of time or attention they were craving from him.

I knew it all too well.

Later that evening, Keaton was doing his homework in his bedroom and Whitney and I were baking in the kitchen. My parents had gone out to dinner with friends, so we had the house to ourselves. Outside, the wind was whistling against the windows, and the temperatures continued to drop, but inside it was warm and cozy, and the kitchen smelled delicious.

Whitney was more cheerful and talkative than she'd been this afternoon, and I was enjoying her stories about new friends at school, a cute boy from her English class, what color she wanted to paint her room at the new house, what she wanted to name the horse we were planning to purchase. It was just the kind of evening I'd envisioned for our new life.

"Mom, can I ask you something?" Whitney kept her eyes on the mixing bowl as she added more powdered sugar to the frosting.

"Sure."

"Why didn't Aunt April ever get married or have kids?"

"I guess she never met the right person."

"But she's so pretty."

I smiled. "It's not just about looks, honey. You have to find someone you can be your real self around. Someone who finds you beautiful inside and out."

"Does she *want* to get married?"

"I think so. But it's not always easy to find the someone. And sometimes you do, but it doesn't work out."

"Where did you meet Daddy?" she asked.

"In Chicago. I was in college and he was working there at the time."

"Were you in love?"

I thought carefully about how to answer. "We were back then. Yes."

"Is that why you got married?"

I looked down at my left hand, recalling the moment Brett had slipped the diamond solitaire on my fourth finger and asked me to be his wife. In all honesty, I'd been torn—my plan had always been to travel after college. But I'd been in love with Brett, and he'd made me all sorts of promises about the beautiful life we'd have together if I'd marry him and move to California, where an executive position waited for him at his family's investment firm. He said he loved me. He said I'd have everything I could possibly want. He said he'd do anything to have me . . . except *wait*.

Being twenty-two, blinded by love, and dazzled by the dream life he dangled in front of my eyes, I'd said yes. I'd believed him. I'd done everything he'd asked, including set my own dreams aside, and followed him across the country, where we did indeed build a beautiful life—on the surface.

But I couldn't say that to Whitney.

"Yes. That's why we got married. And I'm glad we did, sweetheart. Because as difficult as the last few years were, I'd do them all over again just to have you and Keaton. Being your mom is the best thing I've ever done."

She turned on the electric mixer and didn't say anything else while she beat the frosting. But a few minutes later, as she spread the frosting on top of the marshmallow-covered brownies, she said, "Daddy says he loves me. But I don't believe him."

"Oh, Whitney, don't say that."

"It's the truth. I don't believe him anymore. You know what he gave me for Christmas?"

I shook my head. Brett had given the kids their gifts while they were out to dinner with him and Kimmy, and I hadn't asked for any details.

"The same necklace he got for me last year. The *exact same one.*"

"I'm sorry."

"And he sat there telling me how expensive it is, how I need to be sure I take care of it and don't lose it because it's so valuable. And I was sitting there looking at him, thinking,

Dad, you don't know jack shit about taking care of things that are valuable."

I laughed, although it wasn't funny. "God, Whit. You're exactly right. And I don't mean to make light of it, but you are so *exactly* right. He used to buy me expensive gifts all the time too, when all I really wanted was for him to spend more time with us."

"It made me so mad," she said, setting the bowl of frosting aside. "What kind of person is he?"

"Your father isn't a bad person," I said, willing myself to be generous. "But he's always been the kind of guy who thinks he can buy people's love. His father was the same way. It's the only way he knows. It makes him feel like a big shot, and that's what's important to him."

"It's not right." Her lower lip jutted as she smoothed the layer of frosting.

"No, it isn't."

"I feel sorry for that baby they're having. Because it's not like he's ever going to change."

I took a deep breath. "That's hard to say. But I hope for the sake of that baby, he learns to love less selfishly."

"Me too."

I thought it was a good sign that she had empathy for Brett and Kimmy's unborn child. Maybe I wasn't totally fucking up this parenting thing. Grateful for my precocious, resilient, lovely daughter, I grabbed Whitney in a giant bear hug from behind.

"Mom, you're choking me," she complained.

"Sorry, honey," I said, squeezing her tight. "But you're just so huggable, I couldn't resist. I love your big heart."

"Okay, but can you please let me go?"

"Never."

"Mom!"

"Okay, okay." I released her. "Why don't you go up to bed,

sweetheart? I'll clean up. We'll cut them into squares in the morning, and then I'll pack them in a box for you."

"Okay. Thanks, Mom." She wiped her hands on her jeans and headed for the hallway, then suddenly turned around and rushed into my arms, bursting into tears. "I'm sorry," she bawled. "I don't even know why I'm crying."

I embraced her, stroking her hair and gently rocking her, although she was nearly as tall as me. "It's okay, honey. Believe me, I get it. Happens to me all the time."

"I just feel really bad all of a sudden."

"You don't have to explain it to me. Just let it out. I'm here, and I understand."

She cried for a few minutes, then pulled back and wiped her nose on her sleeve. I pulled a tissue from the box on the counter and handed it to her. "Here. Use this, please."

"Sorry." She blew her nose and threw the tissue away before grabbing another one. She mopped up her eyes and was about to toss that one in the trash when someone knocked on the front door, making us look at each other in surprise.

"It's after nine," I said. "I wonder who that is."

"Do I have to be seen?" Whitney looked scared that anyone might see her blotchy face. "I look hideous right now."

"No, it's okay," I told her. "You go upstairs, and I'll be up soon to say goodnight."

She hurried into the front hall and scooted up the steps, and I waited for her to reach the top before I opened the front door.

It was Henry. "Hi."

"Hi."

Neither of us smiled.

"Chloe said you were sick."

"I'm okay." I forced myself to meet his eyes and realized he knew I was lying. "Actually, I'm not okay."

Henry nodded. "Maybe we should talk."

Resigned, I stepped back, dreading the next few minutes. "Come in."

He stepped into the foyer, and I closed the door behind him. Then I stood in front of it with my arms crossed over my chest.

"What's going on, Sylvia?"

"I . . . I don't think I should work at the winery anymore."

He pressed his lips together. "Why?"

Fighting tears, I told him the truth, like we'd promised each other we would. "Because I'm in love with you, Henry."

He closed the distance between us and took me by the shoulders. "It isn't going to matter where you work, Sylvia. Or where you live. I love you too. And I'll *wait* for you. I'll wait as long as it takes to prove to you that I'm not going anywhere—because you're worth it. You're worth every-thing." Then his lips were on mine in a hot, commanding kiss that broke down all my defenses.

I threw my arms around his neck and felt myself being wrapped in his strong, safe arms and lifted right off the floor. For a full minute, I let myself be swept up in the feelings—in the release of my pent-up yearning for him, in the desire he ignited within me, in the blissful haze of hearing he loved me and wanted me and was willing to wait.

But I couldn't let him.

"No, Henry." Tearing my lips off his, I forced the words out, although I nearly choked on them. "Don't wait for me."

"Sylvia, please, can't we—"

"No!" I pushed against his chest, and he set me on my feet, releasing me from his embrace. Unable to meet his eyes, I turned away from him and stared at the door. "We can't go on like this, Henry. It's too hard. I came racing over to the winery today so excited to see you, and when I got there, I was so desperate for you to put your arms around me and so sad when you didn't."

"I'd have given anything to be able to put my arms around you this morning," he said quietly. "You have no idea how badly I wanted to. But I was trying to respect your wishes, Sylvia."

"I know," I whispered, failing to stop the tears from falling. "I know how unfair it is. And I'm sending mixed signals—even to myself." I finally turned around again. "But I don't want to be sad anymore, Henry. This is too hard."

His eyes held so many emotions—love, heartache, frustration, pain. "Tell me what to do, and I'll do it."

I looked at him, this gorgeous, sexy, strong man so willing to do anything for me, and wondered if it could be possible he was telling the truth. If it was possible he could love me the way he said he did. If it was possible I was worth it.

If it was possible he'd stay forever.

But I couldn't bring myself to believe it.

Instead, I opened the door, letting the cold air rush in. "You need to go, Henry. Forget about me."

He stood still for a moment, his chest out, his hands curled into fists. Then he shoved the door closed again. "I'll go. I just want to say one more thing, Sylvia—something I've been thinking about all day. I grew up in a crazy household with three reckless, lunatic brothers and two devoted parents who managed to stay married and raise us without losing their minds. Did we fight? Hell, yes. Were we rich? Hell, no. We didn't have a huge home or fancy cars, we didn't take luxury vacations, and for me new clothes meant hand-me-downs full of holes that my older brother Anthony had outgrown. But it was a great way to grow up, because we were *there* for each other. We took care of one another. We always knew, no matter what, we had family. *That's* the feeling I miss as an adult. That sense of belonging and loyalty. *That's* what I wanted to recreate. Because what I love more than anything is the idea of taking care of people I love, protecting them, providing for them. And I want to be the one that takes care of you, Sylvia. Because you deserve someone who adores you. Who will put *you* first while you're busy putting everyone else first."

"Henry," I croaked, tears dripping from my eyes.

He held up one hand. "Let me finish. I know you're a mother first and foremost, and I'd never get in the way of that. But I *love* you, and I couldn't walk away without a fight."

His eyes pierced mine so deeply I felt it in my soul. I wanted so badly to throw myself in his arms and say *yes, take care of me, yes, protect me, yes, adore me. You're exactly what I want, what I need, what I wished for. Together we'll show the kids what real love looks like. We'll make them believe in it.*

But the words wouldn't come out—they were prisoners of a fear that ran too deep in my veins.

"You have to walk away, Henry," I wept softly. "I don't know how to let myself be loved that way. And I'm too scared to try."

He stared at me, his jaw clenched. "Okay, Sylvia. You win." Then he yanked the door open, and a second later he was gone.

I shut the door quickly so I wouldn't have to watch him walk away. Leaning my forehead against it, I continued to cry as quietly as I could.

That's when I heard the voice behind me at the top of the stairs.

"Mom?"

I gulped back a sob and tried to speak normally. "I'll be right there, Whit."

She paused. "Are you okay?"

"Yes. I'm fine. I'll be fine." I used the bottom of my sweater to dry my face. "Give me a minute, all right?"

"Okay."

I did my best to pull myself together before going upstairs, but it was a futile effort. Thankfully, Whitney's light was already out when I entered her room. She was tucked beneath the sheets, holding her bear at her chest. I sat at the edge of her bed and smoothed her hair back.

"Who was at the door?" she asked.

"Mr. DeSantis."

"Oh." She was quiet for a minute, playing with her stuffed bear's ears. "Mom?"

"Yes?"

"I knew it was Mr. DeSantis. And I heard you talking."

"Oh." I struggled for the right words. "I'm—I'm sorry you heard us. It must have been very upsetting. But I promise, Whitney, there is nothing going on between us. We are not dating."

"I know. I heard."

"After you and I talked on New Year's Eve, he and I decided we wouldn't get romantically involved."

She hesitated. "Because of me?"

"No! No, honey, it wasn't because of you. It's because it was too soon. I wasn't ready. Ever since then, we've only worked together. But even that is going to stop now."

She rolled onto her side, facing me. "He said he loves you."

"Yes, he did."

"Do you believe him?"

I swallowed hard. "I don't know, Whitney. That's part of the problem."

"Do you love him?"

"Not the way I love you."

"But *do* you love him?"

"That's . . . that's complicated."

"No, it's not. It's a yes or no question."

Oh God, I was totally fucking this up, wasn't I? What was the right thing to do? Tell her the truth and risk her feeling guilty and scared? Or lie to her to make her feel safe? I searched my heart and found myself unable to do either one.

Instead, I tried to think about what my own mother would have said.

"Yes, Whitney. I do love him. But I don't want to. My feelings are all mixed up right now—I'm working on sorting them out. The important thing is, nothing is going to change. All the promises I made to you, I'm going to keep. We're going to move into our new house, fix it up just the way we want it, fill our barn with animals to take care of, and have the best time ever."

She looked at me a moment longer. "Okay."

I leaned over and gave her a long hug. "You and your brother are the most important things in my life," I told her. "You're all I need to be happy."

It was when I was leaving her room, the door nearly shut behind me, that I thought I heard her say, "I don't believe you."

But she said it so quietly, I couldn't be sure she'd said anything at all.

CHAPTER 23

Henry

TWO WEEKS WENT BY.

Two endless, miserably lonely weeks during which I didn't see her at all.

The vineyard seemed lifeless without her at my side. The cellar felt like an inescapable dungeon. But the walls of my empty house seemed determined to close in on me, so I spent more time than ever at work.

For the first few days, I kept hoping she'd change her mind and show up to work at the winery. But she didn't, and when Chloe began emailing me responses to the job listing she'd posted for tasting room manager, my heart sank—she really wasn't coming back.

I went to the gym every morning and sometimes in the evening too, nearly busting my hands taking my anger out on the bag. I was fucking furious with myself for forcing the situation. Why couldn't I have had a little more patience? Given her a little breathing space? Let her come to me when she was ready? Instead I had to go charging over there like a bull in a china shop, destroying everything with my clumsy attempt to win her fragile heart.

And every night, I lay awake yearning to be with her and

wondering how the hell you got over losing someone who was never yours in the first place.

Valentine's Day fell on a Friday, and I decided to spend the evening at the gym. I'd just come through the door when I heard a voice call my name.

"Hi Mr. DeSantis!" It was Keaton. He was standing near the entrance, probably waiting to be picked up.

"Hey, Keaton. How's it going?"

"Good."

"How was your class tonight?"

"Great." He smiled enthusiastically. "I really love it, and the coach says I'm really improving."

"I bet you are." I gave him a grin. He looked healthy and happy, maybe even taller than when I'd last seen him on New Year's Eve. Kids grew so fast.

"Hey, I wanted to ask you about something," he said. "It's for my science fair project."

"Sure, go ahead." I shifted my bag higher on my shoulder.

"I want to do an experiment to test whether music affects plant growth. My grandpa thought maybe you'd be able to help me."

"What a cool idea. I'd love to help you." I paused. "But make sure it's okay with your mom, all right?"

"Okay."

Just then, Whitney came rushing through the door. "Keaton, we've been out there forever! Mom says to come on."

"Oh, sorry," he said, gesturing at me. "I was talking to Mr. DeSantis. He's going to help me with my science fair project."

Whitney's face flushed. "Oh . . . hi."

"Hi, Whitney. How are you?"

"Good." She looked at my feet rather than make eye contact. "We should go, Keaton."

"Okay." He looked up at me hopefully. "Should I come to Cloverleigh to get help? We moved into our new house so we don't live there anymore, but I could ask my mom to bring me."

"Sure. Any time you see my truck in the lot, I'm there," I told him, wondering if Sylvia was going to be upset that he'd asked me for help. I couldn't resist one last question. "How is your mom?"

"She's good," Keaton said, pulling open the door. "Bye."

"Bye." I watched them both exit and hurry toward a white SUV that waited outside. I could barely make out Sylvia's silhouette in the driver's seat, but I knew it was her, and my body's reaction was swift and fierce. My chest tightened. My hands clenched. My skin was hot under my clothes. The weeks apart hadn't done anything to ease the longing in my heart—I still wanted her.

As the kids climbed into the car, she looked over at me. For a moment, I couldn't breathe. Were they telling her they'd seen me? What was she doing tonight? Had she been as lonely as I had the last couple weeks? Maybe she'd wave. But within seconds, she looked straight ahead again, and the SUV pulled away.

The next day, one of her kids came to see me at work—but not the one I was expecting.

I was avoiding the tasting room, which was crowded with guests staying at the inn for Valentine's Day weekend. April was helping Chloe out today, and they'd assured me they didn't need my help, so I was hiding out in my office. At the knock on my open door, I looked up and blinked.

"Whitney?"

"Hi," she said, shoving her hands in her coat pockets.

"Hi." I stood up and looked over her shoulder. "What can I do for you? Is Keaton looking for me?"

She shook her head. "No. I'm here by myself."

"Oh." I was totally baffled. "Is everything okay?"

"I'm not sure. Could I talk to you?"

"Of course. Come in." I gestured to one of the chairs across from my desk.

She entered the office and perched uneasily on the edge of one seat. Her face was makeup-free, and it struck me how much she resembled her mom. "Aunt Chloe said you were down here. I walked over from the house."

"Does your mother know you're here?"

She shook her head. "I just told her I was going outside."

"Oh." I was even more confused. Clearing my throat, I sat down and closed my laptop. "What can I do for you?"

"I want to talk to you about my mom."

My heart beat an erratic rhythm. "Okay."

Her eyes dropped to her lap. "So, this is really embarrassing to admit, and I'm sorry, but I heard your conversation the night you came over a couple weeks ago."

"Oh." I shifted uncomfortably in my chair.

"I didn't mean to eavesdrop, I swear." Now her eyes met mine—they were sincere and worried. "But I couldn't help it."

"It's okay," I said, wanting to put her at ease. "I'm sorry if you were upset by anything you heard."

She opened her mouth, closed it, squirmed in her seat, and took another breath. "Did you mean it? What you said? Do you really love my mom?"

For a moment, I was completely taken aback. But I recovered quickly and looked her right in the eye. "Yes, I meant it. Yes, I'm in love with your mom."

"How do you know?"

"What?"

"How do you *know* you're in love with her?"

At first I wasn't sure how to answer the question—but then I pictured Sylvia, and the ache in my chest intensified. "Because when I think about her, my heart races. Because when she's in the room, I can hardly breathe. Because I want to be with her all the time. Because I want to do things for her that make her smile. Because when *she's* happy, *I'm* happy. Because she's the first person in my head when I wake up, the last person I think about before I fall asleep, and the only person in the world who makes me feel like I'm the person I want to be."

Whitney blinked. "Sheesh."

I ran a hand through my hair, embarrassed. "I'm sorry if that upsets you, but I'm a person who believes in telling the truth."

"I'm not upset. I want you to love her like that."

"You do?"

"Yes. See, when I first saw you together, I was really worried, because of what my dad did. He just *left* us for this other woman, and it ruined our family. I feel like I don't even know my dad anymore. I feel like I don't even *have* a dad anymore, like he was just pretending to care all those years."

"I'm sure that's not true." But I wanted to smash my fist in his face for making her think that.

"Maybe, maybe not. But anyway, the thought of losing my mom the way I lost my dad made me panic. I begged her not to be with you, because I thought you'd take her from us like Kimmy took my dad. And then we'd *really* be alone."

I swallowed hard. "That's understandable."

"But she's *not* my dad. She's not my dad at all." Whitney sat up straighter. "And I shouldn't treat her that way. I shouldn't take my anger at my dad out on my mom. I shouldn't let my fears get in the way of my mom's chance to be happy."

I stared at her in disbelief, my jaw dropping. Was she really only thirteen years old?

She seemed to understand my shocked expression. "I've been going to therapy," she said, as if that explained everything.

"Oh."

"And it isn't that my fears aren't real—they are. But the sadness I feel when I hear my mom cry is worse."

"You hear her cry?" A heavy weight settled on my chest.

Whitney nodded, her own eyes shining with tears. "Just about every night. Last night was awful. After we saw you at the gym, Keaton told us about how you're going to help him with his science project, and my mom went to her room as soon as we got home. She turned on her television, but we heard her crying anyway."

I stared at my hands on my lap. "It kills me to think of her so sad."

"Us too. But I think I know why she was so upset. Our dad never did things like offer to help us with school projects. He bought a lot of fancy gifts, but that's not always the answer."

"No," I agreed. "It isn't."

"But it's not just about our dad. It's because she wants to be with you. She says all she needs is me and Keaton to be happy, but I don't believe her." Whitney took a deep breath. "I was wrong to get in the way before, and I'm sorry. So I came here today to make sure you meant what you said about taking care of her, and protecting her."

"I meant what I said."

"Then you need to be with her. Because she loves you too."

"It's not that easy, Whitney. She sent me away, remember?"

"That's because she was scared."

"But I don't know how to make her not scared," I said, frustrated all over again. "I'm not good at this. I think I know what to say, and then it turns out to be the wrong thing. All I know how to do is be honest, and it backfired."

"Can't you try again?"

I didn't answer right away. "I don't know, Whitney. Maybe she's just not ready for it."

She stood up. "You know, you don't sound like the Mr. DeSantis that knocked on the door that night."

Looking up at her in surprise, I blinked. "I don't?"

"No. That guy was a fighter."

Our gazes held for a moment, then she spoke again.

"My mom deserves a fighter, Mr. DeSantis."

I swallowed hard. "Yes, she does."

A moment later, she turned for the door.

"Whitney, wait!"

She looked over one shoulder.

"It's Henry. Call me Henry."

A smile tipped up her lips, and then she was gone.

I was still sitting there, stunned and confused, a few minutes later when April poked her head into my office. "What was that about with Whitney?" she asked, her eyes wide.

"She, uh, wanted to ask me something about Sylvia."

"Is everything okay?"

I shook my head. "Hell if I know."

April's head tilted in sympathy. "I'm sorry, Henry. I know things have been rough for both of you."

"Yeah." I rubbed my face with both hands. "Hey, is it okay if I take off for the day? My head is spinning."

"Of course. Take the night off, go grab a beer with a friend or something. We've got things covered here."

I stood up and grabbed my coat from the back of my chair. "Thanks. See you Monday."

"Henry!" Mia embraced me, kissing my cheek. "Come on in, you handsome stranger. Lucas told me you were stopping by."

"Sorry to barge in on you like this. I know you guys probably have Saturday night plans."

"We've been married for eight years, Henry. This is what Saturday nights look like." She gestured down at her sweats and bare feet. "But we do have wine."

I smiled. "Of course you do."

She motioned for me to follow her. "Come on, we're in the family room."

Lucas looked up from where he sat on the couch pouring wine into three glasses on the coffee table. "Hey," he said, his face breaking into a grin. He stood up and offered his hand. "Long time, no see."

"I know, sorry. The start of the year has been kind of crazy."

"How are things going in the vineyard?" Mia asked.

"Good. All good there." I rubbed the back of my neck. "I just needed to escape for a little bit."

"You're always welcome here." Mia's face was concerned. "But is everything okay?"

"I think so." I let my arm fall and shrugged. "But there's this certain situation I'm feeling really confused about. I guess I could use some advice."

Lucas handed me a glass and grinned. "Does this certain situation have a name?"

I nodded sheepishly. "Yeah. It's Sylvia."

Mia gasped. "Sylvia Sawyer?" Then she looked at her husband, one eyebrow arched. "You knew about this?"

"There wasn't much to know," Lucas said, settling on the couch again. "At least, not at Christmas."

"Uh, yeah, a few things have happened since then." I sat on a chair across from them.

"Like what?" Lucas asked.

"Like I fell in love with her."

Mia squealed and jumped onto the couch next to her husband, arranging herself cross-legged before leaning forward to grab a glass. "Start at the beginning and tell us *everything*."

I told them the story of reconnecting with Sylvia, how quickly things between us had progressed, how neither of us seemed able—or willing, at first—to slow down, and the disastrous New Year's Eve debacle.

Lucas listened silently and attentively, looking every inch the therapist with an ankle crossed over one knee, his elbow resting on the arm of the couch, his chin in his hand. His wife, on the other hand, reacted with loud gasps, sighs, and sounds of dismay wherever appropriate. Her body language was just as dramatic—she'd clap, rub her palms together, tug at her hair in frustration. I half expected her to get on the floor and start kicking and screaming when I told her that Sylvia had broken it off in early January.

But she only sighed dramatically and nodded in sympathy. "Poor thing. You can't choose yourself over your children. You just can't."

"I know. And I'd never expect her to." I went on to explain

how Sylvia still wanted to work at the winery, and how I'd felt obligated to keep my promise to teach her.

"You felt *obligated*?" Lucas questioned, a knowing smile on his lips.

"Okay, fine," I raised my palm. "It was a way I could still see her and talk to her, be close to her. But I swear to God, nothing ever happened between us. For a solid month, we did our best to just be friends."

"And what happened?" Mia asked.

"What happened was we fell in love anyway," I said, frustrated all over again. "It didn't matter that we weren't sleeping together, or doing anything physical at all."

"Of course not." Mia shook her head. "Because your connection to her isn't just about sex. It goes deeper than that."

"Which is what scares her."

"Do you think it's too soon for her?" Lucas asked, breaking his long silence.

"Lucas!" Mia reached over and slapped his arm. "No, it's not too soon. This woman *loves* him. She admitted it." She looked at me for confirmation. "Right?"

"Right. But she also told me to forget her, like in the same breath." I explained what happened the last time I saw her. "I told her I loved her. I told her I wanted to take care of her. I wouldn't walk away without a fight. And she said I had to—that she didn't know how to let herself be loved like that and she was too scared to try."

Mia had been sliding down on the sofa ever since I started talking, as if my story was deflating her hopes like a balloon losing air, and finally wound up in a puddle on the rug next to the coffee table. "That's it," she said. "I'm dead."

Lucas exhaled heavily. "You'll be okay."

"Here's the last part," I said. I told them about Whitney overhearing the entire conversation, running into them last night, and the visit at the winery today. "So now I have no idea what to do. I'm terrified of fucking this up again."

Mia sat straight up. "I know what you need to do."

"You do?" I asked.

"Yes." She nodded defiantly. "Listen, I get this woman. Maybe I didn't go through everything she did, but I feel where she's coming from. I don't know if we've ever told you this, but right before I met Lucas, I was engaged to someone else who jilted me a week before the wedding. Paris was supposed to be my honeymoon, and I went by myself—the last thing I expected was to meet the love of my life tending bar in the Latin Quarter my first night there, but I did."

I looked back and forth between them. "I never knew that."

"Now, when I walked into that bar, I was angry, depressed, and miserable. I had the worst attitude ever."

"The worst," Lucas confirmed.

"But Lucas saw something in me that even I couldn't see. He made me believe in love. He made me believe I was worth it. He made me believe that anything was possible—all I had to do was trust him."

"But *how*?" I said, leaning forward, elbows on my knees.

"He refused to give up," she said simply. "I tried to sabotage us. I broke it off in a train station, said *au revoir*, and walked away." She looked at her husband. "Remember that, babe?"

He nodded. "You walked the wrong way."

She laughed. "Yeah, that should have been a sign right there. But the point is . . ." She looked at me again. "I thought I was doing the right thing. And even better, I was taking *control* of it. I wasn't going to give some half-French bartender-slash-psych professor the opportunity to abandon me—I was going to leave him first. And I did."

"So what happened?"

"I had to go after her." Lucas leaned forward, grabbed his

wife's arm, and tugged her onto his lap. "She forced me to. And I was a guy who didn't believe in marriage, didn't want kids, never thought the whole traditional family thing was for me. But she'd made me look at myself differently, and I knew I couldn't let her get away."

"And you can't let Sylvia get away either, not if you love her." Mia put her arms around Lucas's shoulders. "It doesn't matter that you haven't been together for very long. What matters is the way you feel."

"I love her," I said adamantly. "And I know I can make her happy."

"Then go get her." Mia smiled at me. "If you know her well enough to love her, then you know what she needs to hear. It's in there, Henry." She put a hand over her heart. "Trust me. Trust *you*."

CHAPTER 24

Sylvia

I WAS HELPING April prepare for the inn's big Valentine's dinner when Whitney found me in the restaurant.

"Hey, Whit." I placed one of the centerpieces that had just been delivered from the florist on a table for four near the bar. "Where have you been?"

"I went to see Henry," she announced.

I looked at her, startled. "You what?"

"I went to see Henry in his office at the winery."

My mouth fell open. "Why?"

"Because I needed to talk to him." She pulled out a chair and sat down. "And now I need to talk to you."

"Okay," I said, pulling out the chair adjacent to hers. My head was spinning. "But since when do you call him Henry?"

"Since he told me to today. So here's the thing." Whitney placed her clasped hands on the table. "He's really in love with you. It's true."

My face burned. "Whitney, what on earth—"

"Listen to me. You said, that night he came to the house, that you didn't know whether he loved you or not. You said that was the problem."

"I said that was *part* of the problem."

"Well, it's not anymore. He loves you for real."

"And how do you know this?"

"Because I asked him how he knows he's in love with you, and he gave me this very long speech that I can't exactly remember, but he looked sort of intense and sad like Augustus Waters when he says that he knows that oblivion is inevitable but he is in love with you and all your efforts to keep him from you are going to fail."

"Who?" I asked, feeling like I had whiplash.

She rolled her eyes. "Augustus Waters! From The Fault in Our Stars?"

I shook my head. "Okay, but Whitney, you said you weren't ready for me to date anyone. You said you were scared of what might happen."

"I know what I said on New Year's Eve, and I'm sorry. It wasn't fair. If you and Henry love each other, you should be together. Keaton and I just talked about it, and we agree."

I placed two palms on the tablecloth, wishing the world would just slow down for a moment. I couldn't keep up. "Wait a minute. You spoke to Keaton about this already?"

"Yes, right after I talked to Henry. We want you to be happy, Mom. I know you say you don't need anyone but us, but that's a lot of pressure—and it's not working. We can hear you crying at night. We think you need something of your own."

I stared at her, openmouthed with shock. "I don't know what to say."

"Say you'll give him another chance. Say you forgive me for standing in the way before. I was scared—I'm *still* kind of scared—but the therapist says you can't let fear get the best of you. She says I'm stronger than I think."

"Oh, baby, of course I forgive you." I sniffed as I rose from my chair and reached for her. "Come here."

She stood up and we hugged for a long time.

"Your therapist is right. You are strong. And I'm so lucky to have a daughter like you," I whispered. "Thank you."

"You're welcome. Are you going to call him?"

"I'm going to think about it, I promise."

"Okay," she said, trying to detach herself from me. "But can I go now? Millie said she was going to be here around four, and I think it's after that."

"Oh. Sure." I released her, and she gladly hightailed it out of the restaurant, leaving me to sink back into the chair and sit there in a stupor.

I couldn't believe it. Whitney had gone to see Henry. Whitney was taking what she learned at therapy and helping *me*. Whitney and Keaton wanted me to give Henry another chance. They wanted me to have something of my own.

Was I strong enough to go after it? Was I brave enough to let myself love and be loved? Was I ready to talk down that voice of doubt in my head and offer my heart to Henry—whole, unguarded, and open?

I was sitting there struggling with it all when he suddenly burst into the empty restaurant. He seemed out of breath, like he'd been running, and when he spotted me sitting alone at the table, he moved toward me with long, purposeful strides.

He reached my side and stood above, his chest rising and falling fast, his eyes pinned on mine. "No," he announced.

"No?" I blinked at him.

"No. I changed my mind. I'm not walking away. *Fear* doesn't get to win." He grabbed my arm and pulled me to my feet. My legs were so weak and rubbery that he practically had to hold me up. "I love you, Sylvia. But more than that, I love us together. I love that you listen to me ramble on about volatile acidity like it's the most fascinating subject in the world. I love that you don't care if my shirts have holes. I love hearing you tell stories about growing up here. I love the way you smile at me across a room. I love the way I can guess what you're thinking by the blush in your cheeks. I love the way you put family first, because that's all I've ever wanted to do too."

I'd started to cry, and he brushed his thumbs beneath my eyes.

"I know you're scared, and that's okay. I know you're not used to someone keeping his promises. And I know it's going to take time for me to break down all those walls, but damn it, Sylvia, you're going to let me try. You're going to let me stick around. And you're going to let me love you, and *prove* to you that we can build something so real and so strong, it's unbreakable."

"Henry," I whispered, shaking my head. "What did I do to deserve you?"

He smiled gently. "You came looking for me. That very first night you were home, you came looking for me. I'll never forget that."

"I must have known." I couldn't help smiling.

"You must have known." He briefly pressed his lips to mine. "And I knew it too, that very same night. When I walked you back home through the snow and stood there with you on the porch, I never wanted to kiss someone so badly in all my life."

I gasped, laughing a little. "Really?"

"Yeah." He chuckled. "You don't recall how fast I took off?"

I tried to think back. "You know what? I do remember that. You said something about being able to give in to a woman, and then the next second, you were gone. But I kept thinking and thinking about what you'd said—I couldn't get you off my mind."

"The feeling was definitely mutual."

"I heard you had a visitor earlier today."

He nodded, giving me a crooked grin. "I did. Surprised the hell out of me."

"When she told me where she'd been, I nearly fell over."

"She's a good kid, she and her brother both. I'm looking forward to getting to know them better."

I looked up at him, searching for certainty in his eyes and finding it there. "This is real, isn't it? The way we feel? Even though it happened so quickly and unexpectedly?"

"It's real, Sylvia. Trust me." Then he smiled. "Trust *you*."

That night, I invited Henry over to have dinner and watch a movie with the kids and me. He stopped on the way and picked up cupcakes for the kids, and he brought me a bottle of wine.

"Thank you," I said, giving him a kiss on the cheek and pulling the corkscrew from a drawer. "Want to open it? I'm just finishing up the sauce for the tenderloin. Then I'll give you a tour of the house."

"Perfect. It's a beautiful house. I can see why you fell in love with it so fast."

"Thank you. There's work to be done, but I'm in no rush."

"So are you coming back to work soon?" He opened the bottle and poured two glasses. "I'm not sure if Chloe has mentioned it or not, but she's interviewing two people this week for tasting room help."

"I definitely want to come back," I told him, stirring the mushroom glaze. "I've missed it. I'll talk to Chloe tomorrow."

I gave Henry a tour of the new house, and the kids proudly showed off their rooms. While they dragged him outside in the dark to see the yard, the barn, and the other dilapidated outbuildings I'd have to deal with in the spring, I sliced the tenderloin and made sure the mashed potatoes were still warm.

They trooped inside again, and Henry asked if I was planning a vegetable garden. "You've got a great spot in the yard that would get plenty of sun," he said, removing his jacket.

"Can we, Mom?" Whitney asked.

"Sure," I said. "I used to love working in the garden with my mom when I was young. But I don't know much about putting one in."

"I can help," Henry said.

I imagined it all—a summer day full of sunshine, a garden full of vegetables, a yard full of kids and animals, boisterous shouts and good-natured teasing, a home full of laughter and life . . . Henry and I, together.

I saw it so clearly, there was no doubt in my mind it would happen.

CHAPTER 25

Henry

ONE WEEK after Valentine's Day, I went to pick Sylvia up for our first official date night. It was snowing pretty hard and the roads were bad, so I was running a little late, but she'd said that was okay because it had taken her a little longer than planned to get back from dropping the kids off at her parents' for the night.

Which I was pretty excited about.

It would be the first time we'd been *alone* since New Year's Eve, and every time I thought about it, I immediately got hard.

But I willed myself to have patience. This date was important to me—we'd always remember it. I figured we'd have dinner in town, maybe catch a movie or just stroll up and down Main Street. It wouldn't even matter what we did—I just wanted to be the one that got to take her somewhere, open the door for her, sit in a cozy booth and hold her hand across the table.

Then I'd bring her home and fuck her senseless.

But when she answered my knock, I suddenly wanted to reverse the order of my plans.

"Hi," she said, giving me a mischievous, cherry-lipped grin.

My jaw dropped.

She wore a red and white cheerleader costume, complete with short—and I mean *short*—pleated skirt, tight crop top that said CHEER across the front, white ankle socks and sneakers. Her hair was pulled off her face in a high ponytail tied with a big red bow, and she carried red and white pom poms in her hands.

I think I tried to say hi, but all I got out was a word that sounded like "hot."

"Would you like to come in?"

Nodding, I stepped into the house, unable to take my eyes off her or close my mouth. My dick was already standing at attention yelling GO! FIGHT! WIN! as I shut the door behind me.

"I know we're supposed to go out for dinner, but with the snowstorm and everything, I thought maybe you'd like to stay in," she said seductively, walking backward. "So I planned a little evening for us here."

As if in a trance, I followed her to the family room at the back of the house, where all the shades were pulled and the only light came from candles set on the coffee table—right next to a box of Krispy Kreme donuts and an oversized Restoration Hardware catalog.

I looked at her in surprise. "What's this?"

"It's your favorite things," she said with a grin. "I know one cheerleader isn't the same as teams of them competing on ESPN, but I thought you'd like the outfit just the same."

I had to laugh. "I do."

"Good. Want to take off your coat?"

I shrugged my jacket off and threw it aside, anxious to get my hands on her.

She had other ideas. "Okay, now you sit down and eat a Krispy Kreme."

"You want me to sit down and eat right now?" I put my arms around her. "What if I'd rather do something else?"

"Hey. I'm in charge here." She tapped her pom poms against my chest.

"I love when you try to get bossy." I buried my face in her neck and inhaled. "But I'm not hungry, Sylvia. Not for donuts, anyway."

She laughed when I tickled her throat with my tongue. "Hey, I'm just trying to make our first official date memorable here."

"Goal achieved," I said, backing up toward the couch and bringing her with me. "Seriously. V-I-C-T-O-R-Y. Now let's see your straddle."

Giggling, she let me pull her onto my lap, her knees on either side of my thighs, and tossed her pom poms over my shoulders. "So impatient."

"I can't help it," I said, kissing her lips as my hands slid beneath that skirt. "You know how I get when you wear a short—" I stopped. "You're naked underneath this outfit?"

Her eyelids lowered half-way as I stroked her. "Uh huh."

The bulge in my pants was almost unbearable as I caressed her tongue with mine and mirrored the slow, sensual motion with my fingers between her legs. She rocked her hips over my hand, growing aroused and restless.

"Now who's impatient?" I teased as she reached for my belt.

"S-Y-L-V-I-A." She quickly unbuttoned and unzipped, reaching inside to free my cock, which sprang up eagerly. Wrapping her hand around it, she gave it several tight, hard strokes, making me groan with agonizing pleasure at her touch. I wasn't sure how long I could maintain control, so I was glad when she lowered her body onto mine inside a minute.

I gripped her hips and worked her up and down my hard length, my eyes practically coming out of my head at the sight of her bouncing on my cock in that cheerleader getup. "Oh fuck, I'm not going to last," I growled. I knew it would help if I closed my eyes, but I couldn't do it—she was so fucking hot, it was mesmerizing.

"It's okay," she said breathlessly. Then she leaned down and whispered against my lips, "And we have the whole night together. You can make me come as many times as you want."

That nearly sent me over the edge, but I willed myself to hang on a little longer. I moved one hand between her legs and rubbed my thumb over her clit the way she liked, and her mouth dropped open, her eyes closing. She made soft little sounds as she circled her hips and dug her fingers into my shoulders. When her cries rose to a fever pitch and I felt her leg muscles tense and her body still, I couldn't hold back any longer. I grabbed her hips and thrust into her again and again, my orgasm thundering throughout my body as she came undone above me.

And as I poured into her, I held her close and felt my heart surging with love for her, and I wondered how I ever thought I could give her up.

"Never," I heard myself whispering fiercely into her ear. "I will never let you go."

Her arms tightened around me, and she laid her head on my shoulder. Our hearts beat hard and fast against one another's. "This is right where I want to be, Henry. In your arms. Always."

A little while later, she got up to use the bathroom, and when she returned, she was carrying a plate. Reaching into the box of Krispy Kremes, she set a donut on the plate and handed it to me. "Okay, now you have to let me do the thing I planned."

"Does it involve eating this donut while you jump around in that outfit with no underwear on? Because count me in." I picked up the Krispy Kreme and bit into it.

She laughed. "No, it's even better." Sitting next to me on her knees, she leaned over and picked up the Restoration Hardware catalog and opened it up. "I am going to read you a bedtime story in my sexiest voice."

I burst out laughing and took another bite. "Do it."

She opened the book to a random page, inhaled, and looked at me with sultry eyes. "The reclaimed rustic oak collection."

"Mmmmm," I moaned. "Tell me more."

Posing seductively, she spoke in a breathy, sex kitten voice. Whenever she got to words related to wood, she'd look me in the eye and arch her brows. "Celebrating the organic beauty of *salvaged wood*, our table is handcrafted of *solid oak* timbers reclaimed from decades-old buildings."

"God, you're making me hard." Groaning, I shoved the rest of the donut in my mouth. "Can I jerk off while you read?"

She was trying to stay serious, but a smile was creeping onto her lips. "*Rough-hewn planks* define a simple parsons style, allowing the oak's rustic character to take center stage. Each one-of-a-kind table displays the nicks, knots, and imperfections that speak to *the wood's* former life."

"You're killing me. This is so hot." I reached for the book and set it aside. "But the imperfections of the wood's former life don't matter."

She laughed. "No?"

"No." I pulled her across my lap, cradling her in my arms. "What matters is here and now, and you know what? Here and now is pretty fucking perfect."

Smiling, she looped her arms around my neck. "I agree."

I pressed my lips to hers. "I love you, Sylvia Sawyer. And I might never be able to give you fancy things, but I'll take care of you. I promise."

"I believe you with my whole heart." She gave me that smile, the one that would melt my insides for the rest of my life. "And I don't want fancy things, Henry. I'll take your time and attention over expensive gifts any day. I just want to belong to you."

"You do. And I belong to you." I kissed her once more, and knew in my heart that with these words, we were putting down roots that would be forever intertwined. "We belong together."

Epilogue

SYLVIA

"I'm sorry. Could you say that again?" I asked Dr. Kelson, a dark-skinned woman with kind eyes and a soft voice.

"The test is positive. You're pregnant," she said firmly.

"I can't be. I'm infertile."

She looked at the results again. "Not according to this."

"But my eggs." I shook my head, feeling dizzy and disoriented and sick to my stomach, which was why I was here in the first place. "My eggs aren't good. They're past their due date."

She smiled gingerly and opened a paper calendar on the counter. "The only due date you have to think about is probably sometime this fall. When was your last period?"

"Uh . . ." I tried to think. "Maybe early December?"

She looked up from the calendar. "So did you miss one in January too?"

My brain was reeling. Had I? I must have. "I guess it's possible. My life has been sort of upside down since the move. And my periods have been irregular for the last year, probably because I lost quite a bit of weight."

She nodded. "That can happen. Your weight is in the healthy range now, but let's see if we can pinpoint when you might have conceived."

Conceived.

Oh my God.

"So today is March twelfth. You know for sure you missed one in February, and you think maybe you missed January."

"I'm pretty sure I did," I said, reality sinking in. "And my best guess is that I conceived somewhere between Christmas and New Year's." Tears filled my eyes.

Dr. Kelson plucked a tissue from the box on the counter and handed it to me. "I take it this baby is a surprise?"

"Yes." To say the least.

"You mentioned you're divorced on your intake forms. Is the baby's father—"

"Not my ex," I said, trying to gain control. "It's someone else."

"Is he part of your life? Would he be supportive?"

I nodded and dabbed at my eyes with the tissue. "Yes, he is part of my life, and he's wonderful. He'll be supportive."

"Good. And you have . . ." She checked my paperwork. "Two other children?"

"Yes." A chasm of dread opened in my stomach. How would Whitney and Keaton take the news? "And I'm a little worried about telling them."

"Well, give yourself some time to adjust," she suggested, patting my arm. "And let's get you scheduled for an ultrasound."

An hour later, I pulled into the lot at Cloverleigh Farms and sat behind the wheel of my car, staring out the windshield but seeing nothing.

September eighteenth. That was my due date.

I was nearly twelve weeks along.

I'd scheduled an ultrasound for the following week, at which I'd be able to see and probably even hear the baby's heartbeat.

Oh my God. I put both hands on my belly. There was a heart beating inside me. A heartbeat that Henry and I had created.

I closed my eyes, feeling joyful and terrified all at once.

At least it all made sense now—the nausea, the crying at every little thing, the dizziness, the sore breasts, the gradual but steady weight gain. I'd been glad for the extra pounds and excited to have some more curves, but I'd also had this odd suspicion something wasn't quite right with my body, so I'd made an appointment with April's doctor.

April—what would April say? As soon as I had the thought, I knew April would be supportive. But what about the kids? My parents? Did this make me just like Brett? And wasn't I too old to have a baby? What if something went wrong?

From somewhere deep within me, a voice spoke up—not a voice of doubt this time, but a voice of strength.

That's enough, Sylvia. Stop fretting about this and go in and tell Henry he's going to be a father. You are not betraying anybody by having a baby—it's an incredible, unexpected miracle that will mean more love in this family and in this world. Be grateful you were given such a gift.

When I opened my eyes, the first thing I saw was the house where I grew up.

Smiling, I got out of the car.

"What's up?" Henry followed me into his office and shut the door.

I spun around and faced him. "You might want to sit down."

"Sylvia, tell me." His face was concerned—he knew I'd had a doctor's appointment this morning. He put his arms around me. "What did she say? Whatever it is, it's going to be okay."

"Well," I said, feeling a laugh bubble up out of nowhere. Good Lord, pregnancy made you moody! "It's actually . . . a baby."

One of his brows shot up. "A what?"

"A baby." I smiled tentatively. "I'm pregnant."

A full ten seconds passed while Henry digested the news. He didn't move, didn't blink, didn't breathe. Then his eyes closed. "Tell me I'm not dreaming."

"You're not dreaming, Henry. I'm—*we're*—having a baby. I'm almost twelve weeks along."

Suddenly he picked me up and swung me around. When he set me on my feet, he took my face in his hands and planted a huge kiss on my lips. His eyes were wet. "And you're sure?"

I nodded. "Those tests don't lie. And she examined me to confirm it."

"Oh my God, Sylvia." He pulled me close and wrapped me up in his arms. "You have no idea how happy I am."

"I've got some idea," I said, coughing. "Careful, you're squishing us."

"Oh, sorry!" He let me go, but took my hands in his and looked me in the eye. "How are you? Are you feeling okay?

Do you need to sit down? Are you happy? Are you scared? How did this even happen? Talk to me."

I laughed, lifting my shoulders. "I'm happy, Henry. I have no idea how this happened, and I'm worried about how Whitney and Keaton are going to handle the news, but I'm happy. Maybe a *little* scared."

"Don't be." His expression was serious and he squeezed my hands. "I'll be there every step of the way, and I'll help you talk to the kids if you want. You have nothing to be afraid of. My God, Sylvia." He took me in his arms again, more gently this time. "I never thought I'd have this moment. Thank you."

At the crack in his voice, my tears were back. I put my arms around his waist and took comfort in his warm, familiar scent, the solidity of his chest against my cheek, even the hole in his shirt. This was *real* love.

He dropped to his knee and looked up. "Marry me, Sylvia. I would have asked you anyway, but I was trying to be patient for once. Clearly, the universe does not want us to take our time. I'm sorry I don't have a ring, but what I do have is a promise—I will love you forever. I will be a good father to this baby. And I will never try to take the place of Whitney and Keaton's dad, but I will be there for them, no matter what."

I nodded through my tears.

"Is that yes?"

"Yes," I said, my heart clanging against my ribs. "Yes."

He rose and scooped me up again, gently rocking me from side to side. "You're the best thing that ever happened to me. And I hope you don't mind, but I'm going to spend the rest of my life making sure you know it."

I laughed and sniffled. "I don't mind at all."

As it turned out, I had nothing to worry about where my kids were concerned. Both Whitney and Keaton were surprised but excited about the prospect of a little brother or sister. Henry and I told them together the following Saturday night. It was kind of a tradition now that we all hung out and watched a movie at the new house. Henry never stayed the night, although I was longing for the day when he could.

"Can I tell Millie?" Whitney wanted to know.

"Well, we were planning to tell everyone tomorrow night at Cloverleigh," I said, linking hands with Henry at the table. "The entire family is going for Sunday dinner because it's Grandma's birthday. Can you wait until then?"

"I guess." She looked glum for a second. Then she perked up. "Can the baby sleep in my room?"

Henry and I laughed. "You won't want the baby in your room at first, trust me," I told her. "But I will need plenty of help, don't worry."

Later, when I was saying goodnight to Whitney, she asked me if Henry and I would get married.

"We want to," I said gently, sitting on the edge of her bed. "How do you feel about that?"

"I think you should." Her tone was confident. "Would Henry live here?"

"Probably. We haven't talked about it yet, but that makes the most sense."

"Good." She snuggled deeper under her covers. "I don't want to move again. I like my new room."

"I'm glad." I smoothed her hair back from her face. "You're sure you're okay with all this? If you're not, it's okay to tell me."

"I'm sure. This doesn't feel like it did with Dad and

Kimmy, if that's what you're worried about. It feels really different."

"Good."

"I'm happy for you, Mom."

"Thank you."

"Can I be in the wedding?"

I laughed. "Sure. You'll have to help me plan."

"Really? You mean it?"

"Of course. You know, if it weren't for you, none of this would have happened. So we should be thanking you."

"You're welcome," she said, her voice full of teenage smug.

Laughing, I leaned over and kissed her forehead. "Goodnight, sweetheart."

"Night, Mom."

The following night, we were all gathered in the great room with drinks at my parents' house before dinner when Henry surprised me by asking for everyone's attention. He definitely wasn't someone who enjoyed all eyes in a room on him, and this wasn't how we'd discussed sharing our news.

Taking my hand, he brought me in front of the fireplace and turned to face the crowd. Everyone was there—my parents and kids, April, Mack and Frannie's family, Meg and Noah, Chloe and Oliver. Even Noah's dog Renzo was lying on the floor at his feet. When everyone was quiet and looking in our direction, Henry glanced at me. "Sylvia and I have something to tell you."

My stomach jumped nervously. My sisters were going back and forth between studying me intently and exchanging frantic eye contact with each other, trying to guess what this was about. I could practically hear their voices in my head. *Do you know? I don't know. Does Mom know? I don't think Mom knows.*

Only my children looked calm and unsurprised, sitting next to each other on the couch with my parents, grinning like mad.

Henry dropped to his knee, and someone in the room gasped. "Sylvia," he said, taking my hand. "You know I'm not a guy who likes the spotlight, and I generally avoid drawing this much attention to myself. But this isn't just about me."

I squeezed his hand, fighting back tears.

"Your family has always been such a huge part of your life, and in the last ten years, they've become part of mine too. From my very first day on the job here, I was welcomed and accepted, and they supported me without question when I needed it. They made me feel like I belonged. So it seemed only right to say this in front of them, and in front of your children, the two most important people in your life."

I glanced out at Whitney and Keaton, who smiled back at me.

When I looked down at Henry again, he was taking something from his back pocket—a ring box.

Another gasp from the crowd, and a whispered, "Oh my God."

"Sylvia," Henry said, his voice quiet but confident, "the way I feel about you is no secret. Since you moved back, I haven't been able to think about anything else. And when I picture the rest of my life, it's impossible to imagine it without you—and without this family." He opened the ring box, and a beautifully classic round-cut diamond solitaire on a pavé-studded platinum band caught the firelight and winked at me.

The next gasp was mine, and I covered my mouth with both hands.

Henry took the ring from its snug velvet home and set the box aside. "I know getting married again was the last thing either one of us thought we would do, especially so fast. I know I told you I would never be able to buy you fancy things. I know there are people in this town—maybe even in this room—who will think I'm crazy. But I also know this." He reached for my left hand, and I gave it to him. "I've never loved anyone the way I love you, and I don't want to wake up without you anymore. You make every single day better. You make *me* better. Sylvia Sawyer, will you marry me?"

I was crying and laughing at the same time as he slipped the ring on my finger. "Yes!" I shouted. "Yes!"

He stood and embraced me, lifting me right off my feet, and the entire room busted out cheering and applauding. One by one, my family members came over to congratulate us, and Chloe opened a bottle of champagne. When I refused a glass, April raised an eyebrow and exchanged a look with Chloe, after which both of them looked at my stomach—after which everyone in the room looked at my stomach and went silent.

"Um, is there something else you guys want to tell us?" April asked, unable to keep a grin off her face.

Henry and I looked at each other, and he pulled me in front of him, wrapping his arms around me.

"There might be one other small thing," I said, putting my hands over his. Then I looked at my mom, whose eyes were misting over.

"This is the best birthday ever," she said.

My dad raised his glass. "To our ever-expanding family," he said loudly, a huge grin on his face as he took my mom's hand. "You make us proud, you make us happy, you make us feel like the luckiest people in the world. Cheers to the next generation at Cloverleigh Farms!"

Everyone but me raised a glass and toasted the future of our family—even the kids had sparkling water in their cups—

and I thought of those eight mimosas I drank just a few months back. How incredibly far I had come since then.

Henry tightened his arms around me and kissed my cheek, and I leaned back against him, completely content. My children were smiling, three generations of my family were together, and we all had so much to look forward to.

Wrapped in Henry's embrace, with new life growing inside me, I understood the blessings of home better than I ever had before.

I was right where I belonged.

THE END

Bonus Epilogue

SYLVIA

It was Christmas Eve.

The Inn at Cloverleigh Farms was closed, my entire family was here or soon to arrive, and the man I loved—the father of my newborn son—was waiting for me to walk down the stairs, where we'd say our vows by the fireplace. Snow had been falling all day, and I loved the way it had blanketed the entire farm in white.

Whitney and I had used a room upstairs at the inn to get ready, but she'd been anxious to get downstairs and see who'd arrived so far, so she'd snuck out to peek over the railing of the grand staircase. I was just stepping into my shoes when she came back into the room, grinning and breathless. "Everyone's here," she said. "The music is playing, the fire is going, and the tree is all lit up. Are you ready?"

"I think so." Standing in front of the mirror, I caught her eyes in the reflection and smiled. "What do you think?"

"You look beautiful."

"So do you." I admired my daughter in the short black

velvet dress she'd chosen for tonight, marveling at how grown-up she seemed with her hair blown out and her first pair of (low) heels. She'd eased up on the makeup in recent months, wearing just a trace of the old eyeliner and a much softer shade of lipstick.

She beamed. "Thank you."

"So everyone arrived, huh? I thought maybe the snow would make some people late." Not that we had a ton of guests—Henry and I had both agreed we wanted a small, intimate wedding, and my parents had graciously offered to scale back their usual Christmas Eve party and host our nuptials instead. We thought it would be a fitting anniversary since it was the night we first kissed . . . exactly one year ago.

"They must have left early."

The door opened again, and April poked her head in. "Hey. Can I come in?"

"Of course," I said.

"I have flowers." April entered the room holding a small bouquet of cream-colored roses for me, and one with red roses for Whitney. "Oh, Syl. You're so beautiful."

"Thanks."

"I mean, you're always beautiful, but tonight you just look so . . ." She took a deep breath, searching for the word.

"Happy," I said. "I'm happy."

She sighed. "That's what it is."

"And the dress," I said, turning toward the mirror again. "The dress helps."

April nodded in agreement. "The dress is beyond stunning."

At first I'd planned on wearing something very plain in a shade other than white—I'd already worn the big white ball-gown at my first wedding, and I wasn't some blushing bride in my twenties this time around. For heaven's sake, Henry and I already had a child together—a three-month-old baby boy we'd named Steffan.

But April and Whitney had convinced me to try on the bias-cut ivory satin dress, which had a cowl neckline, an asymmetrical hem, and a narrow red velvet belt at the waist. On my feet were the red satin heels Henry liked. My hair was loose and wavy around my shoulders, and around my neck was a strand of pearls that my mother had given me—they'd belonged to her mom before her.

I faced my sister and daughter again, running a hand over my belly. "The only thing is that it hides nothing. I feel like you can totally tell I just had a baby."

Whitney rolled her eyes. "Because you did, Mom."

Actually, I liked my new curves—and so did Henry. "Who has Steffan right now? Grandma?"

"Yes," Whitney said. "He's sleeping, but she refuses to put him down."

I laughed. "Typical grandmother."

"Henry looks so handsome," said April, fussing with a few strands of my hair. "And he keeps glancing at his watch, and at the stairs, like he just can't wait for you to come down."

"It's true," Whitney confirmed. "I feel like you better get down there or he's going to lose his mind and race up here to get you."

I laughed. "Okay."

"I'll go back down and tell everyone," April said. "Just give me a minute to make sure a path is clear for you two and get Henry and Keaton in the right spot. Whit, I'll give you the thumbs up when you should start down."

"Got it."

"Thanks, April." I blew her a kiss. "You're the best."

A moment later, Whitney and I left the room and went to the second-floor landing. Below us, the lobby was darker than usual, lit only by candles and the strands of lights on the giant evergreen tree in the corner. "Have Yourself a Merry Little Christmas" played over the sound system, and conversations quieted as everyone noticed Whitney at the top of the stairs. Feeling nervous all of a sudden, I tried to stay out of sight as she looked for April's signal.

"Okay," she whispered. "It's time. Ready?"

I nodded, but my throat felt too tight to speak.

Whitney turned and looked at me, her face growing concerned. "All good?"

I nodded, swallowing hard. "Just a couple jitters."

Her lips curved into a reassuring smile. "This is meant to be, Mom. I know it."

"Thanks, sweetheart. I love you."

"I love you too. Should I go down now?"

"Yes." I took a deep breath. "Let's go."

Nodding, she turned for the stairs and carefully made her way down. When she disappeared from my view, I came to the edge of the first step, and a lovely sense of calm came over me. I practically floated down the stairs, unable to keep the smile off my face. How lucky I was, to find real love after so long. And how wonderful to find it right here in the place I'd always think of as home.

When I reached the bottom, I made my way toward the fireplace, where Henry stood waiting for me, with Keaton behind him and Whitney opposite them. For a moment, I could hardly breathe as I took him in, but it wasn't just the dark suit or the close shave or the fresh haircut. His good looks would always make my heart beat faster, but what I loved best about him was the way he looked at me. No one had ever made me feel as cherished, as beautiful, as safe.

On either side of the "aisle" April had arranged, my family members smiled through tears, wiped their eyes, and murmured words of admiration. I felt the love all around me, but I only had eyes for Henry.

The expression he wore was a mix of adoration, wonder, and disbelief. As I got closer, I saw that his eyes were full of tears.

"My God," he said quietly as I reached him. "This can't be real. *You* can't be real. You're too beautiful."

I laughed gently, happily. "This is all real."

The officiant, an old friend of my father's, stepped out from the crowd. "So," he said, a huge smile on his face. "Let's begin."

The ceremony was short and sweet—a simple exchange of vows, a little nervous laughter as I struggled to get Henry's ring on his finger, a couple tears as he cradled my left hand in both of his after slipping on my ring, and uproarious whistles, shouts, and applause when we were pronounced husband and wife. We shared a fairly chaste kiss in front of our guests, but as Henry embraced me, he whispered in my ear, "I can't wait to get you alone, Mrs. De Santis."

My entire body tingled.

"I've been to many a Christmas Eve gathering here," the officiant said jovially, "but I already know this one's my favorite."

"Mine too," said Henry, taking my hand and bring my fingers to his lips before we faced our cheering family and our beautiful future. "Mine too."

Sylvia's Caesar Salad

2 lemons, juiced
    5 cloves garlic, minced
    2 tsp. Dijon mustard
    1 1/2cups olive oil
    1/4 cup red wine vinegar
    1 1/2 Tbsp. Worcestershire sauce
    2 cups shredded Romano Parmesan
    pepper to taste
    Additional shredded cheese for topping

Romaine lettuce, chopped
    Pepperidge Farm Caesar croutons (actually, Sylvia Sawyer DeSantis would probably make her own, but Melanie Harlow buys them!)

1) In a blender or food processor, combine lemon juice, garlic, mustard, olive oil, vinegar, Worcestershire sauce, pepper and cheese. Mix well. Dressing will be thick—you can add more oil and vinegar if you prefer a thinner consistency.

2) Toss dressing with lettuce at last minute. Add croutons and additional shredded cheese on top. You can also add protein to this salad—grilled chicken or shrimp or salmon works great!

Sylvia's Spinach and Artichoke Lasagna

Ingredients

Cooking Spray
1 1/2 Tbsp olive oil
1 box lasagne (Sylvia probably makes her own pasta from scratch but Melanie Harlow uses the no-boil kind)
1/2 yellow onion, chopped
4 cloves garlic, chopped
1 (14.05) oz can chicken or vegetable broth
1 Tbsp. fresh rosemary, chopped
1 can or jar of marinated artichoke hearts, drained and chopped
1 package frozen spinach, thawed and squeezed dry
1 (32oz) jar tomato sauce
3 cups shredded mozzarella cheese
1 (6 oz) container garlic and herb crumbled feta cheese

Directions

1) Preheat oven to 350 degrees. Lightly spray a 9 x 13 baking dish with cooking oil.

2) If using dried pasta, cook according to package directions. If you're going the Harlow route, pour yourself a cocktail and open the box of no-boil noodles.

3) Heat olive oil in large pot over medium heat. Add onions and garlic and sauté until onion is tender and lightly browned. Add broth and rosemary; stir to combine and bring to a boil.

4) Stir in artichokes and spinach, reduce heat, cover, and simmer for 5 minutes. Stir in the pasta sauce.

5) In the bottom of the baking dish, spread 1/4 of the spinach/artichoke mixture. Top with a layer of lasagne and about 3/4 cup shredded mozzarella. Repeat this two more times, then end with leftover spinach/artichoke mix topped with mozzarella. Sprinkle the crumbled feta over the top.

6) Cover and bake for 40 minutes. Uncover and bake 10-15 more minutes. Let stand 10 minutes before cutting.

Never miss a thing!

For exclusive behind the scenes information, sales and freebies, cover reveals, recommendations, and sneak peeks to what's coming, subscribe to my mailing list using the QR code below!

Also by Melanie Harlow

The Frenched Series

Frenched

Yanked

Forked

Floored

The Happy Crazy Love Series

Some Sort of Happy

Some Sort of Crazy

Some Sort of Love

The After We Fall Series

Man Candy

After We Fall

If You Were Mine

From This Moment

The One and Only Series

Only You

Only Him

Only Love

The Cloverleigh Farms Series

Irresistible

Undeniable

Insatiable

Unbreakable

Unforgettable

The Bellamy Creek Series
Drive Me Wild
Make Me Yours
Call Me Crazy
Tie Me Down

Cloverleigh Farms Next Generation Series
Ignite
Taste
Tease
Tempt

Co-Written Books
Hold You Close (Co-written with Corinne Michaels)
Imperfect Match (Co-written with Corinne Michaels)
Strong Enough (M/M romance co-written with David Romanov)

The Speak Easy Duet

The Tango Lesson (A Standalone Novella)

Want a reading order? Click here!

Acknowledgments

As always, my love and gratitude to the following people for their talent, support, wisdom, friendship, and encouragement...

Melissa Gaston, Jenn Watson, Brandi Zelenka, Hang Le, Devyn Jensen, Kayti McGee, Laurelin Paige, Sierra Simone, Lauren Blakely, Corinne Michaels, Margaret Provenzano, Sarah Ferguson and the entire Social Butterfly team, Anthony Colletti, Rebecca Friedman, Flavia Viotti, beta bombshell Crimson Grey, Nancy Smay at Evident Ink, Julia G. of The Romance Bibliophile, proofreaders Michele Ficht and Shannon Mummey, Stacey Blake at Champagne Book Design, the Shop Talkers, the Harlots and the Harlot ARC Team, Club Harlow, bloggers and event organizers, my beloved Queens, my readers all over the world...

And especially to my family. You are home to me.

About the Author

Melanie Harlow likes her heels high, her martini dry, and her history with the naughty bits left in. In addition to UNBREAKABLE, she's the author of over a dozen additional contemporary romances and a historical duet.

She writes from her home outside of Detroit, where she lives with her husband and two daughters. When she's not writing, she's probably got a cocktail in hand. And sometimes when she is.

Find her at www.melanieharlow.com.